T0385314

THE
EDINBURGH
MURDERS

Catriona McPherson was born in the village of Queensferry in south-east Scotland and left Edinburgh University with a PhD in Linguistics. Her historical fiction has been short-listed for the CWA Ellis Peters award and long-listed for Theakston's Crime Novel of the Year, as well as winning two Agathas, two Macavitys, and four Leftys in the USA. Catriona lives most of the year in northern California, spends summers in Scotland, and writes full time in both.

Also by Catriona McPherson

The Dandy Gilver Series
After the Armistice Ball
The Burry Man's Day
Bury Her Deep
The Winter Ground
The Proper Treatment of Bloodstains
Unsuitable Day for a Murder
A Bothersome Number of Corpses
A Deadly Measure of Brimstone
The Reek of Red Herrings
The Unpleasantness in the Ballroom
The Most Misleading Habit
A Spot of Toil and Trouble
A Step So Grave
The Turning Tide
The Mirror Dance
The Witching Hour

The Edinburgh Murders Series
In Place Of Fear

THE EDINBURGH MURDERS

CATRIONA McPHERSON

HODDER &
STOUGHTON

First published in Great Britain in 2025 by Hodder & Stoughton Limited
An Hachette UK company

1

A CIP catalogue record for this title is available from the British Library

Hardback ISBN 978 1 399 72044 1
Trade Paperback ISBN 978 1 399 72046 5
ebook ISBN 978 1 399 72045 8

Typeset in Plantin Light by Manipal Technologies Limited.

Printed and bound in Great Britain by Clays Ltd, Elcograf S.p.A.

Hodder & Stoughton policy is to use papers that are natural, renewable
and recyclable products and made from wood grown in sustainable forests.
The logging and manufacturing processes are expected to conform
to the environmental regulations of the country of origin.

Hodder & Stoughton Limited
Carmelite House
50 Victoria Embankment
London EC4Y 0DZ

The authorised representative in the EEA is Hachette Ireland, 8 Castlecourt
Centre, Castleknock Road, Castleknock, Dublin 15, D15 YF6A, Ireland

www.hodder.co.uk

This is for Laura and Michael Walker,
anglophiles (who stretch to Scotland) and friends.

Glossary

An' all: too, also
Bahookie: bottom
Bairn: child, baby
Beel: to blush
Besom: mildly exasperated term of address for a girl or woman
Bide: stay, remain
Birl: to whirl round
Boak: retch, vomit
Breeks: trousers
Breenge: barge in confidently
Bunker: kitchen work-top or draining board
Bunnet: flat cap
Chap: knock
Chitter: shiver
Chuckies: jacks
Chum (verb): to accompany
Clap: pet, stroke
Clarty: dirty
Clatter: hit repeatedly
Clootie dumpling: steamed pudding cooked in a cloth
Close: the common entrance and stairway of a tenement
Clype: tell-tale
Cowp: rubbish dump, mess (n). overturn (vb)
Crabbit: bad-tempered, out-of-sorts

Creepie: foot stool
Dae ken / Dinnae ken: don't know.
Daftie: idiot
Dicht: wipe
Dooking: apple-bobbing (lit. dipping)
Easy-osy: easy-going
Een: eyes
Eh: is that not so (positive polarity)
Eh no: is that not so (negative polarity)
Fae: from
Fankle: muddle, predicament
Felly: boyfriend (lit. fellow)
Foosty: stale, rancid
Gadgie: man
Gallimaufry: a muddle
Gey: very
Ginger: any fizzy drink
Girn: to cry
Gob: mouth
Green: shared common area behind tenements
Guising: Halloween tradition similar to trick-or-treating, where children dress up and sing, dance or recite poetry for neighbours in return for sweets
Gutties: gym shoes, cloth sandals
Haver: to fantasise, or lie
Heecher: an extreme example
How: why
Howff: a den, or private retreat
Howk: haul, dig
Jeely pan: large copper-bottomed pot for boiling jam
Keek: look, glance
Ken: know (past tense – kent)
Keen: sharp
Killy-coad: piggy back

Kludgy: WC compartment
Messages: shopping
Michty: God (lit. Mighty)
midden: rubbish dump, mess
Mump: sulk
Neb: nose
Neep: swede (UK), rutabaga (US)
Nippy: sharp-tongued
Nippy: waitress
Oxter: armpit
Pally: intimate, friendly
Peerie: spinning top
Pend: alleyway
Piece: sandwich
Plunk: to steal (esp. fruit)
Po: lavatory (lit. pot)
Poke: paper bag or wrapper around food
Puir sowel: poor soul (rhymes with "spare towel")
Red (up): to tidy, or clear
Room-and-kitchen: a tenement flat consisting of kitchen and living room, both with a box bed
Sair fecht: a hard life (lit. sore fight)
Scaffie: road sweeper or dustman (from "scavenger")
Scullery: kitchen (orig. place where washing-up was done)
Scunnered: sickened, disgusted
Simmet: vest (UK), undershirt (US)
Single-end: a one room dwelling in a tenement
Skew-whiff: awry
Slater: woodlouse
Slaver: drool
Sneck: latch
Steamie: laundry-house
Tattie: potato
That: so (adverb)

The now: right now, just then
This weather: at the moment
Thole: bear, submit to
Thon: that (demons. art.)
Toty: small
Trauchled: disordered, messy
Tumshie: swedish turnip
Wame: stomach
Wean: child
Wee: small, negligible, trivial
Wheen: a few (adj) or considerable (adv)
Wheesh/wheesht: shush
Wifie: woman
Winching: dating, courting

Chapter 1

'I like a guid hard scrub,' Mrs Hogg said for the umpteenth time. 'Dinnae be tickling me.'

Helen Crowther stuck her bottom lip out and blew upwards, trying to lift the damp tendrils of hair plastered to her sweating forehead. She wasn't about to touch her face with the hands she was using to wash Mrs Hogg's back.

She still wasn't sure how she'd ended up washing any bit of the woman. She'd only offered to chum along and glare at the baths attendants if they got nippy.

'You wouldnae ken, whip like you,' Mrs Hogg had said, tears standing in her tiny, curranty eyes. 'They can be very cutting at that Cally Crescent. Airs and graces.'

Helen believed her. Everyone had just seen what a smidge of power could do to the wrong kind of person. There was a blackout warden from Lochrin who'd have had the city's population in chains for a glowing fag end. And Helen had spent every Friday night at Cally Crescent herself, from the day she got too big for the zinc bath on the kitchen floor to the day she moved into her wee palace with its own doings. Mrs Hogg was right; Helen had never been scolded for the reason *she'd* been scolded, but she'd heard plenty about getting the free towel too wet, or soaking for too much of the half hour folk were entitled to, or using too much of the chip of carbolic that had been paid for.

'You should give Mrs Hogg a penny off if anything,' Helen had told the attendant who'd muttered and grumbled them upstairs and into a cubicle.

'Aye!' Mrs Hogg chimed in, pugnacious in advance of the insults she was expecting. 'I'll save water for you. I'm like a brick in a cistern, me.'

She was more like a cork in a bottle, Helen thought to herself as she tried to squeeze the back brush in along the woman's side to wash her oxters.

'Oh!' said Mrs Hogg. 'Lovely! Scrape away, Nelly. I like to step out of ma bath rid raw.'

Helen scraped, and kept her eyes trained upwards on the tiles of the cubicle, tracing imagined pictures in the dark veins on the green ones, wondering why on earth the others were mustard-yellow and cream, instead of a nice clean colour like blue or white, or even pink. None of that had occurred to her back when she used to lie here in her own steamy water but, now she was a householder who chose distemper and curtain fabric, she cared about such things.

'Aye well,' said Mrs Hogg presently, with a sigh, 'my time's near up and I need to leave plenty.' At least she had brought her own sheet from home to wrap up in. The towels you got with the one and thruppenny baths wouldn't have gone near her. Helen held it up above her head and out as wide as her arms would go to give the woman her privacy, praying she'd get her leg over the side and not slip.

When Mrs Hogg was standing safely on the wooden rack that did for a bathmat and kept the bathers' clean feet off the clarty floor, there wasn't a lot of space for both women in the cubicle, so Helen edged round the door and said she'd stay in earshot in case Mrs Hogg needed a hand with—

'Ma nooks and crannies!' It wasn't quite a shout but the acoustics in the tiled alcoves made the most of it anyway. 'Ah've got a system,' she assured Helen, who let the cubicle door fall shut and stepped away before she could be given any details.

It was cooler out on the balcony, fresher too, and Helen had always liked the view from here: the filigree-patterned iron that held the roof and the way the light bounced off the shiny tiles. They were spanking clean, wrong colour or no.

Below the balcony, the swimming pond was crowded with children, splashing and shoving, so many of them that the pool looked like a good pot of bairn soup. Helen shuddered. She'd not go near that water till Monday at least. There was bound to be a fair few of those boys and girls getting clean with a tuppenny swim instead of a nine-penny soak. The Downie family had done it themselves more than once when her mammy was on short wages in the bottling hall, those tight years after the first war if her daddy's pay packet wouldn't stretch to the four of them.

Above the weans bobbing around in the water but below the folk like Helen leaning on the balcony rail, were the acrobats. They weren't really acrobats, not from a circus or anything. They were just local laddies, but they were swinging on rings that hung over the pool, making their way up and down its length, showing off to the lasses watching in wonder. Helen remembered the days when she would have marvelled at them too: the strength it took, the confidence, the courage needed to step off the platform high above the deep end and grab for the first ring, risking a soaking if you missed it. Now all they made her think of was chimpanzees in a jungle. 'Don't get sour, Nelly,' she told herself. 'It's harmless fun.'

But she looked away anyway. She didn't want to be seen gawking at laddies in their simmets, an old married woman of twenty-seven like her who should know better. Besides, she had noticed something on the far side of the balcony that snagged her attention and made her smile. Someone in one of the cubicles had thrown his towel over the door, just like her father always did and just like her mother always gave him

3

wrong for: letting all and sundry see their towels! Showing the world their business! Helen knew what lay behind the scolding. Greet had once caught a neighbour rubbing a piece of the terrycloth between thumb and finger and overheard the verdict: 'You could spit peas through this. Your Mack'll have to stand by the fire when he gets home or he'll be chittering.'

Helen's mammy had that perfectly good towel cut up for rags before bedtime. Helen could remember Greet sitting hemming the squares as if she was sticking pins in Mrs Suttie with every stitch and she was round at the store draper at opening time Saturday morning ordering new.

The towel across the balcony had disappeared when Helen glanced back. Whoever it was was getting dried now. She saw a hand and a forearm above the door, pumping up and down as the vigour needed for drying off in all this steam got underway. She stared and then she squinted. That was ten times worse than watching a set of laddies who were only swinging about to be watched anyway, but Helen couldn't drag her eyes off what she could see above the cubicle door over on the south side. That wasn't another man who had slung his towel over the door, like Helen's daddy. That *was* Helen's daddy. That was Mack's hand, his arm. That was his head, tousled from rubbing his hair dry, his dark curls just like her sister Teenie's, until he put on his hair oil and combed it flat again.

But why was Mack in the Cally Crescent Baths? Ever since Helen had moved into her house a year past summer, the whole Downie clan came round on a Friday to revel in luxury and then sit by her fire with fish and chips. And, even before that, even on the right night, Mack had never had his bath this early. Helen glanced at the clock, steamed up and never quite telling the true time, on the short end of the balcony. Below it, the windows of the attendants' wee howff were muffled with eternally damp, grey-ish muslin so no one out here could

4

ever tell whether someone in there was watching. Until, that is, one of them swept the door open and came stamping out to threaten the bathers with extra charges for 'going over'. One of them was at it now. A thin, crooked man in a white overall and rubber-soled shoes that squeaked like tortured mice on the balcony floor was making his way up the south side peering at the chalked times on the outside of the men's doors and consulting his pocket-watch over and over again, as if the time might have changed more than a second in the second since he'd last looked.

'Give a small man a bit of power right enough,' Helen muttered to herself.

Her daddy – if it really was her daddy – clearly had some minutes left in his half-hour slot, since the attendant went by that cubicle without stopping. At the very next door though, he swiped the chalk away with the heel of his hand and then, making a fist, battered so hard on the painted panels that the children in the swimming pond below all looked up, the single movement of their many heads making Helen think of swallows turning in the summer sky. One of the acrobats, startled, let go of a ring mid-swing and was left dangling by one hand.

The only one not to react at all, it seemed, was the man behind the door.

'Ho!' the attendant called out, a boom of a sound intended to rise above the splashes and shouts. 'You've one minute to get oot or Ah'm coming in!'

With another last glance at his watch, he stalked back to his bothy and slammed the door, making the grey muslin swing once or twice before it settled.

'Somebody in bother?' said Mrs Hogg, appearing beside Helen. She was puffing and panting, rivulets of sweat already beginning to trickle down the sides of her face, minutes after her wash. She fanned the neck of the capacious housedress she had dropped over her head and settled herself against the balcony railings, spreading her drying sheet out along the banister for all the world as if it was the pulley in her own kitchen.

'Thon wee crooked mannie's forgot to do a warning,' Helen told her. 'That's what I reckon. He's found somebody past time and he's taking it out on them.'

'Forgot to do a warning?' said Mrs Hogg. 'Away! That's the only thing that lets them thole this job, Nellie. Getting to shout and stamp at folk for spinning out a soak. Bar that, it's all picking hair out drains and sweeping up toenails.'

'You've a right way with words, Mrs Hogg. I never thought on the hair in the drains till this minute. Boak!'

'Aye-aye,' said Mrs Hogg, nudging Helen. 'Here he comes again.'

The same attendant, taking a strict view of how long a minute lasted, was marching along the balcony, watch in hand and jaw off-set as though he was grinding his teeth.

'What a state to get in,' Helen said. 'Even on the busiest night. Mercy! He's unlocking the door. Oh don't look. The poor man!'

She turned away, loath to see a stranger climbing naked out of a bath, but Mrs Hogg leaned over the railings for a better view. 'Seen one, seen them all,' she said. 'But it does no harm to check, eh?'

'Speak for yourself,' Helen said. She'd never seen even one, and wasn't keen to start tonight.

'Nelly,' said Mrs Hogg, nudging again, in the back this time.

'Leave me be!' Helen said, but she softened it with a chuckle. She liked Mrs Hogg, coarse as a deck brush though she was.

'No, Nelly,' she said again, taking hold of Helen's arm and trying to turn her. Helen spread her feet wide and resisted. 'There's something wrong,' Mrs Hogg said, the quietest she'd

6

been throughout the entire outing. 'Something's no right over there. Look.'

Helen turned, still half expecting a trick and a loud shout of laughter, but Mrs Hogg wasn't joking. Over on the far side of the balcony, the attendant was that minute stumbling backwards out of the open cubicle door. When he reached the edge of the balcony, he turned and his face was whiter than his overall, his lips trembling. He bent over the railings.

'Dinnae you boak in that pond!' Mrs Hogg shouted, her voice ringing out clear and hearty despite the muffling steam. 'Dinnae you dare make a mess on all they weans!'

But he wasn't sick. He was faint. As everyone watched, he pivoted on the polished balcony rail, threatening to topple then threatening to crumple until, with him losing consciousness completely, simple gravity took over and he plunged headfirst into the pool below him, hitting the water with a smack and causing a huge gout of water to rise and wash over the changing booths at the side. His pocket watch followed him down, making a small plop beside him.

'No so bad then,' Mrs Hogg said.

The children in the swimming pool were laughing fit to drown themselves and every adult around the edge at the changing neuks, or up on the balcony at the cubicles, was either trying not to laugh or doing it behind their hands.

'Come on, Nelly,' said Mrs Hogg. 'Naeb'dy's looking. Let's see what's to do.'

Chapter 2

Helen noticed the smell before the cubicle door was fully open. Of course, the baths were always known for smells. Whether Fountainbridge folk worked at the brewery, like Greet, or the distillery, tannery, dairies, stables, the sweetie factory – which few believed was worst of all until they'd spent a shift there – or – like Helen's daddy – the abattoir, they were ready for a good wash by Thursday night. Then there was the carbolic, the thick, the pink floor soap, the drain bleach, whatever they put in the swimming pond and the foot bath, the never-dry mop heads, and the steamy damp rising off all the clothes hung on hooks to be shrugged back on again at the end of the night.

But this was something different. This smell didn't belong at the baths, although it was familiar from somewhere. Helen felt recognition and, on its heels, her stomach lurched just as Mrs Hogg, crowding in behind her to peer over her shoulder, said, 'Faugh! What's that? That's reeking. That's turning my wame, Nelly.'

By then, sight had overtaken smell as it did a moment later for Mrs Hogg too, who fell back with a quiet 'Oh!', sounding quite unlike herself. For inside the little cubicle, through swirling steam, they could see a man not exactly floating on the surface of the water, but braced and bobbing, as if he had decided to halt halfway through leaping out when the attendant banged on the door. He wasn't going to leap anywhere, though, no matter how hard anyone banged, no matter what the threat of humiliation. He was beyond embarrassment. He was beyond cares of any kind.

Later Helen would remember thinking his face was frozen, unaware of how wrong that impression would prove to be. Certainly, he wore a rictus of agony, his eyes and lips wide open and even his tongue seeming to arch like an eel in his mouth. His hands gripped the rolled edge of the bath and his feet were hard against the end panel so that his whole body was bent into an impossible shape. How his back didn't break from such an angle, she couldn't imagine.

'Is he deid?' said Mrs Hogg, still whispering.

'He must be,' Helen answered. She took one step inside and touched his arm. She didn't expect it to be cold, not with him dying in his bath as he had done, but she must have thought it would be cooling. At any rate, it was a shock to find that it was hot under her fingertips. She took another step and laid a palm on his biceps. His whole arm was as hot as . . . Helen's mind turned away from the thought that was forming, even as her eyes took in the blistered look of the skin on the front of his body, and the bright-red, smooth look of the bits of him still underwater, as angry and puffy as sunburn.

'Here,' said Mrs Hogg, nudging once more. 'Poor wee mannie.' She held a face flannel, her own, in her hand and nodded at the dead man's midsection. Helen took the square of cloth and laid it gently over his hips for his dignity. There was something off about how it settled against his skin though. There was something off about every bit of this and again her mind revolted against the growing knowledge of what that thing was.

Still, she bent and dipped the tips of her fingers into the water, then snatched them back with a hiss.

'What's he died fae?' said Mrs Hogg. 'Hert, is it? Something sudden anyway.'

10

Helen couldn't speak. She knew beyond her mind's attempt to deny it that what had killed this man wasn't sudden at all, and she didn't understand what had kept him in his bath while it happened. Why would anyone lie in water as it got hotter and hotter?

Because *that* was what had happened. That poor man's skin was as tight as the rind on a poached ham. That smell that didn't belong in the baths? That smell Helen knew so well – her, the daughter of a slaughterhouse man, brought up on cheap cuts carried home for her mammy to cook up into a stew? That smell was meat.

And the feeling of the flannel against his hips? Every cook knew not to cover skin too close or it would stick. Even his face made sense now, except that the look of his wide-open mouth and his arched tongue had been hidden with a roasted apple whenever Helen had seen it before.

'Oh, Mrs Hogg,' she said, whispering as weakly as had the other woman. 'He's boiled. That poor soul's boiled like a pudding.' Then, before she knew what she was doing, Helen barged past the other woman. If she'd been more spindly she'd have been knocked off balance, but as it was she barely rocked.

'Daddy!' Helen shouted, hammering on the next-along door. 'Faither! Mack Downie! Tell me you're out your bath. Stay out that water. Daddy, it's Helen. Tell me you're all right!'

The commotion from the fallen attendant was still going on below, with yells and laughter, and Helen could hear the sound of the man coughing his guts up too – he must have swallowed half the pond going in like he did – but her clattering the door and shouting the odds was beginning to attract a bit of attention and one of the other attendants called along the balcony, 'Here! You, lassie! Get away fae the men's side, you wee besom. You too, Missus! Get back to your own side.'

11

'Daddy!' Helen shouted again, alarmed at the silence from beyond the closed cubicle door. Then she grabbed the top edge and pulled herself up, scrabbling with her feet just like she used to do plunking apples over garden walls when she was wee.

There was a scuffle from inside and she found herself with her face pressed against a wall of white towel suddenly stretched over the gap to stop her seeing in.

'Get down!' the attendant bellowed. 'Behave yourself! What the hang do you think you're doing?'

'Aw, calm doon,' said Mrs Hogg. 'We're no having an orgy. You'd do better to think about the corpse that's dee'd in your bath here than wee Nellie getting a keek at a bare bum.'

Helen let go of the door and dropped back down, bending her knees and hanging over them with her hands braced. Of course! Her father was out of the bath. She had seen him drying himself. And so he'd held up a towel to block the view. He didn't need Helen's attentions.

She looked up one more time and thought she had to be imagining what she saw. The hand holding the towel, the hand right now lowering back behind the door, wasn't her father's or anything like it. She must have mistaken which cubicle she thought she saw him in. This hand was tiny, belonging to a boy, and it was disfigured, the last three fingers lost to some accident or injury, now no more than twisted nubs.

Helen shook away the threatening swoon – for everything suddenly seemed to belong in a nightmare – and gave her attention back to the cubicle next door. The baths' attendant was inside now and Mrs Hogg had crowded in behind him, the pair of them blocking Helen's view.

'This is—' he said. 'This can't— What— I don't—' Then Helen heard the slither and thump as he fainted, banging himself against bathtub and woodwork on his way down.

★

It took over half an hour to clear the baths completely. No one was minded to accept that their paid-for soak was to be snatched away from them and, up and down the balcony, the same arguments could be heard.

'Boiling? Chance'd be a fine thing. Ma watter's barely warm.'

'Aye, puir sowel, but it's nocht to dae wi me, pal.'

'I'll bide here till they've got him away. Keep out your road.'

It wasn't until the police came, in the person of Constable Pearson, familiar from his many years on the Fountainbridge beat, that any of the grumbling bathers could be persuaded to dress and leave, assured that they'd be given a chitty for a free bath another night as soon as the problem had been seen to. Mrs Hogg slipped away at some point too, which wasn't helpful to Helen, since she had no towel with her and no ticket and could not initially explain to Pearson what she was doing there.

The constable had discovered her in a cubicle two doors down. He thought she was washing her hands, probably, but really she was running the hot tap straight into the open plughole, testing the water. It got uncomfortably warm but nowhere close to the cauldron where that poor man still lay.

Pearson barged past, turned the tap off and set about haranguing Helen about how she had come to find the man, blustering on and hardly giving her a chance to answer before he laid into her again.

'I didn't,' she said, when at last he took a breath. 'I didn't find him. That baths mannie wrapped in the towel out there found him and he fainted and fell in the pool. Then that other baths mannie with the bleeding head saw him next and *he* fainted too. It was only me and the woman that gave me the flannel who coped.'

'And what woman was that?' Pearson asked. He looked green about the gills too. The mention of the flannel hadn't helped. It was stuck fast to the dead man's skin and changing colour in a way that even Helen didn't care to think about too closely.

'Mrs Hogg from Orwell Terrace,' she said. 'You'll know her. She's got five laddies all at the Lochrin wee school and her man's a cooper.'

'Big Bella Hogg?' said Pearson, perking up at the chance to laugh at someone. 'She's your bosom pal, is she?' He had put an emphasis on 'bosom' and Helen felt her face flushing, although she'd have said she was so hot and so upset she couldn't get any redder. She scowled at him and tried not to remember the amount of shifting and hefting it had taken to bathe the top half of Mrs Hogg's torso. It was none of his dirty business what kind of figure anyone had.

'She's my patient,' Helen said, as grandly as she could. He didn't query this out loud but he raised his eyebrows in hopes of an explanation. 'I work at Dr Strasser's surgery on Gardener's Crescent.'

'Aye?' said Pearson. 'Well, we could do with a nurse. Why don't you go in and . . . at least take the plug out and sort him.'

Helen hadn't said she was a nurse. Even *he* hadn't said she was a nurse. And, although every bit of her wanted to go in there and try to find out who that man was and what exactly had happened to him, Constable Pearson should have known better than to ask.

'Aren't you waiting for the police surgeon?' Helen said. 'Shouldn't we be sure not to disturb anything until a detective's seen him?'

Pearson's lip rolled back in scorn, turning him as ugly as an ogre from a fairytale. 'Detective?' he said. 'Police surgeon? You've been reading too many penny dreadfuls and we're far too busy to be making work for ourselves on your say-so. Tonight of all nights.'

'How? What's happened tonight?' Helen said.

14

'I've only just heard this, mind, but there's a dangerous lunatic on the loose,' Pearson said. 'You should get
yourself home safe, Miss Downie, and stop meddling in
things you don't understand. He's made his bath too hot
and killt himself, has this mannie. He needs an undertaker,
that's all.'

'Mrs Crowther,' Helen said, then paused. If this dolt of a
constable really believed that the water came out of the Cally
Crescent Baths' taps hot enough to do what had happened
here then she needed two things: she needed him out of the
way and she needed someone he would listen to. He clearly
wasn't going to listen to wee Nellie Downie fae Freer Street,
even if she was now Helen Crowther of Rosemount. 'Aye, no
bother then,' she said. 'I'll see what I can do for him till they
get here from the . . . it'll be the Co-op, is it? Has somebody
run and told them already?'

'His family should be the ones to do that,' Pearson said. 'So
you just see if you can work out who he is and then *you* run
and tell them. I'm going to stand at the front door and . . .'

Breathe fresh air and not disgrace himself by being the
third man to faint or the first one to boak, Helen finished, into
herself.

'And can I get my boss round too?' Helen said. 'Dr Strasser.
The family'll be happier if a doctor's seen him and not
just a . . .'

'Nurse, aye. Aye, whatever,' said Pearson. He hadn't
quite said it this time either. 'I better go,' he added, quite
officiously in Helen's opinion, as if standing on the steps of
the baths building doing nothing was the big job here, and
going back inside that cubicle to deal with a boiled man
was the easy option.

So, all in all, when she marched downstairs behind him
to put her penny in the telephone at the public kiosk and
tell them round at Gardener's Crescent, she was hoping

15

for one Dr Strasser rather than the other. She was hoping for Dr Sarah, rather than Dr Sam. They were both Helen's bosses, just the same, but Dr Sarah was also her friend and her champion. It was Dr Sarah who had taught Helen the word 'officious', a term she needed to use most days as she dealt with inspectors, ministers, and medical reps who had never met a lady doctor before and couldn't rise to the challenge.

'Have you had your tea?' Helen asked her when she answered the phone.

'Oh God,' she said. 'Is it Mrs Hogg? What have you found? Fungus? Maggots? Gangrene?'

'For the love of Pete. No, it's worse than all of that and it's not Mrs Hogg. Come to the baths, please Doc, and quick too.'

Chapter 3

That was the easy-osey way Helen spoke to Dr Sarah these days. The woman had no sense of decorum so it got to feeling daft, her asking Helen endless personal questions and telling her endless private matters and Helen trying to answer back all polite and respectful, like she'd been brought up to talk to doctors. She was different with Dr Strasser, because he was different with her, being a man and one with a lot of sadness and history hanging about him, but the three of them jogged along not bad together.

Helen was a medical almoner, or a welfare officer as they'd started being called on the official forms lately. She visited folk all over Fountainbridge, up and down stairs and in and out of doors. Front doors, cupboard doors, bedroom doors, even kludgy doors. She dished out leaflets, favours, threats sometimes. Or she sat in her wee office and told them what they needed to know about getting specs and fillings, walking sticks and what Dr Sarah called 'contraceptives'.

So it was probably always going to happen that she ended up a right old nosy-parker and a bit of a bossy-boots, even though she was only twenty-seven and the job had terrified her when she started it a year ago. She copied Dr Sarah as far as not giving herself the trouble of self-doubt. The doc helped people and did it in good faith, never scared to act and never slow to admit when she got it wrong. 'You're fine, Helen,' she would say if ever she saw the younger woman wavering. 'I'm fine,' Helen would tell herself in the bathroom mirror every day. She ignored the voices in her head – Greet and Mack and her cheeky wee sister, Teenie – all saying 'Get you!' and 'Hark at Lady Muck there!'

'I'm fine,' she muttered as she made her way back upstairs to the cubicles to deal with this new trial.

She had never seen the baths like this before: the swimming pond still and glassy, the soaring space silent except for the hollow knock of her own two feet. The attendants had retreated behind their nets again and they barely grunted as she called out, in passing, 'There's a doctor coming and we'll get the undertakers to see to him. Just don't lock us in if it takes a wee whiley, eh?'

Helen wished she hadn't let that thought form. As she marched back along the men's side, she could feel herself shrinking and her steps even faltered briefly before she pushed the door and went inside.

At least she could turn away from the sight of him and start going through the clothes that hung from the hook on the back of the cubicle door. She was hoping for a ration card with a name on it, or a bowling club membership or some such; she could tell from the clothes there wouldn't be a chequebook or a silver case of calling cards, even if it made any sense that a man with cards would be having a wash at the public baths on a Thursday evening. These were the clothes of a working man: boots all broken down with long wear and cheap mending; socks darned and none too clean; underclothes Helen's mammy and even Helen herself would be ashamed to hang out on a line, as grey as they were and as stained in the seams; and trousers and jacket of the coarsest, hardiest wool that was ever spun, but bagging at the knees and elbows and threadbare at the cuffs even so. The jacket pockets – Helen checked several times, for men's coats were always well provided with the things – were empty apart from a filthy handkerchief that took all her nosiness to shake out in case of initials.

18

Digging deep into the trouser pockets, Helen found her face close enough to the rough material that she could smell a very familiar smell: it was the abattoir, she was almost sure of it. It was the smell of Mack's knee when she used to clamber onto it and pretend to ride a horsey. It was the smell of his coat shoulder the times, few and far between, that he put his arms around her and patted her back while she wept for her fiancé away at the war. She was convinced that, whoever this man was, he had worked at the slaughterhouse until his untimely end tonight.

With a practical objective – that of seeing if she recognised him – she found herself able to turn and face the bath again.

She thought it would be less shocking this second time, but a cry escaped her throat as she stared at him. He was cooling, his skin sagging, and the water clouding over. Helen knew what would happen to that water if it chilled completely: there would be a layer of fat on the top to be lifted off, the way her mammy—

But she would be sick if she kept thinking along that line. The best she could do was reach under him and pull the plug out so that it didn't get a chance to happen. But Helen knew that if, somehow, this freakish event had come about by someone's malice, it would be stupid and perhaps even criminal to tamper with the evidence before her. So, instead, she looked at his face and did her best to lay it over her memories of her father's workmates, at the slaughterhouse gates, at the dominoes table in Bennet's Bar, even at the bookie's although she usually tried not to catch anyone's eye the few times Mack dragged Teenie and her in there, when Greet was on a Saturday shift for time and a half and he was spending her wage before she'd earned it.

Soberly, Helen concluded that she had never seen the man in her life. She would swear it on a Bible. For one thing, his hair grew in a widow's peak that would have stuck in her mind.

Unless he was one of those men who hid it under a bunnet. But it was usually baldy-headed sorts who did that.

Besides, he had wonderful teeth, straight and white and strong-looking, and there weren't so many in Fountain-bridge with teeth like that. Or not at his age, anyway, which Helen would hazard to be around fifty, judging by the grey hair on his chest and the youthful bulk of his shoulders. He had started to age in minor ways but had not yet lost his vigour when it was taken from him.

Next, she looked at his hands, shuddering a little as she remembered the scarred and twisted finger stumps of the little boy in the cubicle next door. This man's hands were sur-prising. It was unremarkable that his nails were clean – he was in his bath after all – but they were also neatly clipped all to the same length, neither nibbled nor broken, and there were no tobacco stains on any of his fingers. Then Helen noticed something that sent her back to his clothes for another rum-mage. He habitually wore a ring; there was an indented band around the pinkie of his right hand.

She was still rootling in his pockets for this missing ring – surely it would have initials on it? – when the door swung open, squashing her between the bundle of clothes and the panelled wall.

'Good grief!' came Dr Sarah's voice.

Helen slithered out from her trap. 'What killed him, Doc?'

'He's been boiled like a crab,' Dr Sarah said, stepping forward and putting her hand in the water. 'At least—'

'Oh no, it was too hot to bear when I found him at just gone six,' said Helen. 'Look.' She held up her own hand, bright pink and still throbbing gently from its brief immer-sion. She had been too busy to attend to it but felt it now, as much as ever.

'Hmph,' said Dr Sarah. 'I've got calamine in my bag and some of that aloe. Nelly, what on earth happened here? How could anyone kill himself this way?'

Helen hesitated before answering. The summer before last she had refused to be a good girl and mind her betters when they were set on sweeping a death under the carpet. Her stubbornness had caused no end of trouble for Dr Strasser, for Helen's family round in Upper Grove Place and for her husband downstairs at Rosemount Buildings. But the way Dr Sarah had put the question offered Helen a way out, if she chose to take it.

'Do you mean, how could anyone thole it without changing his mind when he felt himself burning?' she asked. 'Or do you mean how could anyone get the water that hot?'

Dr Sarah had been staring at the man; she had a strong stomach even for a doctor. But she turned now, staring at Helen rather blankly. 'Thank you, Nelly. Your questions have clarified things greatly.' She heaved a mighty sigh and blinked three times in quick succession. 'I have no idea how it was effected,' she said, in a brisk tone.

'It wasn't the boiler going wrong,' Helen said, turning to this question with relief. 'I ran the taps for ages into another bath along there a wee bit and it wasn't even close to that hot. Anyway, it wouldn't have been just him.'

'And it's not . . .' Dr Sarah crouched down and peered under the belly of the bath. Helen bent and looked too, but there was nothing to see.

Dr Sarah straightened again with a sheepish snort. 'I wondered if maybe there was a fire or something.'

'A fire? We'd have smelled the smoke!'

'Not a campfire!' she said. 'Something electrical.'

'There's no plugs,' Helen pointed out. She was beginning to think about it properly at last, though, and knew that *something* clever must have been done. The other bathers, attendants, acrobats and swimming children hadn't missed a procession of men carrying steaming kettles.

'Maybe there's a contraption underneath him,' Dr Sarah said. 'An element of some kind. A heating machine.'

'I don't think we should move him to check though,' said Helen. 'I think we need the police.'

Dr Sarah nodded. 'Because *no one* would choose to do this to himself. And certainly no one could do it to himself and hide how it was done. And even if he did, what you said is right. He couldn't stick with his plan. He couldn't *thole* it. I'm going downstairs to tell that bobby to summon his boss,' she said. 'To get fingerprint men and the police surgeon.'

'Good luck!' Helen said, although the truth was Constable Pearson would probably hop to it if the likes of Dr Sarah told him. 'I'm going to my mammy's,' she added. 'My father was here tonight, Doc. Two doors down. I thought it was next door but it wasn't, turns out. Still, he might have seen something.'

'Meantime,' said Dr Sarah. She shoved Helen out of the cubicle and locked herself in. Helen heard a grunt and saw the doc's head appear above the partition as she clambered up onto the edge of the bath and swung herself over, landing like a cat and waiting until she was sure she was balanced before she straightened. 'And that, Nelly, is why I wear trousers,' she said. 'No matter how many old ladies faint in the waiting room.'

Helen walked behind her along the balcony, waited while she told the attendants not to go back into where the body lay, and then followed her down the stairs to the front lobby, thinking it wasn't just the trousers. It was her short hair, her flat shoes, her Norfolk jacket – just like a man's – and her loud, confident voice. If she hadn't been married, and very happily, no one could be blamed for thinking perhaps she was more than a tomboy.

Helen didn't stay to listen to the doc harangue Constable Pearson into doing her bidding but set off along the crescent, headed for what still felt like home. It was a fine, cold, sparkling night, the kind of night where you remembered that Halloween wouldn't be long in coming and you started to look forward to all the treats. Helen's shoe soles crunched on the forming frost and her nose started to drip from the sharp air as she breathed in and out, panting a bit since she was hurrying. She hadn't exactly lied to her boss; she really did think her daddy might have seen something. But, besides that, the coincidence of him being where he shouldn't have been while something dreadful happened had rattled her. Even if she had been banging on the wrong door, wouldn't he have heard and recognised the voice of his own daughter?

Helen hurried along the quiet street, trying not to think about Constable Pearson's tale of an escaped madman, for he was surely making that up to scare her. Still, she was glad to turn into the dark close, trotting up the familiar steps to the front door of the house she'd lived in since before she could remember up until just last summer. She rapped on the wood and opened it, shouting, 'It's only me!', the words Greet and Teen used when they walked into her house, the words her aunties used when they walked into each other's houses, the same words used all over the city by girls and women who knew where they belonged.

Tonight, for the first time ever excepting the day that Helen had come home to find the door locked and all her belongings out on the landing – but they were over that little spat now – she was met not by her mother singing out, 'Come away in, Nelly!' from the kitchen but with the figure of Greet herself, meeting her daughter before the turn in the hall and barring the way.

'What are you doing here?' she demanded. 'Mack! Nelly's just waltzed in.'

'I love you too,' Helen said. 'Are we knocking and waiting now then, are we? What's wrong?' She could hear her father scuffling around in the kitchen, hastily doing something or other, and the mortifying thought struck her, that she had interrupted them getting pally.

'Where's Teen?' she asked.

'Oh, it's her you're after, is it?' said Greet. 'She's in her bedroom. Tell her to get through and help me like she said she would. *You hear?*' This last bit was shouted through the closed door of the bedroom Teenie and Helen used to share before the wedding. Helen felt her shoulders drop; it wasn't that then. Even if her parents still indulged in a cuddle after all these years, and even if they did it at half-past eight on a Thursday night, they wouldn't dream of it when Helen's sister was at home. It was Mack she needed to talk to, but she told herself it would do no harm to say hello to Teenie too.

She knocked on the door, not wanting another surprise, and edged round it. 'What's wrong with Mammy?' she said. 'She's as flustered as a budgie.'

'Nothing to do with me,' said Teen. She was lounging on the bed that used to be Helen's, the candlewick bedspread rucked up and hanging squint, and again as usual, she barely looked up. But for once she wasn't poring over a picture paper. She read those rags over and over until they were tattered but, as far as Helen had ever seen, she never opened the glass door on the family bookcase or walked along the big road to the library. Helen sometimes wondered what was waiting for Teenie when she left the school come next June, and wondered too why the question never seemed to occur to anyone else.

At least today her sister was sewing instead of daydreaming. A huge cloud of spangled fabric puffed out around her like white candy floss.

'What's that?' Helen asked her.

'Why?' Teenie replied in a tone of deep grievance. 'What's wrong with it, in your expert opinion?'

'For crying out loud, Teen, you could find an insult in a ten bob tip. It's pretty and I've never seen it before. But fine. Don't tell me.'

Sheer cussedness then made Teenie stick her needle through for safekeeping and shake the bale of fabric out so Helen could see it clearly. 'It's my costume,' she said.

'For what?' asked Helen. Teenie had never shown any interest even in the wee plays Pauline Begbie used to get up in the back green every summer holiday, and the only place this fountain of net and glitter belonged was surely a pantomime.

Teen gave her sister a pitying look. 'The church Halloween party.'

'Since when did the church have a Halloween party?' Helen said. 'I mind of Mr Lamont preaching a sermon against it not so long ago.'

'Mr Lamont!' Teenie said. 'It's not *our* church. See them doing a party!'

'Who then?' Helen said. 'Daddy'll string you up if it's the Sacred Heart.'

Teenie snorted. 'Naw. It's not them either. This is a funny wee bunch, likes of they Brethren or the ones with the hats. I can't remember what they're called really, but we call them pee-the-beds.'

'Christine Downie!' said Helen. 'That's no way to talk about any church, never mind what hats they wear.'

'It's their own stupid fault,' Teen said. 'It's on their advertisements and everything. *Continence.* I didn't know what it meant till Belinda Mackie told me. Continence! Right on a pasted-over board in front of the church where you can see it from the bus.'

Helen tried to look stern but it was the way Teenie put things, ever since she had been a wee tot. She had a knack for it. And she had a sharp eye for anyone trying not to laugh too.

'See?' she said, as Helen cheeks started to dimple. 'See, Nelly? Pee-the-beds is their own fault really. Anyway, don't worry about me having my head turned. I sit there but I don't listen to any of it.'

'Don't listen? Have you *joined* this church, Teenie? Does Daddy know?'

Teen scoffed. 'Aye, right!' she said. 'Naw, but you have to show your face a bit to get the invitation. It's worth it. We were told we could go as witches, ghosts or headless horsemen, but I'm not spending a party covered in an old sheet or sweltering away with my face buttoned inside my collar. So, witch it is.'

'How's *that* a witch?' Helen said, nodding at the sparkling frock. Then she twigged and both girls spoke in chorus, 'Glinda, the good witch of the north.'

Teenie preened and said, 'My pals'll be pea-green. Spitting.'

'At a party in a church,' Helen said.

The sarcasm was lost on Teenie. 'Aye, a church. What did I tell you? So even you can't tell me not to go, misery-guts. Mammy and Daddy are fine and don't you go telling them different, eh?'

'Speaking of Daddy,' said Helen. 'When did he get back tonight?' It was no use asking Teenie where he had been. If she knew she wouldn't tell and if she didn't know she would lie for the fun of it.

'How?' Teen said, which told Helen that he *had* been out. It really *had* been him.

'Nothing for you to worry about,' she told her sister.

So of course when Helen stepped across to the kitchen, Teen followed. Trouble was another word for fun in Teenie's world.

'Daddy,' Helen said, going over to where Mack sat with his boots off by the range. He had a paper open, but not at the football or the racing and so Helen didn't believe he'd been reading it. She was sure he had snatched it up instead of being caught . . . doing what? She let her gaze travel around the room. When it landed on the closed curtains of her parents' box bed, Greet started up again.

'And what brings you round tonight, Helen?' she said, slightly too loud and slightly too vehement. 'We'll be seeing you tomorrow anyway.'

'All of you?' said Helen. 'Is everyone coming for a bath and a fish supper same as usual?'

'How?' said Greet, sounding exactly like Teenie. There was no match for them when it came to finding offence, or at least taking it.

Helen looked at her father and was half sure he fidgeted under her gaze. 'I've just come from the baths,' she said, watching him to see what he made of it.

'Oh!' Teenie said. 'Is there something wrong with yours then? Can you not get it fixed in time for tomorrow? Cos I've got a dance on Saturday and I need to set my hair. Mammy, can I go round to Betty's and ask if I can use her spray hose tomorrow?'

She didn't wait to hear the answer but galloped off, apparently coatless since the front door immediately banged shut and bounced open again.

'Mercy, if she'd slow down and listen for one minute,' Helen said. 'There's nothing wrong at my place. There was trouble at Cally Crescent and – I don't know – I just wanted to see you all, try and calm down before I go home. Sandy still gets in a right old state if I talk to him about some things.'

Mack's lip curled. Men didn't get in states as far as he was concerned. Too young for the first war, though, and too old for the second, it was easy for him to scoff at Sandy's nerves.

'What happened at the baths?' said Greet, but she sounded wary, as though she didn't want to hear about it, not at all her usual self: eager for gossip, avid for scandal.

'A murder,' Helen said. 'A man was killed in the upstairs cubicles, right there in his bathwater. That Geordie Pearson came to clear everybody out and he thought it was a heart attack or something but I knew better and I got Mrs Dr Strasser to come. She agreed and she's been getting more polis in to see to it.'

'Drowned in his bath?' said Greet. 'That's a terrible thing.'

Helen didn't nod but didn't tell her mother the even more terrible thing. No one needed to imagine the sight she wished she had never seen.

'How did a lassie and a lady doctor know what happened over on the men's side?' said Mack. 'And what were you doing there anyway?'

Helen decided to skate over bursting in on the man. It had taken a while for her parents to stop disapproving – out loud, at least – of her job and the sights it afforded. She had no desire to set them off again. Instead, she addressed the other question. 'I was there with a patient from the surgery, helping her get a good wash since she couldn't manage it by herself.'

Greet's face softened. 'There's kind!' she said. 'There's a good girl. Nothing like a good soak in rid hot water for a poor old soul with aching joints. Who was it, Nelly?'

'But how did you come to see—?' Mack tried again.

'She's not old,' Helen said, knowing that this would divert the pair of them if anything could. 'It was Mrs Hogg from Orwell Terrace.'

She was right. Mack chuckled and Greet's face twisted up. 'Never!' she said. 'Big Bella Hogg couldn't get in one of they wee baths, the size she is now. She'll need to pay double for her coffin.'

'It was a tight squeeze right enough,' Helen said. 'I'll need to tell her she should get the bus down to Genogle. They've got sprays you can stand under.'

'But how did you come to see a man in his bath?' said Mack, like a dog with a bone. Maybe it was fatherly concern for Helen's delicate feelings. Or maybe it was because he'd heard her hammering on a cubicle door, even if it was the wrong one.

'He had a flannel laid over him, if that's what's bothering you,' she said. It was true, strictly speaking, for Helen had laid it there herself. 'But the thing is, Daddy, I think he was from your work. He hadn't his name on him anywhere but I reckon he was a slaughterman. From his clothes.'

'Eh? How?' Mack said.

'Had he his work clothes hinging?' Greet put in. 'His bloody apron?'

'No,' said Helen. 'I'm not being funny, so don't take this the wrong way, Daddy, but there's a smell. Eh, no?' She turned to Greet for support.

'What smell?' Mack said. 'Are you sitting there saying to your father that he stinks?'

'Not a bad smell,' Helen said, still not exactly lying, for the three others in his family were too used to it to mind anymore. 'Just . . . distinctive.'

'Distinctive,' he said, his voice dripping with scorn. 'Is that a word you've learned at Gardener's Crescent, is it? Or is that something *Carolyn's* taught you?'

'Ptsch!' said Greet. Helen's parents were of one mind about Carolyn, her best friend besides Dr Sarah.

'But one thing I did notice,' she said, ploughing on and ignoring them, 'is that he was in the habit of wearing a ring on his pinkie finger and I was thinking that he wouldn't wear it at work so maybe you'd know who it was that was always taking a ring off and putting it on again, at the shift change. A man in his fifties, I'd say, with a widow's peak to his hair – dark hair still, barely turning – who wears a . . . it would be a signet ring. Who is he?'

Mack's scorn had fallen away and been replaced by a look that made Helen's heart leap up into her throat. His lips moved without sound and he looked at Greet, beseechingly. He definitely knew something. And, just as definitely, he didn't want to tell his daughter.

Greet, like most women, was better at dissembling. 'Widow's peak?' she said, with her lips quirked up to one side as if she needed to chew them to help her think. 'Who would that be then? I can't think on a man with a widow's peak except that undertaker that moved away to Burntisland to run a pub. And a ring? What like of a ring, Nelly?'

'It was missing,' Helen reminded her. 'All I saw was a band of white skin where it—' She stopped.

'Where it whit?' said Mack.

Helen closed her eyes, trying to bring the scene back to mind. She was wrong. It hadn't been a band of paler skin, nor even a band of smoother skin. It had been a dent on the finger of a pale, smooth hand, pinked and stretched by the hot water, it was true, but still she should have known that, in life, it had been a thousand miles from what she was looking at now as she faced Mack: her daddy's hands, callused, work-roughened and scarred.

'Never mind,' she said. 'I think I made a mistake.'

'Telling me!' said Mack, belligerent again. 'Barging in here, shouting the odds. I'm away to Bennet's a wee bit early, get some peace.'

He started towards the box bed, where he was in the habit of flinging his coat when he came home. Helen had to pretend she wasn't watching, pretend she didn't notice how he swerved sharply and made for the hallway instead.

'Cold night like this, you need your *big* coat,' Greet said, following him. Helen heard them whispering fiercely at each other while Greet rummaged in the hall cupboard. Quick as a fish, she nipped over to the bed curtains and parted them.

There on the bed lay her daddy's weekday jacket as well as a rolled towel, still damp to the touch and smelling of the old familiar Cally Crescent carbolic when Helen sniffed it.

Chapter 4

Helen's heart lifted as she turned into her street. It always did. It was a long story how she came to live in her own wee upstairs palace at the Rosemount Colonies, with three big rooms and the bathroom too, a square of garden all her own. It missed out a lot to say it came with her job, but that usually did for anyone nosy enough to ask. It was an even longer story – or a stranger one, anyway – how her husband, Sandy, her childhood sweetheart, came to live downstairs in the lower colony with his friend Gavin, that he met in the Stalag. But it suited the three of them. Suited them to call Gavin his friend, for one thing, and now that Helen had recovered from the shock and the shame and most of the anger, she had come to understand why Sandy couldn't bring himself to stop the wedding after he came back – so changed, so profoundly changed – from the war. She wasn't one to cut off her nose to spite her face, not Helen, and she couldn't deny that a show of marriage for the world and her own quiet life behind her door had a lot to recommend it, even if sometimes she felt lonely.

More often she felt lucky. Colony houses were ideal for folk that didn't really want to run into their neighbours every day and, try as Helen might, she'd have needed to be a saint to relish chatting with Gavin as they came and went. Add the trapdoor under the square of carpet in the middle of her kitchen that let Sandy come up unseen if her family arrived unexpectedly and go back down again unseen to where he wanted to be when they were gone again, and it was hard to imagine a better setup. At least Helen had the bigger house and didn't hear them walking over her head. If sometimes she didn't take her tipped heels off and even made journeys over the floor that she didn't strictly need to, she was only human.

As the garden gate and the outside stair came into view, that dark night when the baths mystery started, Helen was bone-tired and wanted nothing more than a sit-down at her fireside and a good cup of strong tea before bed, but a tangle of questions and puzzles was snarling up in her head, making themselves into a nest there, and so she did something she had only done twice before in the last year and a bit since they all settled down here: she went round to the far side of the two houses and knocked on Gavin's door.

There was a moment of pure silence afterwards, so Helen put her mouth to the letterbox and shouted, 'It's only me. Don't worry.' She heard chairs scraping and the sound of footsteps.

'Nell?' Sandy said, standing there in his shirtsleeves and stockinged feet when he'd opened the door. 'Are you all right? Come away in. Or— Do you want me to come up? Why didn't you knock the floor?'

Of course, they had a signal. Helen knocked three times on the floor with a broom to summon him and he knocked three times with his knuckles on the underside of the trap door to warn her when he was arriving.

'I'll come in,' she said and walked past him to the kitchen, where Gavin sat in his cardigan and carpet slippers – he still felt the cold after his southern home. The remains of their dinner were on the table and Helen itched to clear the plates away and wipe out the brimming ashtray.

'Helen?' Gavin said, half standing. 'Can I get you a cup of coffee – tea?'

Helen smiled at the offer and the hasty correction even while she was shaking her head. She sat down in one of the other two chairs they kept at their table although as far as she knew they never had guests for so much as a plate of soup.

'I need to tell someone what happened tonight,' she said. 'You're the lucky winners.'

'Both of us?' said Gavin. He had stayed on his feet and even taken a step to leave the room while Helen was settling herself.

'He'll just tell you anyway,' she said. She was guessing, but she heard the endless soft murmurs of them talking to each other from morning till night, so different from Sandy's glum silence when he had slept beside Helen in the box bed at her parents' house those first few miserable months of their marriage. Sandy and Gavin were one of those couples who shared everything.

Right now, they shared a look, each wondering – Helen imagined – why she was suddenly so agreeable and accepting. The truth was that when real trouble came to call, old grievances had to step aside, and all Helen cared about right now was getting this off her chest.

'I'm going to tell you everything. Will you listen right to the end?'

After another glance had passed between them, they each nodded. Gavin lit another one of his interminable cigarettes – the man was like a kipper – and Helen launched into her tale.

She fixed her gaze on the wall above their heads and told them about the man, his burns, his missing ring, his working clothes, his gentleman's skin, Dr Sarah agreeing that he was murdered. Then she took a breath and told them about Mack in the cubicle ignoring her, Mack hiding his towel, Mack running away early to the pub rather than stay in the house and deal with his daughter.

'Oh, Helen,' Gavin said. 'But you can't think the two things are related. Surely there's a more likely explanation for why a married man is upset that his daughter caught him out of place?'

'No, but my mammy was helping him get his story straight and see me off. He's not running around with a fancy piece and stopping in to wash her perfume off before he goes home to his wife. My mammy warned him I was there and covered up when he ran out of smooth excuses. Whatever it is that they're up to, they're in it together.'

'It'll be ocht or nocht,' Sandy said. 'You know what they're like. But never mind them. A murder?'

That's what he said, but Helen heard what he meant: *another* murder.

'Dr Sarah's got the police coming and they'll sort it all out,' she told him. 'It's nothing to do with me. If you're right that my daddy being at the baths tonight was a fluke, then I'll forget all about it.'

'You're a brave one,' said Gavin. 'I've only heard about it and I'm expecting nightmares.'

Helen didn't reply. She didn't like thinking about Gavin in his bed. She bade them goodnight and went upstairs, via the two front doors. Helen didn't use the hatch. She had nothing to be ashamed of and no need to be sneaking around like something out of a pantomime.

When her hat was off and her shoes were stuffed with paper – the steam in that cubicle was like to ruin them, she found she had no appetite for tea and no energy to make up the fire and wait until it was a comfort to sit by, so she washed quickly and took herself off to her own soft bed, her bedside lamp, her library book, and the vague sadness that still engulfed her sometimes.

When she lay down in the dark, she repeated to herself the closest thing to comfort she'd ever found: she would rather have her job and this peace than a baby a year and a husband to please. She even repeated to herself the thing she made herself admit against her will: that she had it easy up here compared with them down there, hiding.

★

Fridays were always pandemonium at work, when folk who'd waited all week, expecting to feel better, suddenly decided they didn't want to chance it over the weekend. There was a queue outside on the pavement when Helen arrived at half-past eight, two young mothers with children, three old men, and a granny with a squalling baby.

'Is there anyone here just for me?' she asked. It was another cheerless day and they all looked miserable, standing there in the foggy chill, coughing. Helen didn't have the authority to let them into the doctors' waiting room before nine struck, but they could come and steam in hers.

'Are you a nurse?' said the granny with the baby.

'I'm the welfare officer,' Helen said. Every one of them turned away then and fixed their eyes on the front door up the short flight of steps. It hadn't taken long, barely a year, for the NHS welfare officers to become as tangled up with pride and shame as the lady almoners had been in the old days. No one wanted to admit they needed Helen's help. It was something she meant to talk about with her colleagues from all over the city at their next . . . meeting, she supposed, although that made it sound a bit grander than the reality.

'I'm needing a bottle for my chest,' said one of the old men and then, as if to prove it, gave a deep, rich, rattling cough.

'This one's got worms,' said the younger of the two mothers, jerking her thumb at her doleful child. The granny with the baby edged away a step or two.

'Well, you're all welcome to sit in my wee waiting room if you like,' Helen told them. 'You'll need to come back out and in the right way, mind, when the doctors are ready for you.'

All of the old men and the granny elected to follow her in through the gate and down the area steps to the basement door, but the two young women shared a look and shook their heads. Helen knew what they were thinking: it was notorious now, after the stories in the Sunday papers. Her waiting room was yet another of Edinburgh's dark places, like Mary King's Close, that underground street with the souls of the plague victims trapped forever, like the house of horrors in the West Bow whose residents were hanged and garrotted for the crimes they had carried out there.

She didn't believe there was anything left in her waiting room, no more than she thought that summoned evil could stay in the West Bow walls, or that plague could hang in the air for hundreds of years. It was lit by a bright bulb in a clean shade and the walls were distempered and lined with comfortable seats. There was a rack of useful leaflets and a wee box of picture books to stop the bairns getting crabbit.

Still, she saw the granny look around with an interest far too avid when she showed them in. The three old men settled down into their overcoat collars like owls and started coughing as if they had decided together that's what they should do.

'You can wait in my office if you like,' Helen said to the granny. The baby was getting ready to howl at the noise, which sounding like three bears growling. She held the door open and the old woman, child in arms, followed so readily she was near to trotting by the time they had gained the passage.

'What's wrong with the wee one?' Helen asked, as she was taking off her coat and hat, stowing her handbag in her desk drawer and checking the state of supplies in her work bag.

'He's stopped,' the woman said.

'Stopped what?'

'Nothing for four days and we've tried everything.'

'Oh, stopped up!' Helen said. 'Four days?'

'He's had syrup of figs, castor oil, olive oil and prune juice. I've held him over a bowl of steam till my arms gave out and there's been not so much as a gurgle.'

'Poor wee lamb,' said Helen. 'Has he stopped eating?'

'Not him,' said the grandmother, with something like pride. 'He's taken milk night and morning from my daughter-in-law and had his rice and his rusks just the same for his dinner and his tea. I put stewed rhubarb through his rice yesterday and stewed plums in his rusks.'

'Has he been sick?' Helen asked, eyeing the boy, who was sitting like a dumpling on his granny's knee, looking round with interest. He was about ten months old to her best guess – and she was getting very good at guessing – and was neatly turned out in a knitted helmet with matching jacket and leggings, all in a sturdy grey-blue wool. He didn't have rosy cheeks but neither did he look as turgid and pasty as would have been expected with four days of that diet still inside him.

'So I brought him round to the doctors to see if they could . . . What else is there?'

'They can maybe do a lavage,' Helen said, thinking *rather them than me.*

'A whit?'

'A clean out. With warm water and a bit of tubing.'

'Oh!' said the granny, clutching the baby round his middle in evident dismay. 'Oh no, I don't like the sound of that.' He twisted on her lap and gave her a look of consternation. 'I had that nasty business done when I was having my eldest and it was a horrible, horrible . . . No, I'm not letting anyone do the likes of that to him.'

The baby was still squirming, too hot and not keen on being clasped quite as tightly as his grandmother now held him, squeezing him as though for her own comfort as she relived the indignity of a pre-labour enema from goodness knows how many years ago.

'He's just wee though,' Helen said. 'He'll not know anything's wrong.'

The grandmother winced and pulled the baby even closer to her breast. He was struggling now, clearly finding this vice-like grip too much in his current ongoing discomfort.

Both women heard the sound – a soft 'pffff' like a dry puncture – followed by a wave of the stalest gas Helen had ever smelled, almost bitter in its noxiousness. Unfortunately, the woman's response to the threatened calamity was to hold him up off her lap – to hold him, that is – round his middle. Helen would always wonder if this last application of local pressure was what did it. With a thunderous roar that seemed to go on for five minutes but surely couldn't have, although it was still going on when Helen had got a thick sheet of brown paper laid on the floor underneath him, the little boy's problem resolved itself. His leggings started to bulge and droop and the clean grey-blue colour of his costume began to change in a spreading shape like a blossom.

His granny was helpless to do anything but keep holding him out at arm's length. Helen, on the other hand, while hoping that the knitter of the outfit had had a good tight tension in her pins, gave herself over to a fit of helpless laughter. The baby, riding a tidal wave of relief and far too young to be mortified, joined in and giggled with glee.

★

Dr Sarah's nose twitched when she came in after the morning surgery.

'What's that?' she said.

'Me saving you a job,' Helen said. She opened her mouth to explain but the doc was full of news and launched right into it.

'It *was* murder,' she said. 'Well done you for insisting, when that dull-witted copper was all set to ignore the signs. Not but what they'd have realised when they got him to the mortuary, I suppose. The pathologist there isn't all a-twitter like the police seem to be.'

'About what?' Helen said.

'An escapee from West House,' said Dr Sarah.

'Is that true then?' Helen said. 'I thought the copper was making up stories.' She shivered. West House was the poor wing of Edinburgh's asylum, a place she had visited once during the war, with her mentor, and a place that still intruded into her dreams from time to time. The grounds were elegant, with sweeping lawns and benches under spreading trees, but once inside the door it was hard to believe that the old bedlams could have been any worse. 'Is he dangerous?' she asked the doctor.

'I shouldn't have thought so, poor soul,' Dr Sarah said. 'He thinks he's a warlock, or perhaps a demon, and sometimes when he's at his worst he calls himself Beelzebub.'

'Crivens,' said Helen. 'I don't suppose . . . I mean, the man in the bath. Like we said, you'd have to be off your head to do that to yourself.'

'That would be neat,' Dr Sarah said, 'but I shouldn't have thought so. That deed took a lot of preparation and organising.'

'How was it done?' Helen asked. 'Did anyone tell you?'

'A heating element,' said Dr Sarah. 'Apparently, someone plunged a device into the water.'

'How on earth could they tell? Did they find it stashed away somewhere?'

'Look, do you mind if I have a fag?' said the doc. 'It's terribly . . . foosty . . . in here this morning, Nell.'

'Well done,' Helen said. Dr Sarah's attempts to learn Scots were annoying but she had a flair for it. 'Please, light up, by all means.'

Dr Sarah smoked those short little Capstans, just like so many of her patients, and after a moment the air was blue and redolent of something just slightly better than the morning's adventures.

'It was quite clever,' she said, once she'd had a good couple of puffs. 'They could tell there was something copper in the heater because of a residue on the tin of the tap fittings. Or could they tell there'd been something tin because of a residue on the copper? Well, you get the idea. And it was hot enough to make the enamel paint bubble up and come loose where it had touched too. Then there was a bit of a puddle on the floor, that I thought was water. But they're awfully good at what they do, these specialist policemen.'

'What was it?' Helen said, unsure if she wanted to hear.

'Well, not water,' said the doc. 'Paraffin? Kerosene? A spill, at any rate, of whatever they used to heat the element so far from any plugs. The fingerprint men were quite fascinated by the possibilities. They turned back into the little boys they once were.'

'Did they look for fingerprints too?'

'Oh yes,' said Dr Sarah. She shuddered. 'And found lots. I might have to say something to the health inspectors about the standards of cleaning in that place. There were fingerprints galore on the underside of the roll-top.'

'And have you heard if they've found out who he was?' said Helen. 'There was nothing in the paper this morning.'

'Not a dicky-bird,' the doc said, looking around for somewhere to stub out her fag. 'I'll take this with me, shall I?' She would have liked Helen to keep an ashtray in her office, but stayed just short of insisting.

'I don't mind if you smash it on your shoe sole and leave it in my waste-paper basket.'

'If you'd seen what burning to death looks like, you would.' Dr Sarah said. 'Remind me to tell you sometime about the widow woman and three little children in the back-to-back. That was a snuffed taper in the kindling box, but it's the same principle.'

'I've finished with this cup of tea,' Helen said, holding it out. There were just enough dregs in the bottom to douse a fag in.

'No, it's no trouble to take it with me.' Dr Sarah stood, holding her stub upright to keep from burning her fingertips. 'I say—' she began, in an airy voice.

At the same moment, suddenly realising that all this generosity about a dog-end was very suspicious, Helen said: 'What are you up to?'

'Up to?' said the doc. 'I came to tell you about the murder. Pat you on the back for your good instincts. Then the thought occurred to me that if anyone *has* found out who he is they'll know down at the morgue.'

'Aha!' said Helen. 'I see.'

'Oh, don't go all haughty on me, Nelly,' Dr Sarah said. 'Remember, this is my first brush. I wasn't here last time. And you are right in what you always said. It's hard to account for it, but if you're right there at the start you do feel involved. Besides, after the bumbling last night, I'd be a fool to say, "It's all in the hands of the wonderful bobbies".'

'I see,' said Helen again. 'And you thought flattery would win me over, did you?' She was ignoring the fact that it had, until the doc over-egged it. 'So you want to know the man's name because now you've seen him at the scene of his murder, you can't let go? And you think I've got connections among the morgue attendants?'

'Don't you?'

'Stronger than yours?'

'*Different* from mine,' said Dr Sarah. 'I'm too official. I'd have to go in through the front door and explain why I was there.'

43

'Whereas I can skulk in the back door and finagle my way to the findings?'

Helen was trying to shame her, but all the doc said was, 'Exactly,' and left the office carrying her fag end in front of her like a candle.

The worst of it was that she was right. It was true. Helen could get the back door of the Cowgate mortuary opened up anytime she chose to knock on it. She had a friend there in the figure of one Billy, the morgue attendant whom she had met during her maiden investigation the summer before and whom she had greatly impressed with her strong stomach and sharp wits.

Billy wasn't the only friend occupying her thoughts though, as she contemplated another visit to that gruesome place. She had promised Carolyn Sinclair that if ever she had reason to return, Carolyn could go along too.

It was a friendship that still surprised Helen, when she took a square look at it. Carolyn's respectable family tumbling into shame and seclusion was only one result of Helen's first adventure, and was easy enough to account for. For, while most families had unfortunate relatives to ignore, blankets having two sides after all; and while many families had black sheep to disown and deny, even among their legitimate connections; and while a few unfortunate families had read their name in the newspapers, when policemen's evidence as given in court was quoted there, all three calamities befalling the Sinclairs in one giant scandal had put them far beyond Edinburgh's social pale.

Carolyn herself was blameless and had no intention of hanging her head in borrowed guilt. Indeed, she had turned her ousting from the tennis club and old girls' association into the chance to live a life more useful, if less secure. Or as she put it, 'more fun and less stuffy'. Instead of mourning the land-army uniform of her war years and traipsing around

Edinburgh's drawing rooms, baited to hook a husband, she now worked as a gardener in the Botanics down at Inverleith and lived in a flat carved out of a big house, the whole of which was practically identical to her girlhood home. Carolyn claimed to be happier in her attic corner than she had ever been with run of the grand rooms.

Helen looked at her watch and calculated how to pull it off. Carolyn had no telephone in her flat and nor had Helen in her house either, but if she rang the head gardener's number at just on three, when Carolyn finished her shift, it was usually possible to catch her while she was washing her hands and changing her boots in the cloakroom next door. Then the pair could meet on the High Street well before four and get to the mortuary during the two hours when the day and back shift overlapped, giving Helen a two-in-three chance of catching Billy.

If he was on nights, she would have to wait until next week, since her nerve wasn't equal to visiting the Cowgate in the dark, either the morgue itself or even just the narrow streets and slits of closes where all manner of nocturnal lives were led by all manner of people. Of course, as a welfare officer, she dealt with most of them regularly – tramps, drunks, working girls and runaways – but she made sure to do it on bright mornings. In fact, she needed to get her skates on right now and take herself down to the men's hostel at Grindlay Street, where she was meeting the dreaded Mrs Bonny from the office at Johnston Terrace to see about getting them some new mattresses after they'd succumbed to a bout of fleas and bedbugs that belonged in the Bible, not in any place Helen had a say about.

She belted her overcoat extra firmly, girding herself. Mrs Bonny's philosophy was that no form was ever filled in well enough and no sum was too small to quibble over. You'd think it was all coming out of her pocket, and her with nine starving weans in the house. Helen's view was that the service was meant to keep folk well and make them better and nobody should need smelling salts if she tried to use it so.

★

She made it back by a quarter to three, locked herself in the basement cloakroom, took her blouse off and scrubbed her body until she glowed. Those poor men! Then she went back to her office and got the call put through to the Botanics just as three was striking.

'Oh hello,' she said. 'This is Mrs Crowther, from the welfare office at the Gardener's Crescent surgery. Might I have a word with Miss Sinclair if she's still there?'

'You don't get two cracks at that one,' came the head gardener's voice. 'If you're needing Carolyn to cook up your night out dancing, just say so. Ho! Sinclair! It's your pal. Mind and don't take too long.'

'Does he really call you "Sinclair"?' Helen said, when she heard Carolyn lift the receiver.

'Like the army. Quite thrilling.'

Helen smiled. Carolyn might have left the tennis clubs of Edinburgh behind her, but she still spoke like a bright young thing.

'What can I do for you, Nelly?' she went on. 'If you're really pining for a dance, I need to warn you I've been washing greenhouse glass all day and it's mulching tomorrow.'

Helen heard the head gardener's voice in the background offering Carolyn the chance to plant bulbs instead.

'I should jolly well think not!' Carolyn threw over her shoulder. 'Even Sisyphus didn't have to bend double.' She came back to the telephone. 'A thousand daffs to go in,' she said. 'I'll stick with the mulching. But what *do* you want?'

'Not a dancing partner,' said Helen. 'How about a chum to the morgue?'

'Really?' Carolyn sounded as fresh as paint, for all she moaned about what her job took out of her. 'What's afoot? It's not a baby, is it? I don't think I could stand a baby.'

'It's a man in his fifties. But no treat to behold, I warn you.'

'I'll be at St Giles' in twenty minutes,' Carolyn said, and rang off without a goodbye, certainly without giving Helen the chance to say that no arrangement had been made and they might both be sent off with a flea in their ears by one of Billy's workmates if they were unlucky.

Not though, Helen thought, by Billy himself. She was all alone in the room but she felt herself blushing. Even if she had Carolyn in tow, she knew Billy would be pleased to see her and eager to help. She stopped halfway through putting her hat back on and stared at her reflection in the mirror above her fireplace. She would have gaped if she hadn't a hatpin in her mouth. She hoped he wouldn't think Carolyn had been brought as some kind of a chaperone.

Surely not. Surely he felt the same friendly interest in Helen that she felt in him. He had an unusual job, like she did, and came from the same world as her, the southside tenements. They were near the same age and they had conspired to right a wrong together.

True, when they had run into each other at Christmastime on Princes Street he had gone so far as asking if Helen would join him for a cup of tea. She might have expected a morgue attendant to be keenly attuned to the presence or absence of finger rings – or so Helen's aunties always hinted over cups of tea on Thursday nights at her mammy's – but, if Billy had noticed the gold band on Helen's left hand, he hadn't mentioned it. She hoped it was that: either he hadn't looked or he hadn't noticed. She hoped it wasn't that he didn't care.

She hoped it wasn't that somehow he'd got the idea that she wasn't as married as all that.

'Even if it's true,' she said to herself, digging her hatpin in firmly.

*

Carolyn was sitting on the low wall to one side of the cathedral steps, still wearing her twill trousers and a muffler tied in a knot like Mack wore his, the ends stuffed down inside her donkey jacket. She would have looked like a scarecrow if it wasn't for the bright blonde hair twisted up into a French knot, the gold rings in her ears and the swipe of scarlet lipstick. As it was, no one knew what to make of her. Helen saw people look, look again and then whisper to their companions to look too.

'You've a right knack for getting noticed,' she said, walking up.

Carolyn sprang to her feet – at least she had changed her work boots for brogues – and kissed her friend on both cheeks, before tucking her hand into Helen's elbow and dragging her away. 'Let's go,' she said. 'It's almost time for choral evensong and choirs make me weep. So tell me more about this dead man instead.'

'Evensong!' said Helen. 'It's a church of Scotland. He was boiled in his bath.'

Carolyn's footsteps faltered. 'He . . . got overly hot? He— He died of heatstroke? I thought you could only get heatstroke from the sun? Or why don't train drivers drop like flies?'

'Stokers,' said Helen. 'Not drivers. No, he wasn't "overly hot". He was murdered by someone who put a heating element in the water and left him there until he boiled.'

'And why do you want to see him?' Carolyn's voice sounded thick. She would never make it to the cold-storage room if her gall was on the rise already.

48

'I've seen him,' said Helen. 'I found him. I want to see him again because Dr Sarah's keen to know who he is and there was nothing in the papers.'

'Are you sure that's the whole story?' Carolyn said. 'You sound rather grim, you know.' She was a bit daft sometimes, but she was no fool.

'Isn't that enough?' said Helen, plunging off down Niddry Street, leaving Carolyn to catch up. Perhaps she wanted to outrun the memory of Mack's damp towel and shifty looks. Or perhaps she was simply well aware that this part of town was nowhere to dally.

Chapter 5

'There's a sight for sore eyes!' It was Billy himself who answered the door, beaming from ear to ear. He wore the cotton smock and drawstring trousers Helen had seen last time and the short white wellington boots that made him look like a butcher. Today he also had a mask tied behind his head with tapes, although it was currently pushed down under his chin. 'And two for the price of one, eh?' he said, with a wink for Carolyn. 'Who's this then?'

'Miss Sinclair,' Carolyn said, holding out her hand. 'Yes, *those* Sinclairs,' she added, at his look. 'But not *that* one. Or even *that* one. I'm the *other* one and I feel no shame.'

'Right you are,' Billy said. 'Well, come away in and brighten my day, why don't youse both? It's been a heecher.'

'We know about the boiled man,' Carolyn said.

'Him!' said Billy. '*He's* dropped right off the docket. But, aye, that's what we're calling him too.'

'Haven't you found out his name yet?' Carolyn asked. 'We hoped to learn it from you.'

Billy was ushering the women inside and didn't immediately answer. Once the door was closed, he wiped his forehead with a damp hand, leaving it shining, and said, 'That would still leave us one short. We've two corpses and no names for either.'

'Two!' Carolyn said.

'The boiled man and this new one. We're waiting till someone comes and claims them, which they will. Until then it's Joe Bloggs 1 and Joe Bloggs 2.'

'It's good to know that you expect relatives,' Carolyn said. 'One would hate to think of anyone not being missed.'

'Oh, there's plenty not missed,' Billy said, leading them along the passageway to where Helen knew the attendants' staffroom was to be found. 'Or not wanted, if there's going to be a bill for burying them. But you can tell them apart from the others. These two were both used to gentle living and that sort don't get buried on the parish. Someone'll come for them, sooner or later. Here you go. You wait in here and make yourselves comfy. Help yourselves to anything. I'll not be long.'

Carolyn managed not to grimace until he had gone and Helen managed not to laugh at her face. For there was nothing appealing about the battered kettle piping away on top of the little stove, the collection of grubby teacups, the rusted caddy, the lidless sugar bowl with its spoon barnacled an inch deep in crust, the bottle of milk almost finished and what was left in it looking thin and blue.

'Are you going to be all right?' Helen asked her friend. 'Although I must say, it doesn't smell too bad today. It was summer when I was here before.'

'I'm fine,' said Carolyn. 'I wonder what's come up to put a boiled man in the shade.'

They did not have to wait long to find out. Carolyn hadn't finished reading the many leaflets on the little painted table and the many notices hanging by pins from the felt board – 'They've got a darts team and a cycling club' – when Billy was back, along with a colleague who dropped into a chair and snatched the little cap off his head as if it was full of itching powder. He was a fat man and his bald head shone with sweat, as well as there being dark patches spreading over his cotton costume.

'Nelly,' he said. 'Heard a lot about you. You sorted that poor . . .' Then he glanced at Carolyn and fell silent.

'She was my half-sister,' Carolyn said. 'Nell told me we might have been twins at the time and I see from your face that it's true.'

The fat man shook himself. 'Sorry,' he said. 'It's a curse in this job, having a memory for faces like I've got. I recognise relatives all over the city.'

Helen was only half paying attention. Had he heard a lot about her from Billy? Did Billy talk about her? Or was it merely that she was mixed up in the most notorious murder to have befallen Edinburgh for many a long year?

Billy handed his colleague a cup of tea and sat down, taking a noisy draught of his own. 'At least we're done nice and early, Tam,' he said. 'We're not going back after this, girls. The doctor's that scunnered he's away up Arthur's Seat for a walk.'

'*He's* scunnered?' said Tam. 'It wasn't him had to—' He stopped talking, as Billy shushed him.

'Had to what?' said Helen. If Carolyn wanted to come to the mortuary, she should be prepared for the business that went on there.

'Weigh the stomach contents,' said Tam. 'And pack them, till the polis have been and seen it all.'

'Don't you always do that?' said Carolyn. 'If it's a murder? I've a terrible weakness for the worst sort of Sunday paper and they take great delight in listing the last meal of some poor unfortunate who's been put to death by lurid means.'

'They'll have a field day with this one,' Billy said.

'How come?' said Helen. She had always had what her mentor had called a healthy curiosity and what Greet called a twitching neb. She dearly wanted to know what kind of corpse could send a pathologist reeling off for fresh air.

'We've never seen a man killed like this before,' said Tam. He had got the measure of both the girls – Carolyn with her love of scandal sheets and Helen with her neb – and was teasing them.

'Tam,' said Billy, in a weary voice. He stirred another spoonful of sugar into his tea and took a gulp.

'Was he all there?' said Carolyn, determined to look unperturbed.

'Ocht, aye!' said Tam. 'It would take more than dismembered bits to turn us after all these years, eh Billy?' Billy said nothing. 'One of his pinkies was near wrenched off,' Tam continued, 'but he was all there and then some.'

'What does that mean?' said Carolyn. 'A fat man?'

'Look, d'youse want to see him for yourselves?' Billy said, banging his cup down. He hadn't taken to her friend, it occurred to Helen. He couldn't see the good heart under all that brittle prattling.

'I'm game,' said Carolyn. 'I've never seen a dead body. I was in the Land Army. It was my sister who got the warden's job.'

'I don't think that's nice,' Helen said. 'This isn't a zoo. And the man's relatives wouldn't like to think we'd been gawping at him.'

'Look,' Billy said again, 'if you're squeamish about "gawping" you can tell yourself you're coming to see if you recognise him. You've lived in this city all your life and stranger things have happened.'

So they trooped through to the cold store, Helen with measured pace since she had been before and knew what waited there, Carolyn a bit more faltering but with a determined set to her chin. Billy hauled out one of the metal drawer fronts and waited for the ironing-board legs to drop down before he settled the trolley squarely on the tiled floor with a little nudge or two to still the creaking.

The shrouded shape was mountainous under the green sheet. Helen felt herself go through the same set of peculiar thoughts and emotions as last time. She glanced and saw a person, plain and simple. Dr Strasser had talked one day in the garden about . . . Oh, what did he call it? . . .

the way everyone sees human forms in clouds and trees and splashes of ink. So of course this outline looked that way. But then there was the uncanny stillness of the green hummocks and valleys. Helen's mind slowly began to understand that whatever a person was, that thing was missing from here. Here was something both human and not: a person, undeniably, and not a person, beyond a shadow of a doubt.

'Ready?' Billy said and, after getting a nod from both girls, he folded the sheet back and displayed the man from his scalp to his waist.

Carolyn gasped. 'Oh my God!' she said. 'What happened to him?'

'That's the PM wounds and stitches,' Billy said. 'That's not what he died fae.'

'Oh Lord,' Carolyn said. 'When his family comes, will you . . . do something?'

'We do our best,' said Tam, in a gentler voice than he'd been using.

'And you think they'll come because he's a well-to-do gentleman?' Helen said, remembering Billy's prediction. 'But didn't he have any cards on him? Or letters in his pocket? Isn't it strange that one man so far from indigent would be anonymous, never mind two?'

'It surely is,' Billy said. 'And there's no way he's the one spare man we're half waiting for.'

Helen frowned briefly, then nodded. 'The patient that got out of West House?'

'Oh aye, I'd heard that,' said Tam. 'What was his name again?'

'His name's no business of ours,' Billy said. 'No one in that place ever got so fat and sleek.' He spoke vehemently, almost bitterly, and Helen wondered how often inmates from West House ended up here in the Cowgate. 'Nor kept his hair so neat or got such a good shave,' Billy went on. She gave him a kind smile, moved by his compassion, but was nonplussed to see his face snap shut.

'Yes,' said Carolyn, seeing all of that and stepping in to smooth the moment over. 'He looks very . . .'

'Not trauchled,' Tam said. He was helping too.

'And *how* did he die?' said Carolyn. 'What was it that upset the doctor?'

It was a good question and served to move both Helen and Billy past their ruffled moment. Apart from the rough cuts and workaday stitches in his head and torso the man was unmarked, the great mountain of his belly and the sliding pouches of his chest as smooth and pale as the skin of a baby.

'What was it Slice said?' asked Tam. 'It was a new one on me.'

'Who is Slice?' said Carolyn.

'Dr Sallis, the pathologist,' said Helen. 'Don't laugh! You'll only encourage them.'

'What did he say?' said Carolyn.

'Fag wah?' said Tam. 'Wag frah?'

'Frag wah,' Billy said.

'Oh, good God,' said Carolyn. '*Foie gras*? Is that what you meant about weighing the . . . ?' She turned so sharply on the ball of her foot that her shoe sole squeaked on the clean floor.

'What's fwag rah?' said Helen when the door had stopped swinging.

'Dae ken,' said Billy, 'but how he died was he ate and ate and ate and not by choice neither.' Helen must have looked as puzzled as she felt because he went on, 'He had food shoved down his gullet, with a club or something. His throat's all torn and he had it right in his windpipe and coming down his nose.'

'As well as seven pounds of steak and cream and chocolate cake and all sorts in his bag,' said Billy. 'Seven pounds, four ounces. I should know.'

'I don't blame the doctor then,' Helen said. 'That's a wicked thing to do and what a horrible way to die. But . . . How would you . . . Was he tied up?' Without thinking, she moved the sheet to look at the wrists, unable to understand what could make a man submit to this treatment. It was as ludicrous as lying quietly in a warming bath until it killed you.

When she had his nearest hand uncovered, she remembered what Tam had said about the injury to his little finger, and she stared until her eyes watered.

'What?' said Billy. 'What have you seen?'

'His finger got like that because someone forced a ring off it,' she said. 'Look, you can see the band where it was dug in. He must have got it when he was thinner than he ended up.'

Billy bent close and whistled. 'She's right, Tam,' he said. 'He had a ring on that pinkie.'

'So?' said Tam. He was one of those men who far preferred regaling to being regaled.

'Aye but you didn't work on the boiled man,' said Billy. 'I did and he was the same. A pinkie ring missing. Only, his still fitted him and it must have slid off quite the thing.'

'So it's two respectable professional men,' Helen said, 'neither of them with any identification on them, and what identification they usually wore removed. And they're both killed in gey funny ways, a day apart.'

'Not even a day apart,' said Billy. 'This one was killt yesterday too, just that nobody found him till this morning.'

'Aye, there was that an' all,' Tam said. 'It wasn't fresh steak and cream I was ladling out of him.'

'Did he have clothes on?' Helen said.

'Well, he did and he didn't,' said Billy. 'Nothing in the way of drawers, or a shirt and breeks, but he had an apron on and gloves and a set of gaiters.'

'A butcher's apron?' said Helen, aware that her voice had turned harsh because her throat was parched suddenly.

'Gloves like a slaughterman wears? But . . . What like gaiters, though?'

'No,' said Billy. 'Why— Oh right! That's what the boiled man had, eh no? Naw, this was a smith's apron. Thick all round and mail gloves with chamois inside.'

Helen frowned. Smiths didn't wear metal mail gloves. They would melt. 'That's not a smith's work clothes, Billy,' she said. 'That's a tanner. Those are the gloves they wear for when they get the lime off.' Her uncle was at the tannery and he liked to drone on about his work when he'd had a jar. 'I don't know if they wear gaiters, mind.'

'But he was a tanner no more than he was a smith,' said Billy. 'Apart from that one finger, look at those lily-whites.'

'Just like the boiled one right enough then,' Helen said. 'And on the same day too. But this one wasn't at the baths.'

Tam saw his chance to get back in the game. 'Naw, he was right near your bit, Nelly hen,' he said. 'He was in the gents at Maitland's Chophouse at Tollcross. The poor wee lassie on earlies found him when she went to open up for the bread-man first thing. They'll not see her back again, from what our driver was telling us when he brought the van in. She was still screaming and boaking an hour after.'

'Is this me you're traducing?' Carolyn was back. 'Sorry about that. But I had to go and sick up a slice of foie gras I ate just before the war. All better now.'

'What *is* it?' Helen said.

'It's a kind of pâté they make by tamping grain into a live goose until its liver is fit to bust,' said Carolyn. 'The farmer holds the poor creature between his knees and funnels the stuff down.'

'That sounds really horrible,' Helen said. 'You knew that and you ate it anyway?'

'I've seen the light,' Carolyn said, drily. '*Did* you recognise him, Nelly?'

Helen shook her head. 'Put him away, Billy. I've no idea who he is. Poor man. Let him be.' She was ready to leave and Carolyn was desperate to leave, regretting the impulse to visit the mortuary as she regretted few things in her breezy life, but it seemed that Tam was not done with them. And, from the unconvincingly casual look on Billy's face, Helen got the notion that they'd cooked this up together while the girls waited in the staff room.

'What do you do for fun of a Saturday night, Miss Carolyn Sinclair?' Tam said, with a sort of strained heartiness, as they all stood in the corridor not quite saying goodbye but close.

'Oh, I'm too fagged to get up to much mischief these days,' Carolyn said. Of course, she was practised at this sort of thing: brushing off suitors. Perhaps she always managed it by taking the questions at face value and addressing them with a briskness few men, surely, could withstand.

Tam was bumptious enough for anything, though. 'Floating around as light as a feather with a good strong arm to guide you, though?' he said. 'You'd manage that, wouldn't you?'

'Eh?' said Carolyn. Her mother would have fallen into a faint if she'd heard.

'Have you ever been skating?' Tam said. 'Ice skating, I mean. Not slogging round a back green with a set of wheels strapped to your gutties.'

'Ice skating?' said Carolyn. 'Um, certainly. I've skated on ponds at St Moritz when the weather was too bad to ski. Why do you ask?'

This was a different ploy: making him declare himself. Helen thought it might work too, because Tam swallowed hard and shot a look at Billy as if for guidance, or rescue maybe.

'Well, how about the four of us go to the Haymarket rink after work tomorrow and you show us how it's done in France.'

'Switzerland,' said Carolyn, but even that didn't stop him.

59

'Grand,' he said, clapping his hands together and elbowing Billy in the ribs. 'Right then, we'll meet you in the Haymarket Bar at six o'clock and make a night of it. Alright, Billy-boy?'

Helen couldn't meet his eyes and, even keeping her gaze on her own feet, she could feel her cheeks warming. Surely, *surely*, Carolyn couldn't mean to accept?

But Carolyn threw back her head and let out a trill of laughter. 'What a treat! What a jape! Do I need to go out at lunchtime and buy a pair of blades?'

'Ocht no, you can hire skates,' said Tam.

'Rented shoes,' said Carolyn, her voice beginning to burble as a proper fit of giggles threatened to overtake her. 'I can't wait. Until tomorrow, then.'

'Is that all right with you, Nelly?' Billy muttered, as Helen turned to follow her friend out.

'Um, eh, I'll. Aye!' Helen said then shot out of the open door like a rabbit.

She closed her ears against the sound of Tam's guffaws behind her, but she couldn't do anything about Carolyn. 'What a good friend he is!' was the first thing *she* said, when she finally stopped laughing. They were back in the High School yards by this time, scuttling past the men who whiled away the afternoons there till the Sally Annie opened.

'Who?' Helen said.

'Tam!' said Carolyn, starting to jog along Infirmary Street at the sight of two buses waiting near the stop at the far end. 'He can't possibly want to squire me around on his precious Saturday night, but to help his pal Billy get a date with you, he's willing to make the sacrifice.'

'What are you on about?' said Helen. 'The only reason for Mr Tam . . .'

'Oh Lord, You're right! I don't even know his name!'

'. . . for Tam *not* to ask you out would be if he had any sense of his place and didn't dare to. Why did you say yes, for the love of Pete?'

'Oh, come off it,' said Carolyn. The second bus was a 45, which would take Helen near enough to Tollcross and carry onwards to the leafy Grange. Carolyn swung up and paid both their fares before Helen could stop her. 'You can't deny there's something ruggedly irresistible about him. Those strong hands and that tuft of red chest hair above his smock!'

'Wheesht yourself!' said Helen, cringing as she heard a couple of titters from the other passengers. 'Behave! You'll be on ginger tomorrow night if this is you stone cold sober.'

'I'll be on ginger tomorrow night lest I fall over and break an ankle,' Carolyn said. 'The one and only time I came home from St Moritz in plaster, it was the skating pond that did for me, not the slopes. What are you going to wear, Nelly?'

'Padding,' Helen said. 'Thick stockings and a thick skirt and a thick jumper.'

'A skirt?' said Carolyn. 'You're more confident than I. You better put your long drawers on then.'

'Will you stop?' Helen hissed, but she had a point. Unlike Carolyn and Dr Sarah and even Teenie, Helen didn't possess any slacks, but the thought of sprawling on the ice with her skirt round her ears was enough to get her into her first pair. 'Can I come up to yours and try some trousers on?' she said, as the bus drew in to her stop. 'Or can you come to mine a wee bit early and bring some with you?'

'Hallelujah!' Carolyn said. 'At last. How are you going to broach it, by the way? At home, I mean. If I bring the trews down, can I help you?'

Helen managed to work herself up to high dudgeon on the short walk back to the surgery. Broach? She muttered to herself. *Broach?* Why exactly would she have to even *tell* Sandy

61

where she was going the following evening, much less *broach* anything?

'You look fierce.' Dr Strasser was coming along the crescent from the other end, swinging his medical bag. In her fume, Helen hadn't seen him.

'I've been at the Cowgate and I've got lots to tell,' she said, knowing this would distract him. Knowing too that he would be up to date with all of Dr Sarah's thoughts and feelings about the boiled man. It seemed to Helen that they must talk non-stop from the moment the last patient left at night to the first of them showing up in the morning, because not the slightest little titbit could be told to either without the other finding out.

'I've been at the other end,' said Dr Strasser. He ushered Helen up the main stairs and opened the front door.

'The Grassmarket?'

'Ha!' said the doc as if he thought she was joking. 'No, the other end from the morgue. I've been at a birth. Mrs Coulter has a fine big boy and her milk's in.'

'After all that,' Helen said. Mrs Coulter, not quite nineteen years old, had been at the surgery begging for nerve pills every week for the last nine months. Helen had no excuse to visit her – the district nurse would see to everything – but she'd pop round anyway to share in the happy outcome.

Dr Sarah had heard their return and came to interrogate Helen, after the usual kissing and cooing with her husband. Helen walked away into the dining room where the tea was usually laid out on cold or wet days, although both the docs had a mania for fresh air.

'And how did you get on?' Dr Sarah asked, as they came in arm and arm while Helen was pouring.

She told them everything up until the moment the ice skating discussion began and both of them listened in rapt silence, chewing and sipping but adding nothing.

'So it's two different methods,' she finished up. 'But in another way, it's two methods with a lot in common.'

'In terms of their oddness,' said Dr Strasser. 'Yes, I see what you mean. And that's not all, either. It's two men of the same age and the same station in life, is that right? Both murdered in public places, albeit quietly, and left either naked with another man's clothes nearby or wearing another man's clothes, and both with a signet ring removed.'

'Marvellous precis, darling,' said Dr Sarah. 'I wonder what's happened to the owners of the clothes, though? Will *their* bodies turn up somewhere with pinstripes and pearl cufflinks?'

'It's the rings that bother me,' said Helen. 'They must have had initials on them, but how big a coincidence it is for both men to have initials on their rings? I looked at every man's hand all the way back on the bus and not a single one of them had a ring on at all. Well, one old gentleman had gloves on, but no one else for sure.'

'Maybe the two men are related and their name starts with a Z,' said Dr Sarah. 'That would make them easier to identify and, obviously, whoever killed them doesn't want that to happen.'

'So you definitely think it's one person who did both murders?' said Helen. 'One wicked and twisted mind that came up with both those nasty plans?'

'I'm sure of it,' said Dr Sarah. 'I bet you half a crown.'

Dr Strasser laughed and Helen tried not to let the shock show on her face. Of course, being Jewish, Dr Sarah had never had the benefit of a minister thundering from the pulpit about the evils of gambling. Neither had Dr Strasser but he had lived in Edinburgh long enough to know better than opening a book on anything that moved.

'I suppose we shall find out when the police catch the rascal or rascals,' he said. 'You know you can leave it to them this time, Helen. Don't you?'

Chapter 6

She did, she did. But, on the other hand, she was a welfare officer in the Tollcross and Fountainbridge ward and the poor wee nippy who'd found the fat man in the gents might still be at work right there in the chophouse and would surely need a bit of friendly sympathy. So, instead of crossing the crescent towards home at five o'clock, Helen took the top road, heading for Maitland's. She had never been inside before. Meals out weren't a feature of life in the Downie family, then there was the war, and once she had her own place she'd hardly spend a tanner on tough meat and lukewarm mash when she could have better piping hot from her own kitchen.

She was surprised the place was open, truth to tell, and as she looked around the tables, full of men tucking into loaded plates, she wondered if they knew a corpse had lain in the place overnight, even if it was in the gents and not the scullery.

The manager or whoever he was – he had a bow tie on and a superior look to go with it – was bearing down on her where she stood on the doormat.

'Meeting someone?' he said, for all the world as if she might be a working girl come to ply her trade in his establishment.

'I'm Mrs Crowther, the welfare officer from the Gardener's Crescent surgery,' she said. 'I'm looking for the wee girl who found the—'

The manager about covered her mouth with one of his gloved hands, trying to shut her up. In the end he settled for dragging her through the back by the elbow and hissing at her all the way to button her lip, give it a rest, watch her step and most ominously of all 'not push him'. To what, Helen couldn't imagine and didn't want to guess.

'Is she here?' she asked, when they came to rest in a tiny pantry-cum-office occupying the short corridor between the dining room and the steamy, clattering kitchen.

'I had to send her home,' said the manager, tugging his cuffs. 'She was no use and like as not to tell a customer why. Youse girls have no sense of discretion. Just open the mouth and let it fall out. We'd be ruined.'

'You've never met me!' Helen said, bristling at being swept up with the waitress this way.

'Aye well,' said the manager. 'She's hardly the crème de la crème. It's all very well, but who's got to work beside them, eh? Muggins, that's who.'

Helen decided there was no point trying to pick her way through this man's grievances. 'What's her address?' she said. She opened her nurse's bag to find a bit of paper and a pencil. It was a sore point, this bag; she thought it looked like giving herself airs since she wasn't a nurse, but it had been a present from the docs and it was right handy. The manager was eyeing it now and it mollified him or at least set him down a little.

'Gardener's Crescent *medical* surgery?' he said. 'Aye well, I suppose she might need a wee powder to help her sleep, state of her this morning. She's the last stair on Lady Lawson Street and I tell you what, if she's *not* there, you come back and tell me. I said I wouldn't dock her wages but if she's out gallivanting, she's in for a shock.'

'And what's her name?' Helen said. She didn't need to write down Lady Lawson Street and she knew which end he meant. Lady Lawson Street led down towards the Grassmarket from their little patch so, for Fountainbridge folk, the last stair was at the bottom.

'Jessie Gibb,' said the manager. 'You'll tell me?'

'I'll use my sense of discretion,' Helen said, making an enemy for life and instantly kicking herself, for he'd not answer any more of her questions now. But then she thought of a way to trick him.

'Did you hear they've found out *his* name?' she said.

'Oh?'

'But then you probably knew who he was anyway if he was a regular customer.'

'I did not!' The wee pantry place was shelved all around and those shelves were full – bags of flour and meal, drums of lard, bottle after bottle of what Helen suspected was wine – but he managed to make the air ring anyway. 'I'd never clapped eyes on the man before in my life! Now get away with you and don't let me see you here again. I've a good mind to tell your bosses how you're going on.'

Helen shrugged. Let him try. Any time a patient had complained to one of the doctors about something she'd done – or not done, more likely – they'd got nowhere fast.

He didn't like being shrugged at, this manager man. He turned on his heel and battered through the swing door into the kitchen to take it out on someone there.

Helen turned the other way and marched back through the dining room towards the front door. Before she got there, though, her eye was caught by a small brass sign in the tiled area that served as a vestibule. 'Ladies', it said. Helen pushed the door open and found, not a common area with sinks and a couple of cubicles, but a single pan and basin squeezed into a room the size of a cupboard. She went back out to the little lobby again and looked at the door opposite. 'Gentlemen', said the sign. Dared she? She glanced around but no one was

67

paying her any attention. The two waiters were busy and the diners were either starving hungry or greedier than average, all their attention fixed on their plates.

Before she could talk herself out of it, Helen tried the door and, finding it unlocked, ducked inside and shot the bolt behind her.

It was slightly bigger than the ladies' facilities and had the benefit of a window, high in the wall and less than two-foot square. It also reeked of bleach, unlike the faint scent of ladies' perfumes and Izal across the way. It had clearly been scrubbed from lightbulb to floor drain after the morning's discovery.

For that reason, Helen felt no qualms about touching the lavatory lid to close it, so she could hop up and have a closer look at the window. It really was tiny and made even smaller by a cumbersome hinge. Helen could probably squeeze through, but the murderer would have to be a very slight man.

All in all, she would have concluded that the window was a red herring if it weren't for the long and obviously fresh scratches in the paint on the windowsill and, as she saw when she balanced one foot on the sink and hoisted herself up, the flattened docks and nettles at the bottom of the drainpipe outside. Of course, that might have been from the policemen but why would they have stood around right there unless they believed the murderer had passed that way?

Helen was still there, pondering, when someone rattled the door handle and made her all but overbalance. She jumped down, pulled the flush, ran some water and then shot the bolt back and opened up to find a red-faced man still with his napkin tucked into his collar.

'You're at the wrong door,' she said, stepping back with a hand at her breast as though she was shocked.

'Eh, excuse *me*,' he said, 'but I think you'll find it's *you* that's wrong.' He jabbed a finger at the 'Ladies' sign, opposite.

Helen giggled. 'Ocht, well,' she said. 'No harm done.' Then she fled.

A stranger come to Fountainbridge from another district would have been hard pressed to find the outside of the gents' lavatory window, but Helen was born and raised on these streets and she knew without thinking that it was past Fleming's yard, in by the butchers' bins.

Her feet took her to the spot within minutes. There were the flattened docks and crushed nettles and there was the wee window propped open. The tin lid was right there on the outside paintwork. For, beyond the reach of the bleach bottle and scrubbing brush that had obliterated all traces inside, she could clearly see a dusting of fine black, smeared in places and thick in the corner of the sill. It was fingerprint powder.

Helen set off again with a swelling pride at her detecting skills. She now knew that the murderer was slight and thin, as well as knowing a great deal about his two victims, if not their names. There was still much to puzzle out, though. A slight, thin murderer could have left by way of the gents' window, and might have entered that way too, but how was the body brought in? And where was it hidden until after closing time? Or, if he killed the fat man in the chophouse, where did *both* of them hide until all the cooks and waiters and the manager were gone? Well, perhaps Jessie Gibb could unravel the mystery. Helen picked up her pace and scuttled across the main road with a tram bearing down on her and the driver waving his fist and dinging his bell to get her to hurry.

The manager's cynicism was completely unwarranted, Helen discovered, when she had climbed the stair at the bottom of Lady Lawson Street. She was shown into a neat room and kitchen by a tall, thin woman in her forties, worry etched into her gathered brow, and there was Jessie Gibb, a little round person looking like a clootie dumpling the way she was tucked up inside a blanket on a chair near the range. Helen forgot about the case entirely and was only a welfare officer, in her ward – or near its edge anyway, – finding a patient in dire need of succour.

'I'm Mrs Crowther from the Gardener's Crescent surgery,' she said.

'We're under Doctor Paulson at Bristo,' said Mrs Gibb.

'Aye, but it was Fountainbridge it happened and it's all one,' Helen said. She shrugged out of her coat and sank down on the creepie at Jessie's side, taking hold of one of her plump little hands and trying to pour all of her kind concern into her eyes. 'You poor wee sausage,' she said.

Jessie gasped and let her breath go in a wail. Her face was sodden from crying, crumpled about the eyes and swollen about the nose.

'Would it help to talk about it?' Helen said. 'I know it was a terrible shock for you, but nothing shocks me, things I've seen.'

Jessie gave her mother a wary look and shook her head, biting her bottom lip with tiny sharp teeth like chips of ice. She would have a pretty smile, to go with her curls and her bonny figure.

'I'm needing to step out, as it goes,' Mrs Gibb said, whether because she dreaded to hear what her daughter had to say, or couldn't bear to hear it again, or maybe even because she knew her presence was like a blockage in a roan pipe and guessed that Jessie would only speak freely once her mother was out of earshot. 'I'm only running a message to the store. Twenty minutes is as long as I'll be. Thank you, Mrs Crowther.' And she was gone.

'Oh, Mrs Crowther!' burst out Jessie as soon as the front door had banged shut. 'Or – it's Nelly Downie, isn't it? You were years ahead of me at the school but I remember you. Oh Nelly! I wish I could pluck my eyes out and scrub them with soap. Every time I turn my head I see it again. I'm scared to go to bed tonight in case he comes in my dreams.'

'It must have been terrible,' Helen said. 'I saw him at the mortuary and I heard about all the food.'

'I don't know how I'll ever eat another bite!' said Jessie. 'My maw tried to give me chicken broth but it had these wee pearls of fat on the top and—' She pressed a hand to her mouth and swallowed hard, her eyes wide and staring.

'You poor wee button,' Helen said. 'Don't worry about it. It will fade. And it could have been worse, you know.'

It was a gamble, trying this. But it worked. Jessie was that put out at the suggestion of her having it easy that she dropped Helen's hand and, for the first time, got an interested look – not bleak and beleaguered, not strained and aghast – on her face.

'How?'

'He had an apron on, didn't he? So, you didn't have to see him naked.'

Jessie gave the tiniest little giggle. 'I've never seen a naked man.'

'So I should think!' Helen said. 'Well, he didn't have the apron on when I saw him and it was no treat.' There was another giggle, slightly bigger. 'Had you ever seen a dead person at all before?'

'Oh aye, but that was my granny, and she was in a coffin nice and tidy.'

'Aye, it's easier when it's someone you know. A dead stranger is always a jolt.' She waited. If Jessie knew the man, now would be the time to say so. When the silence continued, she tried another gambit. 'You know what I think would help? If you tried to work out how it was done.'

'How it—' The horrified look was back. 'He was choked with food. Good food from our own kitchen that I serve up every day. Oh, what am I ever going to do? I'll have to get a different job! I'll never be able to serve a steak and watch a customer put it in their mouth. I'll faint.'

'Not that, not that,' Helen said. 'How he got in there, I mean. They know the murderer came and went through the wee window because they've been at the sill with their finger-print powder.'

'Finger—?' Jessie gave a strange gasping cluck. Helen couldn't tell if it was a shriek or the start of laughter. 'Finger-prints? They've got *fingerprints*?' Then she bent over her knees and buried her face in the blanket, still laughing or shrieking, until her breath was spent and her voice was no more than a croak in her throat.

It was a pure pity that this should be the moment Mrs Gibb came back in with her messages. She thumped her basket down on the kitchen table and flew to her daughter's side, spit-ting words in Helen's direction from the corner of her mouth as she passed.

'Go and git!' she said. 'You were meant to be helping!'

Helen beat a hasty retreat, making a beeline back to the surgery, through the five o'clock tide of workers all surging homewards. She had to step off the pavement again and again, into the path of the trams, in order to keep moving.

'Docs?' she called out as soon as she was in the basement door and halfway up the back stairs. 'Are you still down here?' Both of the consulting rooms' doors were closed and the ground floor had the still, cold feeling of a done day. Right enough Dr Sarah's head appeared over the banister on the floor above, joined by her husband a moment later.

'Helen? Is everything all right?'

'Can I come up?'

'Of course, but should we come down? Is there an emergency?'

'See there, I've done it again,' Helen said, trotting up the stairs. 'You think I'm talking about what I should be concen-trating on instead of . . . Oh, what a mess!'

'Come in, come in,' said Dr Strasser. 'What on earth's wrong?' He led her, without ever actually touching her for he

72

was scrupulous that way, into the drawing room at the front of the house where the pair of them had been sitting with the newspapers the way they did every evening and with a drink because it was Friday. Also because it was Friday, the table by the windows was laid with a white cloth, crystal glasses and heavy candles for later.

'I've been to see a Mrs Gibb at Lady Lawson Street,' Helen began, sitting on the edge of the small sofa opposite the fire. Each of the doctors took up their places in the armchairs. She saw the two frowns and the shared look. 'No!' she said. 'They're not our patients. That makes it even worse. But her daughter, Jessie Gibb, is the waitress at Maitland's Chophouse that found the man this morning. I got her name and address and I went to see her and . . . I've not helped her. I said I was from here and I even said I was there to see if she was over her upset and then I upset her worse than ever and her mammy's raging. So she'll probably be round here tomorrow and get you to sack me.'

'How did you upset her?' said Dr Strasser. 'Asking questions?'

'No,' Helen said. 'The questions helped. The puzzle, you know. They gave her something else to think about.'

'So what set her off?' Dr Sarah asked.

'It was . . . hmph,' said Helen. 'That's queer. It was me mentioning fingerprints. She took hysterics suddenly.'

'She did it!' Dr Sarah exclaimed. 'She's the murderer and she hadn't thought of fingerprints until that very moment. Helen, you have cracked the case.'

Helen shook her head. 'She's too round. The murderer escaped through a wee tiny window but, if Jessie Gibb had tried it, she'd be there still. So it wasn't that but, anyway, what I'm trying to tell you is I'm sorry I used your name – the surgery's name – to go meddling.'

'Pooh and pish,' said Dr Sarah. For all her attempts to learn Scots, she still had plenty of these Southern sayings left that made her sound like a daftie. 'We'll deal with Mrs Gibb if she cuts up rough, won't we Sam? Tell us more about the puzzle.'

Helen took a deep breath and began.

'Well, it's easy,' said Dr Strasser, when she was done. 'The murderer – let's call him the thin man – scrambled through this window into the gents', then opened up the door from the inside and let the fat man enter.'

Helen sat back, letting her breath out in a huff. 'Of course,' she said. 'And then, after the fat man was dead, the thin man left the same way?' It was very straightforward suddenly. 'But we still don't know what's wrong with Jessie.'

'She must know who the thin man is,' said Dr Sarah. 'Why else would the thought of fingerprints bother her?'

'Of course,' said Helen again.

It was on her lips to tell them about Mack being at the baths and trying to deny it, for wouldn't they be able to clear up that mystery too? Before she could summon the nerve to broach it, though, Dr Sarah clapped her hands. 'Sam,' she said. 'I'm going to turn the oven off. We can have it tomorrow.'

'What?' said Dr Strasser. 'Where are we going?'

'For a cutlet at Maitland's Chophouse,' she said. 'I'll inspect the inside of the front door for deadbolts and mortice locks and what have you and you can cast an eye on the window in the gents.'

'But it's Friday,' said Dr Strasser.

'Mercy!' said Helen. 'It *is* Friday. What time is it? I'm needing to go.'

She scolded herself across the road and along the lane. Two men had died and the city police would solve their murders like they solved all the others that were committed in Edinburgh. That business last year was the exception that proved the rule and she had more than enough on her plate with her job, her house, her marriage and the barrage she was just about to get from her mammy for not being in when the family came for bath night.

Half an hour later, though, when she had been roundly scolded, told she was neglecting Sandy, and asked how long this silly job was going to carry on, she was irritated enough that she couldn't resist poking a finger in last night's lies.

'So what's the order tonight?' she said. 'Daddy, I know you're usually last seeing you work the hardest and get the muckiest but you look as clean as a whistle today. Do you want first go instead tonight?'

Sandy, sitting there as if butter wouldn't melt like he did every Friday, boggled at her. Greet shot to her feet and stamped off to run the bath. She sometimes still took a cloth round it before she let the water in, same as Cally Crescent, and Helen could never decide if it was habit or she meant to be rude.

Mack took a while to think of what to say but settled in the end on, 'Are you telling your daddy he doesn't do an honest week's work and end with an honest week's sweat?' It was a good riposte and if only he hadn't looked so relieved to have thought of it, it might have set all of Helen's concerns at bay.

Teenie, who had been quiet so far, now looked round them all and said, 'What's wrong with youse tonight? You could cut the air with a knife in here. I wish I'd gone to the dancing like I asked to.'

Chapter 7

One of the worst things about Helen's new life was that she couldn't get her washing started on a Monday before she went to work then nip back on her dinner to see to it. It wasn't the distance; it was the serge skirt and pressed blouse. It was the sheer stockings and high heels and wee hat. She couldn't bend over a copper and return to her office, flushed and damp.

But one of the *best* things about Helen's new life was that she had the drying green in her garden all to herself seven days a week and could wash on a Saturday with no neighbours looking on and sharing their opinions. She boiled her biggest pot as well as both kettles and the jeely pan, each full to the brim, as soon as she opened her eyes and, after taking out just enough for a cup of tea, she dressed in a crossover with only a petticoat underneath and fitted the mangle onto the edge of the sink. Then she threw the windows open front and back, and all the doors too, and set to it. It rankled that she still washed Sandy's clothes, but it would have looked gey queer else if Greet or Teen came knocking.

She was downstairs with the first basket before ten o'clock, pinning her sheets into sails to billow in the wind, her pillowcases and towels ice-white and as cheerful as a string of bunting. She heard Sandy's window sash go up and turned to greet him.

'I was going to give the grass its last cut later,' he said, carefully balancing a teacup on the sill and leaning his elbows on the frame.

'It could be dry by dinnertime, day like this,' Helen said. 'Can you believe it, in October? Anyway.' She looked down and wiggled her bare toes into the lush tussocks of grass. 'I like it like this, with the last of the daisies and dandelions.'

'You shouldn't stand at the sink in your bare feet,' Sandy said. 'You could slip on the wet floor.'

'I don't wet my floor when I'm washing,' said Helen. 'I'm Greet's girl, remember.'

Sandy laughed and for a moment they looked frankly at one another, acknowledging a small trickle of the great river of feeling there between them. Then Gavin closed a door somewhere inside the ground floor house, Helen's face shut down and the moment was over.

'Oh by the way,' she said, as she was turning back to the washing rope. 'I'm going out tonight. Ice skating with Carolyn.' It was true and he accepted it with barely a nod. He was turning away too.

*

By five o'clock, with the last of the damp washing draped over the pulley and the kitchen fire built up to finish it off by bedtime, Helen was standing in front of her open wardrobe, hoping to find an outfit Carolyn would agree was too chic to abandon, and thus to escape her first outing in trousers. Or perhaps the pair Carolyn brought wouldn't fit.

She was holding up a longer than usual woollen skirt against her pinny – wondering if its tight cut, while allowing her to fall down without displaying her all, would actually let her skate – when the familiar ump-tiddly-aye-lah of Carolyn's knock sounded.

'Good Lord,' Carolyn said, when the door was open. 'You weren't thinking of wearing that, were you? Billy will run a mile.'

'Shut up!' said Helen, grabbing her friend's elbow and hauling her inside. She pointed a fierce finger downwards and hissed, 'I haven't mentioned Billy. As far as them down there are concerned you and me are going out for a bit of fun and exercise. I was all set to tell him I wanted to do a recce before I recommended it to convalescing patients, but he wasn't interested one way or another.'

Carolyn sailed past the kitchen and straight into the living room, which was also Helen's bedroom. She eyed the open wardrobe door and raised one eyebrow before beginning to pluck trousers out of the carpet bag she had brought with her. There were at least four pairs. The chance of escape dwindled to a point and snuffed out. 'I've brought different sizes,' she said. 'If the small ones fit, you can keep them. Double digging has been a calamity for my *ligne*. And I've brought some socks too. Do you even own socks?'

'Bed socks,' Helen said. 'And knitted ones for inside my wellies.'

Carolyn rolled her eyes and settled onto the small sofa, all set to watch. 'Start by putting that pink jersey on top,' she said. 'You know the one.'

Three pairs of the slacks fitted, one snugly, one loosely and one, like Goldilocks' porridge, just right. These were pale grey with a herringbone pattern and a waistband exactly like a man's suit trousers, all hooks and buttons and belt loops.

'I haven't *got* a belt,' Helen said, but Carolyn was already rummaging in the carpet bag again. 'Put your black shoes on to match,' she ordered.

When Helen was belted and shod, she finally looked at herself in the long mirror on the inside of her wardrobe door.

'Oh no,' she said.

'What? Rot! You look lovely.'

'They're so . . .' Helen twisted this way and that, unable to take her eyes off the way the material clung to her hips – all the way to where her legs began. As she moved, it got even worse. 'It looks as if my bahookie's *winking*!' she said. 'I can't go out like this.'

'Exactly, and of course you can,' Carolyn said. 'You've got a lovely bottom, Nelly. Make sure and don't let Billy take your arm on the ice right away. We need to skate together for a while, ahead of the men.'

'Will you stop!' Helen said. 'This isn't funny!'

Carolyn sobered up. 'I agree,' she said. 'It's delicate and serious. Look in the pocket.'

Helen slipped both hands into the side pockets of the slacks, so much deeper than skirt pockets that she could only touch the familiar little square packet with the tips of her fingers. She snatched her hand out again and clapped it over her mouth.

'So you know what it is then,' Carolyn said. 'That's a start.'

'From work!' Helen said. 'How on earth did *you* get a hold of it? Please tell me you didn't march into a barber's.'

'Even I'm not that bold,' Carolyn said.

'And what if it was to fall out of my pocket and go spinning across the ice?'

'I didn't mean you to take it with you!' said Carolyn, springing up and coming to stand next to Helen to check her lipstick in the mirror. 'Pop it in your bedside table. I won't be picking up the carpet bag until late on tomorrow, after church. So don't worry about me disturbing you.'

'If you don't stop this right now, I'm not going to come at all.'

'Poor Billy!'

'And then Billy and Tam will be free to pick up another pair of girls, more their type,' Helen said. 'It'll take them ten minutes.'

'I'm not sure there's another girl more Billy's type in the whole of the city,' said Carolyn, sounding serious all of a sudden.

'Tam is a different story, I grant you. But I'm willing to put up with him, for your sake. How bad can a night out skating possibly be?'

These were words that would come back to haunt her.

★

The Haymarket Bar was seething with the Saturday early crowd when the girls arrived an hour later. Only the unfamiliar flapping of the trouser cuffs at her ankles had disturbed Helen on the journey down from Fountainbridge but when Billy slipped behind her and put his hands on her coat collar to help her shrug out of the thing in the crush, she felt her stomach flip over. She hadn't even had her tea, since Carolyn had scoffed and said they would all have pie and chips from the rink cafeteria later.

The wolf whistle came from Tam, but when Helen turned back Billy's eyes were warm and his mouth was open. 'Well, would you skate in a kilt?' she said, embarrassment turning her brusque. He smiled and went off to the bar to fetch their drinks, a half of shandy for her and a gin and lemon for Carolyn.

There was no chance of a seat. Laughing groups of boys and girls had commandeered all the booths while pairs, trios and quartets of men were hunched around at the small tables, smoking the air blue and glowering. So, after their glasses were drained, the men helped the girls back on with their coats and the four of them stepped out into the sparkling darkness to dart across the breadth of the junction, dodging cars, carts, trams and buses as the five busy roads met at the station. Just beyond, there was another press of people, children, girls and boys Teenie's age, young men and women, and a few older couples too, some carrying their own ice skates slung over their shoulders with casual swank.

'Good,' Carolyn said. 'If it's as busy as this on the ice there'll always be someone nearby to break my fall.'

'I won't let you fall, hen,' said Tam. 'Or at least I'll fling myself down for you to land on.' Carolyn giggled and joined the back of the queue.

Helen and Billy became separated from the other two by a crowd of girls in pleated skirts and short socks, pushing ahead in their eagerness. 'Ach, leave them,' Billy said. 'Only young once.'

'Says Grandad!' Helen retorted. She didn't mean to be pert, but she was unsettled by this outing that felt more and more like a date and couldn't help acting like Teenie who, whatever else she might be, never found herself flattened by life.

'Wait till you hear my joints creak when we get going round,' Billy said. 'It'll drown out the band.'

'Band?' said Helen, but then the crowd in front of them gave way suddenly and they were in the door, getting tickets, swapping their shoes for pairs of skates – dark-brown leather boots for the men but thrilling, white-patent bootees with pink laces for Carolyn and Helen. It looked as though she had chosen her fluffy jumper especially to match, Helen thought, looking down at herself before she tried standing up on the scarred floor by the changing bench. Billy's hand came into view as he leaned down to offer her a steady arm and, concentrating hard and laughing nervously, they stalked and staggered towards the archway that led to the rink.

'Whooft!' said Helen, when she stepped through. There was indeed a band, with trumpets and a piano and a drum kit that took up half the stage. There were also pillars and panels and a high, domed ceiling with painted plaster friezes and emblems. The spectator seats all around the edge of the ice were posher looking than the balcony at the Dominion picture house and Helen thought she could spend a very pleasant evening sitting there watching the skilled skaters whizz around the middle of the gleaming oval, while the children tottered and tumbled at the edge, looking like puppies. But, with a firm grip on her elbow, Billy stepped down from the wooden slats onto the ice and Helen had no choice but to follow.

'Bend your legs a wee bit,' he said. 'Let me pull you till you get your balance.' She wasn't the only girl, rigid as a sledge, being hauled onto the rink by her companion, but there were others, pairs with arms linked as if for the Gay Gordons, sweeping their legs out to each side in turn and flying along. Billy saw her looking, drew her into the edge and let her take hold of the wooden rail.

'Try to walk on the spot to see how it feels,' he said. Helen dutifully churned her feet out behind her, feeling as though they might shoot back and land her flat on her face.

'See?' Billy said. 'It's the same as swimming. You need to keep moving.'

'I can't swim,' Helen said.

'Well, there's *next* Saturday sorted,' said Billy. 'But we're here tonight. How do you feel about a turn? Nice and slow and I'll have hold of you.'

Working in a doctor's surgery, Helen had seen her fair share of broken legs and fractured wrists, women bearing down Gardener's Crescent with some well-grown boy or hefty girl that she hadn't carried for years but was now cradling in her arms with no effort at all as she brought the precious bundle to the doctor to get seen to. Three weeks back, Mrs Kinson had given her fifteen-year-old son a killy-coad all the way from the canal side, right up the steps and through the waiting room, and only started panting when she had set him down and sunk into a chair.

So Helen felt a good lot of wariness as she let go of the side and pushed her left foot forward, slicing into the ice with her blade. Billy had one hand under her elbow and the other across her back, and she leaned slightly in towards him as she lifted her right foot and pushed it forward in turn.

'Faster's easier,' Billy said. 'Like going a bike.'

'I can't go a bike,' said Helen. 'I've never had a bike.' But she picked up her left foot again and moved it more deliberately, not leaving so long this time before she switched to the right this time. Soon they had crossed the short end of the rink and Billy was steering her gently round the curve to keep going.

'You're a born skater,' he said. 'Here, take my hand. It's more stable that way.'

Helen turned to give him a look, suspecting him of tricking her, but this caused her to wobble so much that she snapped her eyes forward again and clutched his hand in hers, feeling the strength of his crooked arm like a beam of wood. Besides, it was her left and his right, like dancing, not like holding hands at all.

Picking up speed and gradually relaxing, which made it easier, they made three complete circuits, even overtaking a pair of shrieking girls who were clearly hoping a pair of lads would come and help them.

'It's murder on your – calves,' Helen said. She had started to say *thighs* then lost her nerve.

'We could sit out a bit and have a poke of chips and a ginger,' Billy said, turning towards the rail again.

Helen took hold of it thankfully, hauling herself up through a gap and collapsing into the nearest free seat. 'I feel like I've been carrying coal,' she said.

'You sit and rest and I'll away and get the doings,' said Billy. 'Do you see Tam and your pal? I'll get for them too and you flag them down when they pass, eh?'

But even though she spotted them, Helen couldn't wave them over because Tam and Carolyn weren't anywhere near the edge with other wary wobblers. They were whizzing around on an inner track, slicing and surging so fast that Carolyn's hair streamed out behind her. Only the acrobats doing spins and jumps were closer to the middle and Helen craned to see if Billy was near enough to call back. He shouldn't waste money buying chips and ginger to go uneaten, but no way was she going to clamber after him and twist an ankle.

The two of them were hungry enough and thirsty enough to finish the lot, as it happened. And, when Tam and Carolyn finally stopped, cheeks pink and chests heaving, they headed for the opposite side. Carolyn waved but didn't seem keen to give up the two seats together she had found. She fanned herself and mugged blowing her hair off her face and Helen nodded back and raised her bottle of ginger in salute.

'Ah, now for the good bit,' Billy said. He was wolfing down his chips, but he wiped his hands on a clean hanky, not on his trouser legs like some men, and not on his hair which always turned Helen's stomach to see. It was half-past seven now and the bairns were leaving, while the pairs of middling skaters all seemed to be joining Helen and Billy, Tam and Carolyn, in taking a rest from their exertions. That cleared the way for the experts, who were more than happy to put on a show. Dressed in bright, knitted garments that stretched along with them, they raced around, leaping and switching like butterflies, like salmon in a river, then they suddenly stopped and crouched, making themselves spin faster and faster by some magic Helen couldn't begin to understand, before breaking free in a great wheeling arc and beginning to race again.

At the edge of the oval a black-haired man stood, swaying from side to side, clearly planning something big along the expanse, waiting only for a girl in the centre to finish a set of spins before he set off. She waved at him and he began to plough towards her, pumping his arms.

85

Helen would never be able to say what happened next. It was all too quick and too muddled. The girl fell, everyone knew that, because when it was over there she still was on hands and knees on the ice, screaming. But some would claim that she took her tumble because the black-haired man made a beeline for her, whereas Helen was almost sure that she fell first, distracted by something under her feet, and that he knocked into her and went down onto his back, spinning away like a sycamore seed because the sheet of ice he had expected wasn't there for him and he couldn't stop in time.

'Help! Help!' screamed the girl on all fours in the middle of the rink and then, maybe because she was bonny and lithe, there was a crush of lads converging from all sides, knocking into each other, slipping and falling, competing to help her to her feet and only managing to send her sprawling. 'Get off me! Leave me alone!' she shouted, kicking out with her skates. 'Help *him*! Help *him*!'

The would-be saviours turned to look at the black-haired man who was back on his feet and skating towards her again. 'I'm fine, Jeanette,' he said. 'What's wrong?' The crowd in the rink-side seats had started to twitter but silence fell at that, for everyone wanted to know.

'Not you,' said Jeanette. She was sitting on her bottom on the ice now, with her legs stretched out to either side and her feet pigeon-toed under the weight of her blades. 'Him!'

Helen couldn't see her point a finger anywhere but all the lads gathered around suddenly looked downwards, as if they were scolded bairns. One whistled and one reeled away turning green.

'Somebody get the police,' said the black-haired man.

'I'm off-duty,' came a voice from near where Helen sat. Constable Pearson stood up and lumbered towards the nearest break in the barrier. Then he stopped and shouted, 'Somebody go and get me a curling kipper, eh?'

Helen was mystified but Billy stood and clumped away on his skates in the direction of the shoe counter.

'Youse lot get back,' Pearson shouted from the edge, where he was tugging off his skates. 'Get off the ice, the lot of you. You too, hen,' he added in a gentler voice. Jeanette clambered to her feet, helped by a willing volunteer on each side, and the three of them skated slowly towards the seats.

A man on the rink's staff had finally realised something was going on and came marching and shouting the odds towards Constable Pearson, only to be headed off. Then Billy was back with a sheaf of what looked like shoe soles and, Helen saw, were indeed just that. Constable Pearson fitted one onto his left foot over his sock and stepped onto the rink, paddling along with his right foot as if he was rowing with one oar.

Billy dropped Helen's shoes and his own boots down at her feet as well as two more of the 'kippers'.

'Get this on and come over with me to see what's what,' he said. 'They might need your kind of doctor and they might need mine. I've an awfy feeling about this, Nell.'

Helen unlaced the skates and got her own shoes on in record time, then snapped the extra sole on top and followed Billy down onto the ice. It was even colder through her smart brogues and the sticky sole took a bit of concentration before she could get going.

'You again,' said Pearson as he saw her drawing near. 'And who's this?'

'I'm from the—' Billy said, then he fell silent and stood staring down. Helen came to a halt beside him and steeled herself before looking downwards too.

The ice was not quite white anywhere. There were grey and yellow shadows running through it, some deep and some shallow, and then the busy Friday night had turned the very top layer to slush and powder under all the blades. But still it was clear enough to see what Helen was staring at now: a small dark blob, a much bigger pinky-blue blob beside it and, deep below both – or perhaps not deep below at all, as there was no way to tell how deep the ice was, same as water – but, in any case, beyond the two blobs, the dark one and the pinky-blue one, there were three columns sticking out, bent like tin chimneys. And then closest to the surface than all of that – the three columns and the two blobs – was another column, straighter than the rest and tapering into fronds that almost broke the skin of ice encasing them. And one of these fronds – these *fingers* as Helen could no longer deny – was thick and discoloured with a white dent all around from the rough removal of a signet ring. Helen blinked. Two arms, two legs, a dark head and a pink, naked torso.

'It's another one,' she breathed to Billy. 'A third one.'

'A frozen man,' Billy breathed back. 'You're going to need all the big guns up here, Pearsy,' he added, louder. 'You should get on the blower to them right now.'

'A body frozen in the ice?' said a voice behind Helen. She turned to see a small man in a jersey and flannels with his muffler tucked in at his V-neck. He had a notebook in one hand and a stub of a pencil in the other. 'Is that what you just said?' he demanded. 'What's your name and who are you?'

'Who are *you*?' said Constable Pearson.

'Reg Maitland, from the *Evening News*,' said the man. 'And I'm never off-duty, me.'

Chapter 8

Edinburgh went mad for the story of the frozen man at Haymarket ice rink and when news of the boiled man and the choked man leaked out and the three stories got joined together, reporters came through from Glasgow and down from Dundee. Everyone in Upper Grove Place agreed that they wouldn't be surprised if press was on its way from London, stymied by the Sunday trains, but not to be stopped for long.

After dinner, Teenie was packed off to her pal's house with money for ice cream, although the weather had taken a bitter turn and no doubt she would save it up to spend at Woolworth's bargain counter on Monday morning.

Helen had explained away Sandy's absence by saying he'd a bad foot from standing on a nail at work and was keeping off it for the day. So it was Greet, Mack and Helen only who sat in the kitchen turning the thing over and over, round and round. At least, Helen did. Greet and Mack tried every way and then some to change the subject. Helen ploughed on.

'And they still don't know who any of these poor souls are,' she said. 'But somebody must miss them, eh no?' This was met with a determined silence. 'Don't know who they are and don't know whose clothes they were found with. I mean, the frozen man didn't have any clothes on at all, but that's at least five lots of people keeping quiet when they should be speaking up.'

'Where d'you get five?' said Mack. 'It's onl—'

Greet shushed him.

'The family of the boiled man,' Helen said, making as if she hadn't heard her father's slip or noticed her mother's attempts to cover it. 'The family of the choked man, the family of the frozen man, the working man who left his clothes in the baths and the tanner who's lost his apron.'

'They aprons and gaiters are dear too,' said Greet. 'They're a big outlay when a laddie starts his apprenticeship. I mind when my brother—'

'Daddy,' Helen said, 'You'd notice quick enough if any of *your* clothes went missing, wouldn't you?'

'Me?' said Mack, startled out of the silence his wife had just shoved him into.

He didn't quite manage to look innocent and Helen didn't quite manage not to look accusing. The memory of that damp terry towelling under her fingers made her rub her hand on her skirt as if to wipe it dry. And suddenly she was tired of hinting round it all. It wasn't as if her daddy could actually be mixed up in any of this. 'Look, I know you were at the baths on Thursday night,' she said, making her voice as strong and stern as she could get it, like when she had to tell a proud woman to wash her weans or get a nit comb. 'I saw you, Daddy. And I know *you* know he was there too, Mammy. I'm turning inside out fretting about what's going on.'

Greet folded in on herself in a way Helen had never seen her do before. Mack took another tack; he started to bluster. 'Oh, and was I at the ice rink too?' he demanded. 'Was I stuffing my gob in Maitland's Chophouse yesterday? Was I—'

'Wheesht!' Greet sent the word out like a spear and Mack reared back from it, making his chair creak.

Helen stared, aghast, first at one of her parents and then at the other. 'There's a fourth, isn't there?' she said. 'That's why me saying "five" surprised you there. You were going to say "It's only four", weren't you? And then you were just about to say something about the fourth one till Mammy stopped you. Oh, you're not cut out for this, Daddy. You might as well tell me now.'

'Don't you speak to me like that under my roof,' Mack thundered.

Helen remembered him saying that to Teenie once about a dance or a perm or somesuch and Teen snapping back at him, that it wasn't his roof, it was the landlord's, and he should have said 'under my ceiling'. She never understood where Teenie got her nerve. Right now, *her* throat was dry as she answered him and her voice wavered.

'How come you're not shouting at Mammy for saying "Wheesht" to you? It's cos she saved your skin, eh no?'

'Get out of my house!' Mack said, standing up and pointing towards the door.

'And here's me thinking maybe family feeling should stop me from reporting what I saw,' said Helen. 'Shows what I know.' She was shocked to hear this coming out of her mouth and, as her father stood up, she cringed as if she might be about to feel the back of his hand.

'Nelly, maybe you should go on home,' Greet said.

'Oh, so you're flinging me out too, are you?' Helen demanded. 'For being right? For knowing something's up?'

'Let your father and me talk,' Gret said. 'Promise me you won't say anything about this to anyone, at least till tomorrow. There's a good girl, eh?'

Helen's eyes filled with instant tears. Greet had never spoken to either of her daughters like that in their lives – wheedling and craven – and, hearing it, Helen realised she had somehow gone across and was now aligned with factors and landlords, folk who had to be handled gently. She flushed and was shaking as she stood. 'If you won't treat me like one of the family and tell me, then why should I treat you different from anyone else keeping secrets?' she demanded, trying to lash out at her own shame. 'It's three murders and youse know something about it, don't you? You can't have it both ways.'

Mack jabbed a finger at the door but neither of them said anything.

Helen was close to tears now. Dr Strasser and Dr Sarah never spoke to anyone like that, nor Carolyn neither. And Gavin would never let words so sharp and mean pass his lips. She had let herself down, for all her airs. She had proved that she'd left the tenements and now sat behind a desk in her own office, but she was as rough as any other Freer Street wean if scratched, and always would be.

She kept her head down, avoiding neighbours' greetings as she hurried to the road end and turned for Rosemount. Gavin's windows were lit behind his drawn curtains and there was a burble of music from his wireless as well as the usual scent of the never-ending cigarettes wafting through the cracked sash beside her front steps. She crept up as quietly as her shoes would let her and eased the key round in the lock. She would honour her mother's request and say nothing to anyone, but it would be that much easier if there was no one around to tell.

*

Waking in the morning, it was impossible not to feel a bit brighter. The sun was up, sending shafts of light along the curtain hems in her big room, and it was Monday – the start of another week of work and purpose. Besides, Helen couldn't ever wake, alone in that big box bed, with the smooth sheets and the plump pillows, without feeling as if she was wrapped in luxury. She swung her legs round and wriggled her toes into her slippers, then swept her

warm dressing gown round like a cape and belted it firmly. It had been a Christmas present from the Strassers,
this dressing gown, and Helen had never seen the like of
it. With its quilted lining, not to mention the braid on both
cuffs and pocket, it was more like an evening coat than
something to wear while building up the fire and bringing
the milk in.

As she bent to lift the bottle from the step today, she happened to glance along the length of road, her eyes drawn by
the sight of two figures advancing. Folk usually *left* the street
in the morning, since there was nothing back here for them to
come to, and none of the neighbours worked nights or did a
shift of early cleaning.

But these weren't neighbours. Helen jerked upright, only
just managing not to let the milk bottle slip through her fingers. She turned on her heel and fled inside, banging the door
behind her. Then she took her broom and thumped hard,
three times, on the kitchen floor. It was her signal to get Sandy
upstairs in a hurry. She prayed they were awake to hear it.

Rather than wring her hands, she got the kettle on and
spooned tea – too much for her, just right for them – into the
big pot, set the fresh milk down on a doily in the middle of
the table and let down the pulley to loop the last of Saturday's
wash up out of the way, listening all the while. One ear was
trained on the outside steps, dreading the tramp of clogs and
boots approaching the front door, while the other keened down
through the floor for Sandy's tread on the rungs of the ladder.

She waited as long as she could bear to, feeling her colour
rise, and then rolled back the carpet and was flooded with a
wave of relief to see the trap door dislodge and begin to rise.

'Hurry up!' she said. 'Mack and Greet!'

Sandy came up the rest of the ladder like a monkey and
Helen had just got the carpet rolling again when the front
door opened and Greet called, 'Yoo-hoooo!'

'What do they want?' Sandy said. He went to loop his braces up over his shirt sleeves but Helen mimed at him to leave them and shooed him out the door into the hall to greet his in-laws.

'This is a surprise,' she heard him say, then she turned to tend to the kettle, just beginning to spit.

'You never told Sandy?' Greet said, coming in and choosing the best chair, near the fire and handy to put her feet up on the spar of the table.

'You asked me not to tell anyone,' Helen said.

Greet shook her head and sucked her teeth. 'You've no idea how to be a wife,' she said. 'Don't think you weren't seen.'

Helen's stomach dropped, but she kept her eyes trained on the stream of peat-coloured tea she was pouring into the four cups and said nothing.

'Seen doing what?' Sandy was back. 'Didn't tell me what?' He was making a good job of his lines.

'Two different things,' Mack said, settling into the next best chair on the other side of the fire. 'Although no doubt she never told you what she was up to on Saturday night either. Take a look at one of the papers you sweep out of the gutter today, Sandy lad. She was right there.'

Sandy blinked and raised his shoulders at Helen in a bewildered shrug. 'They think you don't know I went ice skating with Carolyn,' she said.

'And the rest of it,' said Mack. 'Is that right what Mamie Tourock told your mammy at the close-mouth the now?'

'What was that then?' Helen said. She seized the milk bottle back from Greet, who had been about to pour the top into her cup. Helen shook the cream through and handed it back to her mother with a sweet smile that fooled neither of them.

'She was gallivanting,' Mack said. 'I bet she never told you she was canoodling with another fellow.'

94

Sandy's face went through a set of different expressions as fast as the wind chases clouds across the sky. He landed on a stony look. 'What fellow would this be?' he said.

'I wasn't canoodling,' Helen said. 'Carolyn and I ran into a lad I've met through work, and his pal. They're good skaters. They took the pair of us on. Probably saved us breaking our necks.'

'And what were they saving you from when youse were sitting out together?' Greet said.

The memory swept back to Helen of her salty, greasy fingers picking hot chips out of the poke and the feel of them slipping when she lifted the cold bottle of ginger. 'What?' she said. 'It was packed on Saturday night, Mammy. There was no space to sit on your todd with an empty seat on either side and, aye, there was a lad to one side of me, but not the same one.' Greet's face clouded with uncertainty. 'Mrs Tourock's no changed then, eh?'

Sandy laughed and stretched his hands above his head. 'What's on my piece today then, Nelly? Usual Monday, is it? Cold fae yesterday?'

He could have been on the West End stage, Helen reckoned. He was the picture of a husband with not a thing to worry about, sure that his wife would pack a nice dinner to keep him going all day. Mack looked on approvingly, giving a series of slight nods.

'So what about the other thing?' said Helen. 'Now you've got me back on the straight and narrow and stopped me eloping with Billy from the morgue!'

'Is that who you were skating with?' Greet said. 'Oh I wouldn't like those hands on me.'

'He washes them, Mammy,' Helen said, biting her lip on a comment about her father's job. 'The other thing?'

'You've to promise to keep quiet about it,' Mack said. 'Like you told us you would.'

'I didn't and it depends what it is,' said Helen. Even Sandy looked shocked and he opened his mouth to argue. She cut him off. 'Mack was at the baths on Thursday night, in the next but one cubicle to where that poor man died. And he didn't want me to know.'

'It's not my fault they put me next door along to that business,' Mack said. 'You get what you're given in thon place.'

'Remember, Nelly?' Greet said. 'You, me and Teen packed in like pilchards halfway along and then some wee slip getting the big one on the corner. No amount of pleading.'

Helen nodded. These were happy memories from before they got too big to get in together and had to pay double and go alone. 'I'm glad you've finally admitted you were there,' she said to her father. 'Why the big secret?'

'I needed a good wash,' Mack said. 'And I didn't want to do it at the slaughterhouse. No more did I want to bring it home.'

'You could have come here a night early,' Sandy said. 'We wouldn't have minded.'

But Helen understood what he was getting at. Once in her childhood, before Teenie was born, Mack had come home, early and furtive, and washed himself from head to toe in the scullery sink, with Greet and Helen banished to the other end of the kitchen, there being no second room there on Freer Street for them to wait in. Then Greet set to, grim-faced, with her scouring powder, working quick and silent, before putting half the dirty pots back in the sink and filling it with scummy water from the slop pail, even letting the cloth float in the scraps, getting greasy, which was a thing she prided herself on never happening in any house of hers.

That first time it was just another one of the bewildering things the big people did and never explained to wee ones. The second time, on Grove Place, despite the separate room they sat in, Helen knew from the smell what had happened.

96

Her daddy had ruined a beast, nicked its guts and wasted the whole carcass and, rather than get his wages docked, he had hidden it and come home to sluice away the evidence.

That second night, the knock they dreaded came. As Helen and Teen were getting their hair twisted into rags for bedtime, two strange men were suddenly in the kitchen, looking at Mack and nosing round the place, sniffing and checking the sink in the offshoot.

'What's to do?' Greet had said. 'Are you saying my man here has stolen meat fae ye? I'll tell you this: Mack Downie is as honest as the day is long and you can look in my larder and my slop pail as close as you like, you'll find nothing.'

'Mrs—' one of the men said.

But Greet was just getting going. 'We had beef mince,' she said. 'Look at the plates in the sink if you're that mistrusting. Mince! See? If you've got cows coming into the abattoir that mince their own meat without a butcher, you'll be millionaires by Monday.'

'I see your dirty plates,' said the other man. 'And right enough you're not looking all that fresh, Downie.' That was when Helen noticed that after his strip wash, her daddy had put yesterday's shirt back on and had somehow got his clean hands grimed all around the nails and knuckles, like Teen and her in the back court when they made mud pies.

'Let's go,' said the first man. 'There's no point asking you for a name,' he said, as a parting shot. He waited. 'Naw, I didnae think so.'

It hadn't occurred to Helen to worry, that night when she was a child, but it struck her now. 'Are you sure no one will tell on you, Daddy?' she said.

'It wasn't me,' Mack said. 'I was just helping.'

'Helping who?' said Helen.

'A p—'

'Naeb'dy !' Greet spat at him. 'You did it yourself.'

97

'Once,' said Mack. 'Once in all these years. But not on Thursday.'

'Twice, Daddy,' Helen said. Then she shook her head to drive off her own quibbling. 'Whether you were helping someone else or not, what makes you so sure no one'll tell?'

'Not us. *We're* not clypes for the bosses.'

'But you surely took a chance going into the baths, did you not?'

'It was fine,' Mack said, which was barely an answer. 'And now, look. I'm needing to get to my work and your mammy's not even started her whites yet. We'll away and we'll say no more about it, Thursday *or* last night. No need to apologise to me, Nelly. Water under the bridge, eh?'

'So you'll not tell me what was on the tip of your tongue there when Mammy wheeshed you?'

'Water under the bridge,' Mack said again, and far more finally.

Greet retied her shawl tighter around her body as she stood and Mack buttoned his jacket lapel over his neck as if there was a raging storm outside. Helen wasn't the fan of alienists that Dr Sarah had turned out to be, always reading some guff out of her medical magazines, like double Dutch with some Greek for good measure, but even *she* could see that closing all your buttons and tightening all your knots for a wee stroll to work and wash house on a sunny day was a strange way to be behaving.

'And about *Saturday* night,' Greet said, 'since you've so much to say about family feeling, you'll take your sister with you next time.'

'Oh aye, she'll thank me for that,' Helen said. 'Teen's got more treats in her diary than me any day. You might as well give her a stair to scrub as a night out with her sister!'

'Is that supposed to be clever?' said Mack in a voice so doom-laden that Helen shot him a look of stark surprise.

'What's wrong?' she said.

'Her wee party's been cancelled,' Greet said. 'She's been bent over that needle for weeks and she was going to be a right smasher, but they've went and said it's not safe to have wee ones out at night when that devil's on the loose and the whole thing's off.' She threw Helen a filthy look, as if she personally had wrecked her sister's plans.

'The poor soul who got out of West House?' Helen said.

'Puir sowel?' said Mack. 'You've a strange idea of who gets your sympathy, Helen Downie. Have you forgotten that this maniac once managed to make twelve women dance around naked at midnight.'

'In the Pentland Hills that time?' said Helen. 'Is that who's out then?' She remembered the reports in the news and Greet throwing out perfectly good pages of newspaper that could have lit their fire, not wanting filth like that burning in the grate of a good Christian family like the Downies.

'Spoiling Teenie's treat. *She's* the poor soul. Not that her sister cares!' Greet glared and stalked out of the room.

Helen trailed back from the front door after seeing them off, fully expecting to find Sandy rolling the carpet back all set to go home, but he was still sitting where she had left him.

'Something's not right,' he said. 'Mack would never have gone to the baths covered in— And that's not all either. Did you notice that you said "next but one" and he said "next"?'

'Eh?' said Helen, her mind once more on the question of a fourth body. 'Do you mean a fifth?'

'What?' Sandy said. 'I mean the baths. You said two along and he said right next door. I don't think he noticed the slip.'

'That's right,' Helen said. From old habit, so as not to waste milk, she poured what was left of Greet and Mack's tea into her own cup and nursed it. 'I was sure it was the next one along. He hung his towel over the door like my mammy always tells him not to. But then, when I went over there and tried to tell him to get out, it was someone else. A boy, I think. Or a tiny wee man, anyway. Someone with twisted fingers, or not even that. Stumps, it was.'

'But do you agree?' said Sandy. 'Mack wasn't clearing up after a gut nick?'

'I agree.'

'So why was he there?'

'Well,' said Helen, 'I'll tell you this much. Last night, when I had made him so angry he was sounding off like nobody's business, he goes "the baths, the rink, the chophouse, the—" and then didn't my mammy jump in and shut him up before he could say the next bit.'

'What next bit?' said Sandy.

'Exactly. I reckon there's another one, somewhere. Still waiting to be found like the choked man was and the frozen man too, because I bet when they thaw him they'll say he was killed on Thursday like the others. And I bet sooner or later they'll find this fourth. If Greet hadn't stopped him, my daddy was just about to let slip where he is.'

'You don't think Mack . . . did it, do you?' Sandy said. He had stood up and bent to roll the carpet, but now he dropped it back and gaped at her.

'He couldn't fit through any size of lavvy window,' said Helen. Sandy's blink reminded her how little he knew of the tale. 'And he knows nocht about plumbing. Besides, how could he get into Haymarket ice rink and plant a man in there? If the body had been hanging from a hook in the killing room, it would be another story. But no, it wasn't him that did any of it.' She shook her head. 'He knows something, though.'

Sandy rolled the carpet without answering, then lifted the handle and hauled the trapdoor open. 'I'm sorry your night skating got cut short,' he said. 'Do you think you'll be taking it up, Carolyn and you?'

It was a good way off from the question he wanted to ask and Helen didn't think she was under any obligation to answer, but her reply was heartfelt anyway. 'Naw,' she said. 'It'll be a long time before I go back inside that place. And I won't be the only one, I daresay.'

Chapter 9

'Have you heard the news?' said Dr Sarah, trotting down the basement stairs. She must have heard Helen running the tap in the kitchenette.

'About Saturday night?' Helen said. 'The frozen man? I can do better than that, Doc. I was there.'

Dr Sarah stopped dead on the bottom step, curling her stockinged toes round the edge as if she needed help to balance. Her mouth hung open and above it her eyes danced, even in the low light of the cellar passage.

'And that's not all. If I tell you something, but I can't tell you how I know, will you trust me without badgering me? Because I do know but I really can't explain.'

'Of course, Nell,' the doc said. 'Good grief, what woman alive could respond to that by saying "No, no, you keep your own counsel". I'm agog.'

'There's a fourth one,' Helen said. 'Undiscovered, or maybe not even committed, but one way or another it's not finished yet.'

'How do you kn— Sorry. Really and truly, though?' Helen nodded. 'Sam!' said Dr Sarah, turning and racing back up the stairs. She spoke to Helen over her shoulder. 'Come up and tell us as much as you can. We've got time before morning surgery. Sa-am! Are you ready? Come down and hear this.'

The baize door at the top of the stairs slammed closed and bounced open. Helen caught it on the rebound and marched towards the main stairs as if into battle.

The air in the breakfast room stank of the coffee the doctors drank all morning until the sherry came out of the sideboard. Helen had tasted it once, to be polite, then filed it away with stout, whisky and marzipan as yet another substance people pretended to enjoy for the swank of it. She could just about thole the smell these days but she was glad the pot was cleared and neither doctor looked like fetching another one.

'Someone was running through the bodies so far,' she said, when Dr Strasser had been brought up to date by his wife's breathless summary. 'Don't ask me who. I won't tell you. But they said "baths, rink, café" and they were going to add another one, another place, until someone else stopped them. And the thing is, they understood exactly why they'd been interrupted and it took the longest time for them to come up with a story. You see?'

'More details would help,' said Dr Strasser. 'I know, I know,' he added, holding up both hands to ward off Helen's protest. 'But tell me this much: are you in any danger? Do these people, whoever they are, know that you suspect them?'

'No, I'm not,' said Helen truthfully. She decided it would be better to tell a white lie in answer to the second question. 'No, they don't.'

'But the thing is, Sam,' said Dr Sarah, 'imagine if we could work it out and stop it happening.'

'I think it's happened already,' Helen said. 'I know what I said about "not committed" but hand on heart I think it all happened on Thursday. Two did, for sure, and how long does it take to freeze a block of ice as big as a coal bunker?'

'A boiled man, a frozen man, a choked man . . .' said Dr Sarah. 'And . . . ?'

'What's the opposite of choked?' said Dr Strasser.

'Or,' said his wife, 'who's to say it's just *one* more. Perhaps the set will include . . . well, I have no idea, off the top of my head. What *is* the opposite of choked?'

104

'The opposite of stuffed would be starved,' Helen said. 'And that would explain why he's not been found yet. If they started starving someone on Thursday it'll take . . .'

'Three weeks if there's water,' said Dr Strasser. 'Three to five days dry.'

'Tomorrow at the latest to save him then,' said Dr Sarah. 'Or it might be over already.'

'I really hope I'm wrong,' Helen said. 'I'd hate to think there was a man starving somewhere and no one searching for him.'

Dr Strasser nodded. 'Perhaps if they manage to identify one of the men today, they'd be able to draw a connection and find the fourth one, if there is a fourth one.'

'With a day to spare,' said his wife. She glanced up at the clock on the mantelpiece. 'But we shall have to leave it to the police. It's time to get to the pithead. Are you busy this morning, Nelly? Or can I waft anyone down your way that might need you?'

'Paperwork, Doc,' Helen said. She supposed Dr Sarah was right about the police, but Constable Pearson hadn't even thought the boiled man was murder; it had taken Dr Sarah and Helen herself to get the investigation started. Mind you, Billy would have known as soon as the man got to the Cowgate – Billy and Tam. Well, Billy.

'Nell?' said Dr Sarah.

'Eh?' she said. 'Oh! Sorry. Yes, certainly, Doc. Waft away.'

★

The paperwork was like to bury you alive, she thought, as she tackled another wedge of it. It was too finicky to keep up to date by the day, but her old practice of leaving it till last thing on a Friday had meant that she used to slog through it with flagging energy, creasing her carbons and twisting her flimsies into rags, making it twice the bother. So, recently, she had taken to keeping her diary free on a Monday morning and tackling it while she was fresh, even though she shivered at the thought of Mrs Bonny dropping in before she was done.

'Care of child,' she wrote in her neatest hand at the top of a fresh sheet, 'observations and recommendations.' These home reports had taken her hours of sweat and struggle a year ago, but she was a dab hand at them now. She could paint a picture, accurate but kind, full of understanding as well as clarity, and could frame her recommendations just so, to give the mother a fair chance but leave the inspector in no doubt about the need for supervision.

She worked uninterrupted – no waftings, as it turned out – until the last of the morning's patients had left the clinic, their boots and clogs ringing out as they came down the front stairs above her head. She heard first one doctor and then the other leave on their house calls and went to boil herself a kettle for a cup of tea. She had finished it, with her cup rinsed and draining and her pile of papers satisfyingly thin, when she heard Dr Sarah return, enter, pause, and then advance down the basement steps towards her.

'Nearly,' she muttered, but it was no worry. Thanks to her habit of putting the newest work on the bottom of the pile she was up to date as far as Friday already and even Mrs Bonny couldn't have an argument with that. So she was looking up with a smile on her face as the doc tapped her fingertips against the half-open door and entered. She sat in the chair opposite Helen with a groan.

'I've got a job for you, if you're willing,' she said. 'Nasty business though.' She ran her hands through her hair and Helen saw that they were nothing like as clean as a doctor's hands should be, dark lines around the nailbeds that looked suspiciously like blood.

'Doc?' she said, frowning at them.

Dr Sarah took them out of her hair and stared at them, a tear slowly building in the corner of each eye. 'I was nipping over Tollcross,' she said. 'An accident on the tramlines.'

'Bad?' Helen knew the answer, for the doc would hardly weep over a bump or a scrape.

'A little girl, only three, got out of her granny's grip and ran to go and pet the dairy pony on the far side.'

'Oh no,' Helen said. 'Did you—? Could you—?'

Dr Sarah shook her head. 'There was nothing I could do. It was over before the traffic stopped and I got to her side. Oh, Helen.'

'Is it one of our patients?' Helen said.

The doctor nodded. 'The third youngest of the Morrisons,' she replied, naming a family of nine children who lived across a pair of top-floor two-room-and-kitchens in Thistle Place with their parents and grandparents. Helen had wondered at first about the wee ones toddling over the landing between one house and the other, nothing to stop them tripping and falling down the stone stairs, but she had come to see what a happy home it was for all nine of the little ones, from the oldest girl proudly bringing home her wages from the sweetie factory to the eleven-month-old baby, sleeping in a pulled-out drawer under his parents' box bed, top and tail with the youngest but one. There were families of nine she might think would hardly miss a mouth to feed, but the Morrisons weren't among their number.

'Is old Mrs Morrison all right?' she said.

'Hysterical,' said Dr Sarah. 'I gave her a powder and sent her up to the hospital, more to keep her away from home than anything, if I'm honest. A nice woman who knows the family went with her and promised not to breathe a word until the parents have been told.'

'And that's what you want me to do, is it?' Helen said. 'Tell them?'

Dr Sarah looked up with a jerk. 'Goodness, no,' she said. 'I went and broke the news straight away. Told Mrs and got a neighbour to run to the stables and tell Mr. Oh, Nelly. That poor woman.'

'Aye, she's a grand wee mother,' Helen said. 'There's a lot of love on that landing. It's going to be hard for them.' She paused. 'So what is it you need me for? Do you think the other children need to get away?'

'Absolutely not,' said Dr Sarah. 'They will be all the better for being together once Granny rallies and young Mr Morrison gets signed off his work. I'm going to go and write a line for him right now.' She grimaced. 'No, I'm afraid I'm going to ask you for more than form filling. Someone has to go and identify her little body, you see. I have forbidden young Mrs Morrison. Did you know she's pregnant again? The last thing she needs is a shock that loses her the new baby. So I'd like you to go with young *Mr* Morrison. His father will no doubt offer but, with his heart, I think it's a very bad idea. I would go myself but I've got an ulcerous leg coming in in half an hour.'

It was a moment Helen would never forget, and one that would haunt her. She never told the doctor – either doctor – or Sandy or Carolyn or her family that, alongside the pangs of sympathy she felt for the Morrisons and the pressing feeling of dread about having to go and see the child, she felt a little leap of eagerness about getting this chance to share her thoughts about a fourth man. Even worse than that, she felt a surge of warmth at the prospect of seeing Billy.

★

The neighbours had descended upon the Morrisons by the time she got across the canal and up there, after stopping off at home to change into a less jaunty hat and put a black armband over her coat sleeve. In the midst of bustling, stricken-looking women cutting sandwiches and making tea, young Mrs Morrison sat blank and pale, rubbing her swollen belly and apparently seeing nothing that passed before her. Her husband was standing out of the way, leaning back against the closed door of the press as if he had been propped up there and then forgotten.

'Nelly,' said one of the neighbour women. Helen vaguely recognised her from meeting her mammy at the brewery gate.

'Where are the bairns?' Helen said.

'They've left them in the school,' said another woman, a youngster and a stranger. 'No point telling them what they'll have the rest of their lives to know.'

A third woman shook her head and then gave a pointed look at the side of Mrs Morrison's head. 'It's nearly three,' she said. 'They'll be home soon enough.'

'What about the wee ones?' said Helen. This house had never been so quiet, so still. Even the family cat was sitting bolt upright on the fire mat, staring at his mistress.

'Through by,' said Mr Morrison. His voice sounded weak and strained. 'Helping my faither no brek his hert. Are you the wan the lady doctor said wis comin?'

Helen had never met the man before, her business and the Strassers' being with Mrs Morrison and the children. He had the rough tongue of Glasgow and it was hard to tell how stern he was as a rule. In this moment, he looked and sounded as unbending and merciless as a tent preacher.

'Nelly Crowther, Mr Morrison,' she said. 'I'm here to go with you whenever you're ready. But there's no hurry. Why don't you sit down and have a cup of tea before we even think about it?'

'I need to see her,' the man said, his voice breaking.

'*I* need to see her,' said his wife, still staring straight ahead, but speaking so loudly that the closest of the neighbour women startled.

'Dr Strasser didn't think that was a good idea,' Helen said gently, crouching down and putting a hand over one of the other woman's. She was ice cold. 'Will you hold a cup, just for the warmth?' she said. 'You don't need to drink any.'

A steaming cup, without a saucer, appeared over her shoulder as one of the neighbours proffered it, and Helen managed to wrap both of Mrs Morrison's hands around it before Mr Morrison was there at her elbow, nudging Helen aside.

'You *will* see her, Nora,' he said. 'You'll see our wee Angela when she's all nice and tidy, all clean and comfy. She'll be right here till she goes to the church. But let me go and see her now, eh? Let me take care of her for the both of us.'

His wife's gaze finally shifted as she caught his eye, giving a faint nod and an even fainter smile. He stood, using Helen's arm to help him straighten, like an old man.

'Right then,' he said and turned away to leave the room, with Helen following.

★

'I mind ae the first time I saw her,' he said, when they were down on the street. 'She was as red as a berry and screaming blue murder. Waving her arms like she wanted to start a fight and kicking her legs as if her blanket was full of ants. She's been the same way ever since. Never stops.' His voice broke on the last word. He took two or three big breaths that didn't quite turn into sobs. 'My poor maw. This'll kill her. And losing *her* will kill my faither.'

'How did all three of you end up through here?' Helen said. His accent was too thick for him to have been in Edinburgh since boyhood. She knew how quickly a West Coast twang

110

or an island lilt got teased out of children's mouths at the Fountainbridge schools.

'They came through when my faither retired off the ships,' he said. 'Nora's lot are all away and when we had four, my mammy decided she wasn't missing out on them.' His eyes crinkled up as he grinned. 'Or that's what I told Nora. Really, she didn't reckon anyone else but her could manage them.' He had been lost in his memories of happy days, but as the hammer of the day's calamity came down on him again his face darkened. 'It'll kill her.'

'You've eight needing her more than ever,' Helen said. 'And soon it'll be nine. She won't leave you. If she knows you don't blame her—'

'Blame?' said Mr Morrison. 'Angela climbed out the window and sat on the sill waving down to her mammy on the back green when she was two. I was right there in the kitchen and never noticed till Nora screamed. She crawled down two landings before that, when she smelled a cake baking in Mrs Glenn's, and we never even missed her till the Glenn lassie brought her back up again. And she loved every animal that walked the earth or flew in the air. If she'd ever been to the seaside she'd have wanted to clap the fish too. I don't blame my maw for anything.'

'She sounds like a right wee . . .' Helen said, before realising she couldn't possibly finish the thought.

But Mr Morrison only laughed. 'You're not saying anything we haven't said before you. Even at her christening, folk were making cracks about giving her that name, of all the names we could have chosen. But there wasn't an ounce of bad in her. My wee Angela.'

They were headed up Viewforth towards Gilmore Place now, Helen having decided to lead Mr Morrison on a round-about route to the Cowgate, one that didn't pass the site of the accident. 'I'm not meaning to pry,' she said, 'but since you mention a christening, do you have a priest you could send for? For a bit of comfort. For succour.' They had reached that right strange wee crossroads of Gilmore Place and Viewforth that Helen had always thought was neither one thing nor another. There was a church there, tucked in beside a funeral director, in what looked like an old meeting hall. It struck her that there was a dog collar missing from the crowd in the wee house.

Mr Morrison gave a mirthless laugh. 'A *priest*, on account of all the weans, is it?'

'Or a minister?' Helen said, hastily, waving at the church they were passing.

Mr Morrison pointed a jeering thumb in its direction. 'Cold comfort from that lot,' he said.

Right enough, when Helen looked where he was pointing she saw a big notice posted under glass outside the church door, thick black letters like a newspaper stand and exclamation marks after every word: CLEANLINESS! HARDINESS! ABSTINENCE! THRIFT! She decided that maybe neighbours making sandwiches were more use to the poor Morrisons today.

As if to confirm it, the young man went on, 'I tell you this, Mrs Crowther, if any priest or minister came coiling round us talking about God's will, after this here, he'd leave with a fat lip.'

Helen had no argument and in silence they made their zigzag progress through the side streets all the way to the Grassmarket then beyond its hustle and bustle of barrow boys and cartmen into the mouth of the Cowgate where an even deeper gloom settled over both of them until there was no sound except their footsteps and Mr Morrison's occasional gasps as he fought against the pain that threatened to overtake him.

At the mortuary, minutes later, it was odd for Helen to go in at the front gate and up the steps to the visitors' door.

She had never seen the public bit of the place before. If she had guessed before today, she would have expected a foyer like the library or a big police station, but the lobby and desk of the morgue were as grim and dour as the basement, only slightly warmer and with the unmistakable smell a bit fainter. There was a clerk at the desk who looked up, wearing the sort of hangdog expression that suited the place but not the task of comforting and welcoming the visitors.

'Name?' he said, looking over a list in the open ledger before him.

'Morrison,' said the young man. 'Angela Morrison, my wee girl.'

The turned-down mouth and half-shut eyes softened a little, and the man cracked a smile as he spoke again, revealing long grey teeth with big gaps between each of them. 'They're ready for you, Mr and Mrs Morrison,' he said. 'Take a seat and somebody'll come and get you.'

Helen opened her mouth to correct him, but then closed it again pursing her lips over her teeth. If the morgue was anything like hospitals and jails, they'd have an endless rule book about what and who were permitted, and she didn't want to be told she couldn't go with the poor man.

She sat down and waited until the clerk had disappeared before speaking again. 'What's your name?' she said. 'I'm Helen. Nelly.'

'Jack.'

'Have you ever seen a person who's died before, Jack?' She was flooded with the memory of asking Jessie Gibb the same question on Friday and the answer she got now was a variation on the same one.

'Aye, but an auld dear,' Jack said. 'Nora's maw. Then her paw. All nice in their coffins. That's how come I knew what to say to Nora back there.'

'You're a kind man,' Helen told him. 'A good man.'

'Ach,' he said, pushing the compliment away.

They both turned as the door opened and the clerk reappeared followed by the familiar grey uniform and even more familiar head full of crisp curls. It was Billy.

'Nelly!' he said. 'What—? Is she your—?'

'What?' said Jack.

'I'm here in a professional capacity,' Helen said, 'to accompany Mr Morrison through the ordeal.'

'Where fae?' said the clerk, confirming everything she had feared about the regulations.

'She's fine,' Billy said. 'Gardener's Crescent Surgery.'

'Ohhhh,' said the clerk, his doleful face lifting into a travesty of a leer, '*You're* the one Tam was saying—'

'Mr Morrison,' Billy said, cutting across the clerk and earning a frown. 'If you're ready.'

It was another bit of the morgue Helen had never seen but here some attempt had been made to make it less grim than the other rooms. There was a lamp on a wee table with a linen runner and two leatherette armchairs, only they were side by side against the far wall, clearly meant for sinking into if your legs gave way, not for relaxing. The only other piece of furniture in the room was the trolley, its metal legs and chipped enamel wheels sitting in grooves on the floorboards that had been worn out of the varnish over the years, as burdened trolleys were pushed in and hauled out again, stopping in just that spot every time.

This morning's burden wouldn't have spoiled the finish on the floor. On top of the trolley, under a white sheet, there was a pitifully small shape, reaching nowhere near either the head or the foot of the flat expanse it lay upon. Mr Morrison started to gulp and sway and Helen led him over to one of the armchairs, steering him so that he dropped into it instead of onto the floor.

Billy caught her eye and shook his head, anguish etched on his face. 'Can *you* look at her, Mrs C?' he said. 'She's peaceful and there's nothing bad to see.'

'Gie's a minute,' said Jack. He stared down at the floor with his hands clasped together as if he might be praying, then suddenly stood up, cleared his throat and nodded at Billy.

Helen watched Billy's deft hands fold back the sheet, same as she'd watched him do before, but this time the face revealed was round and chubby, with bow lips that were still pink and soft lashes that looked as if surely, any minute now, they must flutter open.

'Angela,' said her father. He stepped forward and cupped her cheek in one of his big hands. 'She looks perfect. What happened?' He made as if to lower the sheet further to see more of her little body and Billy's hand shot out, grabbing him by the wrist and prising his arm up and away.

'Her injuries are nothing you need to remember,' he said, calmly but firmly. Mr Morrison dropped his arm to his side again and, with one last deep drinking look at his daughter's face, he turned away.

'You go and wait out front,' Billy said. 'I'll send Mrs Crowther through to you when the papers are ready for you to sign.'

'I'll need to go with Jack,' Helen said. She had quite forgotten her own plan to kill two birds with this visit and was shocked at Billy thinking he could get her away from the poor man and speak to her of other things.

'I'm fine, hen,' the young man said. 'I'll wait outside in the fresh air, though. You come and get me, eh?'

As soon as he had left, Billy turned and began to speak with urgency, laying a hand on Helen's arm. 'Listen,' he said.

But Helen wrenched free and stepped away from him. 'She's still lying right here,' she said. 'At least take her poor wee corpse away before you move on to whatever it is, eh?' She reached out and touched the leg shape under the white sheet then started back at the strange rustling sound that came from the still, tiny form. 'What—?'

'There's not much of her,' Billy said. 'That's straw.'

115

The next thing Helen knew was a swirling feeling she recognised from the summer shows, lights and sound and a weightlessness, and then a pair of strong arms holding her up as she scrabbled to get her feet back underneath her.

'Oh Billy!' she said. 'If he'd pulled the cover back!'

'Shoosh, shoosh, I was ready for him,' Billy said. 'It's not the first time. You sit here till I get Angela back safe.'

The emptiness of the little room once Billy had wheeled the trolley away was eerie in a way Helen couldn't account for, like her granny's stair on a moonless night, or the space under the bed when Teenie used to take too long to find her on rainy days, playing hide and seek in the house. Helen couldn't help thinking about how many restless souls might be gathered in the corners like cobwebs, left over from all the unclaimed bodies that passed through.

Billy opening up the door made her jump.

He sat down in the other chair and took her hand. 'Sorry,' he said. How could he not notice a wedding ring when his own fingers were touching it? 'Look, Nelly. There's something not right here. Slice and the Fiscal were shut in his office for nearly an hour this morning, muttering away, and then the face on the doc when he came to cut the man from the rink! Something's troubling him.'

'Did he speak to you?'

'Not him,' Billy said. 'I'm just an orderly. I scrub guts and mop blood, me. But that's not all. You're going to think I'm daft, but . . .'

'You know there's another one,' Helen said.

'I wouldn't say I *know*,' Billy whispered. 'I didn't catch enough of it to be certain sure. But, from the tone of it . . . From the *urgency* . . .'

Helen leaned forward. She wanted to understand but couldn't catch his meaning.

116

'Likes of, if I'm down here,' Billy said, 'and folk come in to the front desk, I can't hear what they say, but I can hear how they say it. I can tell if they're dreading to find out about a death or if they know already. Urgent, like I said. Or else . . .'

'Bleak?' said Helen. 'Resigned?'

Billy nodded. 'Resigned. Exactly.' He had been looking into space but now he threw a sharp glance Helen's way. 'But what makes *you* think there's more to come?'

'We're short the starved man,' Helen said.

Billy's eyes widened. 'I was thinking drowned,' he said. 'Killed with food and then killed with water.' He paused, chewing his lip. 'But you're right. Burned, chilled, stuffed and starved. Aye, it could be.'

'The thing that's bothering me,' Helen said, 'is that we might still be in time to save him.' Billy nodded his encouragement for her to go on. 'At least, could the doctor tell when the man from the rink died?'

'It was tough,' Billy said. 'He had to thaw first and the warm water we thawed him out in threw off all the calculations about post-mortem changes. But Slice got on the blower to a pal in London and talked it over – left the bloke lying there wide open until he got a clue what to check for. This pal worked in Russia at the tail end of the war and had plenty to say about "deterioration in sub-zero temperatures". Anyway, eventually Slice came down on Thursday.'

'Same as the other two,' Helen said, thinking that, for all his modesty, Billy didn't sound like an orderly. He had picked up more about the work done here than that doctor gave him credit for. 'Except there were no working man's clothes with this one.'

'Not exactly,' Billy said.

'Eh?' said Helen. 'He was naked as a newborn baby. I saw him as clear as— Well, I mean the ice wasn't *that* cloudy.'

117

'The ice *wasn't* that cloudy,' Billy said. 'Some of the "clouds" you saw were thin white linen, soaked, clinging round him.' He paused as if he had said enough.

'Thin white linen like a shroud?' Helen said.

Billy shook his head. 'A pinny. He was wearing a housemaid's pinny. Or a parlourmaid, or a lady's maid – I wouldn't know. But frilly and fine with ribbons to hold it on at the back.'

'So . . . working *women's* clothes,' Helen said. 'That's . . . So could *this* one be the poor wee mannie from West House? Because wearing a maid's apron is gey queer if you ask me.'

'No chance at all,' Billy said. 'That lost soul is still on his toes, out there somewhere.'

'Slaughterman's clothes and tanner's clothes and a house-maid's pinny?' said Helen. 'Could *that* help us find the fourth one maybe? Because what I was saying, what I was getting at, is the Strassers told me it takes as much as five days to starve, if you're held without water. If whoever it is – whatever black-hearted devil is doing this – started on Thursday then number four might still be hanging on to life. Somewhere.' She gave Billy her most grave look. 'Are you sure you didn't hear anything the Fiscal and your boss were saying?'

'I did catch something,' Billy said. 'Made no sense, mind.' Helen gave him an encouraging look. 'They mentioned a dentist.'

Helen waited for more but there was none. 'Likes of . . . named him?' she said. 'Which dentist? Why?'

'No, not like that. They said "a dentist" and more than once too.'

'Had one of the men maybe just had something done to his teeth?' said Helen.

'Aye, that's what I thought too,' said Billy. 'But I had a right good look in their mouths for new fillings or new holes where they'd just had one howked out and there was nothing to see.

The first one had good teeth. The second one had plenty fillings right enough but no new ones. And the man from the rink's teeth were just like anybody's, right squint but not . . . what would you say?'

'Remarkable enough to make a dentist worth finding,' said Helen. 'So it must be that one of them *was* a dentist, d'you not think? Maybe Dr Sallis's dentist or the Fiscal's dentist. But they're keeping it quiet for some reason.'

'For some reason,' Billy echoed. 'Aye, that'll be the size of it.'

It took Helen a moment to understand his wry tone, but she got there. They were well-to-do men, the three of them, with soft hands and good teeth, but all had been found naked or near-naked, and surely not in any place they'd frequent when alive. So somewhere or other around the edges of this case, this mystery, there was a scandal lurking. And she knew what Edinburgh did with scandals: buried them.

'Here we go again,' Billy said, confirming that his thoughts had taken him down the same path.

'Aye,' Helen said, with a sigh. Then she stirred herself. 'Or maybe we're too hard on them. Maybe they said dentist for some other reason. Or maybe they didn't say dentist at all. What other word sounds like "dentist"?'

Before Billy could answer they both jumped as the door opened and Tam put his head round the door. 'Not where I'd go winching,' he said, with a wink, as he handed over a thick piece of grey paper to Billy. 'Takes all kinds, I suppose.'

And so embarrassment carried Helen away without another word spoken, when a little more discussion might have led to enlightenment. But then, by the end of that long sad day there would be much more to occupy them, the morgue orderly and the budding detective both.

Chapter 10

Helen was at home, in her housecoat, enjoying fried egg and potato. That was her usual Monday tea if there was no meat left over from Sunday, and few were the weeks when her family didn't polish off all she'd made, Greet checking the empty dishes as if to tell her daughter she'd kept them on short rations. If Sandy and Helen went round to Grove Place, on the other hand, Greet thought nothing of wrapping a good pound of lamb or beef in wax paper and setting it aside for Mack's pieces through the week, sending her daughter and son-in-law home empty-handed.

Helen swirled the small teapot out with warm water, watching her eggs clouding as they cooked in their dish, her potatoes dancing and fizzing in the big pan. Where would a person who killed in the baths, a café and the ice rink, choose to hide a man while he starved? Or what was missing from a set where an abattoir, a tannery, and a well-to-do house were the others? There was no pattern at all. The fourth one could be anywhere, not least because the murderer seemed to have the key to more buildings in the city than it made any sense for one person to hold, unless he was a policeman or on the council. And even a policeman couldn't be alone at the Haymarket rink long enough to . . . How *was* it done? Maybe she would go down to Sandy and Gavin's later and ask them if they knew anything about making that much ice.

She glanced back at the frying pan, tutted to see her chipped tatties browner than she liked them, then put everything out of her mind except her dinner and her library book, sitting over it at the table long after the dregs of the tea had got cold, promising herself every time she turned a page that she would soon go to bed, but unable to help herself gulping down chapter after chapter.

She was still there when a timid knock at the front door made her jerk upright. She checked the clock on the mantel and frowned. It was gone nine o'clock, late for anyone but family to be here and that wasn't a family knock, either Mack's pounding, Greet's rap, or Teenie's sharp rat-a-tat. It certainly wasn't Carolyn, who knocked once then marched in, and the doctors would have called out, surely, the same way they did when they came to her office. It wasn't Sandy either, who had developed a knock that was closer to a coded message than a simple summons. It could be Gavin, she supposed. He might feel tentative about disturbing her but if something had happened that brought him to her door it would be urgent enough to make his knock a more determined one than that.

Or, she suddenly thought to herself, it could be the knock of a poor soul who'd been out on the streets since escaping the madhouse on Thursday past. Her house was at the end of a dead-end street, exactly the kind of hidey-hole someone would crawl to. But would he knock? This Beelzebub, this demon, this bogeyman?

The knock sounded again as Helen made her way along the passage. 'Who is it?' she called, trying to sound bolder than she felt. She hadn't realised this difference between Upper Grove Place and Rosemount Colonies until now: all the aunties and neighbours she *had* been used to, the solitary life with its quiet evenings she was getting used to now. 'Who's there?' she said, managing a bit more mettle.

'It's me, Mrs Crowther,' came a girl's voice from outside. 'It's Rita.'

Helen couldn't bring to mind a Rita, but she knew the sound of someone in trouble and she unlocked the door without another moment's hesitation. On her step stood someone she did vaguely recognise but was nevertheless astonished to find visiting her. Rita was one of the working girls from the notorious street at the back of Haymarket, a girl Helen had first run into over a year ago when she ventured down there, her heart banging in her chest, to talk to the women about 'health and hygiene'. She had been roundly laughed at and had had to listen to a lot of mucky talk about what her leaflets would be useful for, but the visit served its purpose. All the Haymarket girls now knew that Mrs Crowther from Gardener's Crescent was someone they could turn to. And now, here tonight, was Rita turning.

'Come away in,' Helen said. 'You're shivering.' She thought it was more than the skimpy wee skirt and thin lacy blouse that was causing it too; Rita had had a shock. She settled the girl in her own chair at the kitchen table and set about making fresh tea.

'Are you hurt?' she said. 'Are you ill? Is it a doctor you're needing?'

Rita shook her head. Her curls were that stiff with setting lotion that they didn't move and Helen tried not to let thoughts of uncleanliness cross her mind as the girl laid her head back against the cushion and closed her eyes.

'You know there's a nice lady doctor at my work, don't you?' she said. 'She hasn't a harsh bone in her body so if you need her help, you can just ask.'

Rita shook her head again. 'I'm fine. Can you put three sugars in my tea? And no milk. I'll be fine. If you help me, I might be fine. Somehow. Maybe.' With that she burst into tears, sobbing and gasping while her nose ran and her mouth drooled. Helen hurried over and handed her a tea towel along with her cup.

'I don't want to go to jail!' she wailed.

'What have you done?' said Helen, hoping she sounded less alarmed and more capable than she felt.

'Nothing!' It came out like a yelp. 'But look there – even you suspect me. I can't go to the polis. They'll never believe me!'

'Why don't you tell me what's happened,' Helen said, 'and if you've truly done nothing, I will help you. I promise.'

'I *haven't*!' Rita said again.

'Well, that's good then,' said Helen. 'Have a drink of tea and start at the beginning, eh?'

'There's a man in my room,' Rita said, after taking a draught that made Helen think either the tea was cold or the girl had a mouth of iron. 'And he's dead.'

'Oh!' Helen said. 'One of your . . . callers died?'

'Callers!' said Rita, with a bit of spirit. The Haymarket girls could always be relied on for scorn. 'Naw, I've been out. Working, you know. And before that— Well, it doesn't matter where I was, but when I came back to my room he was there and he's as dead as a doorknob. What am I going to do? Oh, what am I going to do?'

'Do you share your room?' Helen said.

'Naw, it's just mine and I keep it locked. How did he get in?'

'Do you know him?'

'I don't know!' Rita said, on a rising note. 'I can't tell. He doesn't look like anything you would believe!'

Helen felt a chill creep over her shoulders and wished she had made a hot cup of tea for herself too. 'Is he— Is he awfy thin and gaunt?' she asked, proud that her voice did not tremble. 'Does he look like he's starved?'

'I don't know!' said Rita again then, just as had happened with Jessie Gibb, the task of thinking it through calmed her. 'I couldn't really see— Hing on. Thin? Naw, not so's you'd say so. It was hard to tell, mind. He could be.'

124

For a moment, Helen felt relief, but then the thought struck her that she didn't know if the flesh melted off a man's bones in the five days it took him to starve of food and water.

'Is he naked?' she said, unsure which answer she hoped for.

'Sort of,' Rita said, still calm as she used her reason instead of being lost in panic. 'I mean, he's got clothes on but they're not his, I can tell you that much.'

Helen shivered again. It was the fourth man; she was sure if it.

'Are they working clothes?' she said, unable to keep the note of doom from her voice.

Rita gave her a sharp look. 'Now how the hangment did you know that?' she said. 'Do you know what's going on? *Can* you help me? Like you promised. Oh, Mrs Crowther, *can* you?'

'I need to see him,' Helen said. 'I will help you. But I need to see him before anything.' She wished she knew where Billy lived and that she herself still lived up a tenement stair where there was always a laddie who'd run a message for a penny. She felt very much alone as she went into the other room to get dressed. So perhaps it was to summon for herself a bit of Carolyn's vim that she chose to put the trousers on again.

'My, my,' said Rita, when Helen reemerged. 'Fancy a game of flats?'

'What?' Helen said.

'Ocht, never mind me. I'll take your arm gladly, kind sir.'

'I'm doing you a favour, you wee besom,' Helen said, caught between gladness that Rita had stopped shaking and annoyance at the cheek of the girl.

'Aye, right,' Rita said. 'You're straining like a whippet to get a sniff of him. You can't hide it.'

Helen said nothing, just locked the door behind her and set off through the dark streets, as the clocks struck ten, wondering how her life had become what it was and how much more she would have to face this evening.

Apart from the maniac on the loose, who could be anywhere really, it wasn't a bad time to go wandering the city. It was far too late for weans, just too late for women coming home from visits, and not quite closing time. So they had the streets to themselves. Ten minutes brought them to the station and the lane behind the yards where Rita and the rest of them plied their trade. There were no men to be seen, but quiet voices came from two or three shadowed doorways as the pair passed.

'Got yourself a good one, Reet!'

'Aye, you keep your heid doon, Mister. Spare your beels.'

Only one woman, an elder of the district, saw past Helen's trousers and cap. 'Evening, Mrs C,' she said. 'Everything awright?'

'Wheesht,' said Rita and the woman, already invisible, drew farther back into the dark with a rustle of her old-fashioned petticoats.

Near the back of a pub that Helen couldn't place on a mental map of the front street – perhaps it had no formal entrance at all – Rita drew her by her arm along the narrow pend that served as a barrel yard and through a gateway that seemed no more than a hole in the fence, since the girls had to step over a foot-high lintel to get to the other side. 'This is me,' she said, disappearing into a doorless entryway and trotting up a flight of wooden steps.

Helen followed, taking in a smell of rot so sweet it would have been pleasant if she hadn't known it came from mushrooms growing in the wood and not from the cake it smelled like. She heard a baby squalling behind one of the doors and a hacking cough from inside the room opposite.

'Like something from Dickens,' she muttered to herself. It was what Dr Sarah sometimes said, after a visit to one of their poorest patients.

'What's that?' Rita said, half a flight ahead.

'How long have you lived here?'

'Since I was fifteen,' Rita said.

Helen decided not to ask how long that was in case the answer was unbearable. Rita's heavy make-up couldn't disguise her round cheeks, the spray of spots on her chin and the light, feathery eyebrows. If she was older than seventeen now, Helen would be pleasantly surprised.

They met just one neighbour on their journey up the stairs. A woman opened her door as they passed, but drew back and waited. Helen kept her head down and scurried by. She was trying not to be recognised, but it occurred to her that most of the men Rita led up these stairs would be trying to escape recognition just the same. She felt herself flush in the darkness. What would her mammy say?

'Right,' Rita said, stopping at last at the top of the stair. 'Brace yourself.' She was breathing heavily and Helen thought she would dearly love to have the girl under her wing for a few weeks, to get some food into her and make her go for walks in the fresh air. Maybe she could even get a bed in one of the retreats that various do-gooders had set up around the outskirts of the city, although they were usually for miners and factory girls, not for Rita and the like, whose work was every bit as dangerous and whose living conditions were, if this place was anything to go by, even worse.

For, as was usual on the last landing in tenements where neither the factor nor the tenants were all that fussy, this had become a cowp, piled high with old clothes and broken sticks of furniture, reeking of mice and the cats they attracted. Helen did indeed brace herself for what lay behind the door.

Rita opened it with a key she evidently kept in her stocking-top, then struck a match on the door frame and lit a candle that was sitting on a table just inside. She walked into the middle of the little room and Helen followed, surprised and relieved by what she saw there.

There was a sink under the window, with a cloth folded over its front edge and a tin bath hung over its bunker. Three shelves off to the side held tins of food, one or two pots and a few pieces of crockery. The fire was swept and laid ready for lighting, and the floor was clean, the boards almost white from bleach. On the other hand, there wasn't so much as a rag mat over them. Nor was there a seat except for two wooden stools at a small table. No more was there a cushion, or a curtain, or a picture on the walls. The one soft place in the whole single-end was the bed, where an eiderdown far too big for the mattress reached the floor all around and a mound of pillows obscured the headboard.

Helen stared. On top of this eiderdown and with his head propped on the pillow mound, was a man as dead as any she had ever seen in a coffin or on Billy's trolleys at the morgue. He lay like a stone saint on a church tomb, his noble face casting a haughty shadow onto the wall behind in the candlelight and his hands crossed over his stomach as if in prayer.

There the saintly resemblance ended. As Helen's gaze travelled over him, she felt an outrageous desire to laugh starting to rise up in her. She knew it was half horror but some of it was the absurdity as well. To stop it bursting out, she bit down hard on her lip and forced herself to keep studying him.

He was not wearing many clothes: no shirt, coat, trousers or shoes. All he had on was a pair of stockings made from black diamonds that criss-crossed all the way up his legs, letting the hairs poke through, held up by a suspender belt made for a woman's body and cutting into the flesh of his hips like a tourniquet. He wore a scrap of lace that might have been a pair of cami knickers and was bare-chested except for the trailing fronds of a feather boa wound round and around his neck. *Above* his neck was a sight from a nightmare. His face was purple and his tongue protruded from his blackened mouth just as his dark eyes bulged from their sockets. He had been strangled. But before that, he had been hit on the side of the head, hard enough to cut his temple, and there was blood smeared over his cheek and clumped in the feathers of the boa.

Helen stepped closer and looked at the hands folded so peacefully over his torso. The left was on top and the right obscured, so she took her handkerchief from her pocket and tried to move his left fingers gently. To her horror his whole arm swung free on the hinge of his shoulder and waved stiffly, still bent at the elbow. She grabbed it through the cotton of her hanky and replaced it where it belonged, noticing two things as she did so. There were bloody smudges on both his arms from where the killer, wearing gloves or with a cloth over his hands, had arranged the pose. The other striking detail was the right hand, clearly showing where a ring had been wrenched off the pinkie.

'This is nothing to do with me, Mrs Crowther,' Rita said.

'Oh I know,' Helen said. This man had no more connection to the back of Haymarket than the first one had to the baths, the next to the café or the third to the rink. Or maybe she was being naïve. Certainly when she'd been here before talking to the girls, some of the men who slunk past had seemed ordinary enough and not from the rough end. 'Did you know him though?' she asked, checking.

'Never seen him in my life.' The girl sounded definite and even a little affronted.

'Are they your clothes?'

'Chance'd be a fine thing.' That was an even heartier sound. 'Can I strip them off him and keep them anyway?'

Helen decided to pretend she was joking. 'I've got one last question,' she said. 'Why did you come to me before raising the alarm and getting a constable?'

'Before?' Rita said. '*Before*? Don't tell me you're going to get the polis to me now? You said you would help me! I told you I didn't want to go to jail and you promised!'

'But you didn't do this,' Helen said. 'Why would anyone, even the stupidest bobby ever born, think you were strong enough to throttle a man, or silly enough to kill him in your own house?'

'Oh aye, right,' Rita said. 'They'll go, "Yes, Miss, you are innocent, please carry on your business and sorry we disturbed you." How daft can you get? They'll sling me in the jail as soon as look at me. They might clear out the whole stair and carry on down the street.'

Helen opened her mouth to argue, then remembered how she had had to get Dr Sarah to make Constable Pearson listen on Thursday night, her with her respectable job and a ring on her finger. She had to admit that Rita was probably right.

'Pack what you need,' she said. 'You're coming away with me for a few days. But you can't work, mind.'

'What'll I live off?' Rita said.

'Bounty,' said Helen, a word she hadn't used since the wartime when her mentor was called 'Lady Bountiful' behind her back. 'Get packing,' she said again. 'Quickly.'

'Pack whit?' said Rita. 'I've nothing to pack.'

'Your toothbrush and powder. Clean drawers and vest. Your brush and comb. Your ration card and purse. Come on, Rita. Look lively.'

The girl darted here and there, gathering little items and laying them on the tabletop on a shawl she clearly meant to tie into a bundle.

'Or wait a minute,' Helen said. 'Maybe you shouldn't pack. Maybe you shouldn't leave a clue that you've cleared out.

Or . . . No, that's wrong! You need to pack more. You need to pack up all the evidence that someone lives here. Leave it looking like a . . . I don't know the word . . . but like a place that's only used for . . . business.'

'A basket, you mean?'

'What?'

'Smaller than a cathouse, ken. Just a basket made for one.'

'Right,' said Helen. 'Make it look like a basket. But only if what you said is right enough. Your neighbours are all your . . . colleagues? So they won't clype on you?'

'Colleagues!' said Rita. She was gathering up the bread-knife and the tin opener, a small Bible and a drawerful of neatly folded clothes. 'But, aye, you're right. They are and they'd never turn me in.'

'All of them?' Helen said. 'There was a bairn and an old woman coughing.'

Rita sent a scornful look over her shoulder. 'It's an old man,' she said. 'Peg Harrold's old pa. He's in his bed till he's done now. And there's more than one bairn, Mrs Crowther. Just one screaming tonight is all.'

Helen was helping now, casting her eyes around and wondering what the telltale signs of occupation were. The salt and pepper shakers would have to go. Even if visitors to a basket had a cup of tea and perhaps a bun, they wouldn't season food there. She looked under the sink and took all but one of the folded rags there, swiping the block of clothes soap too.

In no time at all the little room had lost what few crumbs of Rita's personality it ever contained and looked merely functional. Except for the bed and its occupant, it looked like the houses the factor used to show to Greet when Freer Street had got unbearable and the Downies were ready for flitting.

Each with a bundle over their shoulder, they left. Helen stopped Rita from pocketing the key, then stood pondering on the crowded and smelly landing for a good long while. Should they lock it up and throw the key in the canal? Leave it open with the key on the inside? Lock it up and leave the key behind? In the end, she rubbed it clean on her trouser leg and, once again using her hanky, she threw it into the pile of rubbish by the door.

Then the two girls made their way down the stairs, stepping carefully in the middle of the treads to stop their bundles from banging against the walls.

'Where are we going?' said Rita. 'Your place?'

'One of them,' Helen said. 'Which one though? Wheesht and let me think it through, eh? Keep your een peeled and your wits about you.'

Chapter 11

She could take the girl home, but then she would have to tell Sandy what she was doing. If she was going to tell Sandy, she might as well billet Rita down at Gavin's to save Greet or Mack stumbling over her. Or she could ask Rita if she had a friend who would take her in. These were Helen's musings, but deep down she knew where she was headed as soon as her feet hit the street again.

She left the girl waiting on a secluded bit of wall on the crescent, guarding both bundles, then nipped home, changed into a skirt, gave detailed instructions to Sandy through Gavin's letter box, crossed the park and marched up the surgery steps, steeling herself to see this clever plan through to its conclusion, or perhaps lose her job, depending how it panned out.

'Nelly?' Dr Sarah looked over the banister. Her hair was scraped back in kirby grips and her face shone with night cream, but she still had a cigarette in her hand so at least Helen hadn't got her out of bed. 'Who's that with you?' She trotted downstairs in her dressing gown and flapping slippers and gave Rita her usual look of friendly interest. She had seen the bundles too. 'Here for the night, I take it,' she said. 'Do you need medical attention or just shelter.'

'Patricia McMunn,' Rita said, bobbing a curtsy as if Dr Sarah was the Queen. 'I'm not needing anything except somewhere to curl up.'

'And where better?' Dr Sarah said. 'Nelly, would you like to show Patricia up to the little room on the top floor and then join me in the drawing room?'

'I can find it, I'm sure,' Rita said and, dropping one of her bundles, she hauled herself up the stairs, hanging onto the banister as though it was the railing of a boat on a stormy sea.

'Well?' said the doc, when the fading footsteps suggested the girl was out of earshot.

'A fourth man,' Helen said. She jerked her head upwards. 'In *her* room. She knows nothing about it but she's a working girl and she thought she'd get slung in the jail willy-nilly. Probably right, eh?'

Dr Sarah went to lift the bundle and frowned in surprise at the sound of clattering knives and plates.

'She's cleared out so they don't go looking for whoever lives there,' Helen said.

'Good idea,' Dr Sarah said. She opened the broom cupboard and shoved the bundle inside. 'What now then? Are we supposed to wait until someone finds the body?'

'I've taken care of that,' said Helen and no sooner had she spoken than the telephone bell rang out. Seeing this was a doctor's house with telephones all over the place, it always sounded like a calamity when they rang in the hallway, in both surgeries, in the drawing room and beside Dr Strasser's bed.

'I've got it!' Dr Sarah called up the stairwell at the sound of her husband's groan from above. 'Strasser,' she said crisply, lifting the receiver. Then after a pause, 'Who is this?' Then, 'Hello? Hello?'

Helen couldn't help but smirk. Her plan had worked.

'That was an anonymous call,' said Dr Sarah, 'telling me that a man desperately needs medical attention at a certain top floor flat in a certain stair on a back street not far from here. He told me to hurry before it was too late.'

'What are you going to do, Doc?' Helen said.

'We must attend, Helen,' the doctor said. 'It's our oath. Well, it's my oath and your vocation. We must attend. Give me two minutes to dress and I'll join you in the car.'

A policeman passed on his beat while Helen sat shrinking into the passenger seat, glad that Dr Sarah had parked it in the darkness between two pools of streetlight tonight. He was almost at the end when the front door slammed and the doc came tripping down the steps and across the pavement. The copper turned and shone his torch but, when she raised a hand in greeting, he simply raised his back at her, switched off the beam of light and turned away.

'Excellent,' Dr Sarah said. 'A corroborating witness in case this turns on me and bites.'

She started the car and, perhaps because they had got used to the doctors setting off to emergencies at all hours, not a single neighbour twitched a curtain to see her go.

In the time since Helen and Rita had left Haymarket, last orders had rung and the drinkers had flooded out and scattered for home. Now only stragglers too drunk to hurry or with nowhere to hurry to were still on the streets. One or two looked up as the car passed but it was a cold night and most were hunched into their collars, facing down.

'Turn up Dalry Road and then hook back,' Helen said, when the great broad junction was behind them. 'I'm not sure how far down you'll get the motor, though. These lanes get right narrow.'

When the way through began to be blocked by dustbins and piles of rubble left from wartime, now with docks and nettles growing through them, Dr Sarah drew into the kerb and brought the car to a halt. 'I think I'll make extra sure the car's locked,' she said, which was a thing that never troubled them up on the crescent. She checked the three passenger doors and the boot then locked the driver's door with her key and turned to Helen. 'Lay on, MacDuff.'

Helen retraced her steps along the street, but this time not a single one of the women she knew were there ventured to greet her or show themselves.

It was quieter on the stair now, the baby settled and the old man with the cough having found some relief or fallen asleep. At the top, Helen paused, said, 'Don't worry if you want to laugh, Doc. I nearly burst trying to hold it in,' and opened the door.

'Well, he's not starved,' said Dr Sarah, after she had had a good look at the man, holding the candle over him and spilling a long drip of wax onto his bare stomach. 'He's been strangled.'

'Look at his right hand though,' Helen said. 'He's short a ring, just like the rest.'

'Not to mention being short his own clothes,' said Dr Sarah. 'Do they belong to—?' She bit her lip, as Helen's eyes flashed.

'This room doesn't seem to be anyone's house, does it?' Helen said. 'I reckon it's a basket.' She was showing off, but the doctor only nodded, unsurprised by the term.

'I wonder who pays the rent,' she said.

'It's cash down and no papers,' said a voice from behind them, making both women jump. 'Who are y—? Oh, it's yourself, Mrs Crowther. What—?' As Helen moved away from the bed, no longer blocking the view of the corpse, the woman's voice died in her throat.

'Aye, it's me, Lila,' Helen said. 'And this is Dr Strasser. Here! Sit down before you fall down.' For Lila had paled and was swaying.

'Who—? Who—?' she said, unable to rip her eyes away even as she turned green at the sight.

'I take it from your shock that you didn't hear anything?' Dr Sarah said.

'I heard nothing that sounded like that!' Lila said. 'Coming and going, same as ever, but I didn't hear *that*.'

'We're going to fetch the police now,' Dr Sarah said. 'Would you mind telling your neighbours to stay inside and out of the way. I wouldn't want any of you to get mixed up in this.'

'Where's . . . ? I mean to say, Where's . . . ?' Lila said, chewing on her lip and glancing anxiously between Helen and the doctor.

'Do you use this "basket"?' Helen said, giving the woman a drilling look.

'Eh?'

'Do you know the names of any of the girls who come in and use this "basket"?'

'Whit? Oh! Right. Naw. I've my own room,' she said. 'I've no need for baskets. And I couldn't tell you anything about this one.'

'Not even who pays the rent?'

'Not a dicky bird and I'll away up and down the stair and make sure no one else knows either.'

'And you're certain sure the factor won't have a name?'

'Factor!' said Lila. 'Aye well, mister man that owns here might use a factor for his other places, his posher places, but round this bit he's got a big laddie with an even bigger pal.'

'Edinburgh is as Edinburgh does,' said Dr Sarah.

'You're a quick learner, doc,' Lila said.

The two women stood for a moment in shared understanding, until Helen started to fidget.

'Aye, you're right,' said Lila, noticing. 'I'll better get on with it.'

'That's my girl,' the doctor said, as though Lila wasn't ten years the senior. 'We'll give you fifteen minutes while we find a bobby, shall we say? Then home and doors locked.'

Lila – although Helen wondered what her real name was, if Rita was Patricia whenever she wasn't working – stopped in the threshold and said, 'Thanks,' before hurrying away.

★

137

It was that same copper they had seen outside the surgery, in the end. They spied him halfway up Palmerston Place, strolling along beside the grand, quiet buildings, with his hands behind his back and his boot heels clacking. He had a rare knack for avoiding anywhere there might be trouble, Helen thought to herself as she broke into a trot to catch him up before he could turn off onto one of the side streets, even quieter and more pleasant for a moonlit wander.

'Miss?' he said, turning at the sound of her steps. 'Doctor?' he added, as he saw that there were two of them. 'Are you needing an ambulance?'

'We're needing you and more than you,' Helen panted.

'There is a dead man in a little flat up by the distillery there,' said Dr Strasser. 'We need your help.'

'Aw michty!' said the constable. 'A man's died on the— I mean, a man's died where he never should have been, has he? Where's the prozzer?'

'I will thank you to keep a civil tongue in your head,' Dr Strasser said. 'And no, he didn't die "on the job" as you were so crudely about to say. He has been murdered. Strangled. So we shall need your superior officers and at least a fingerprint man and a photographer.'

The copper had been sulking since the word civil hit his ears but he couldn't argue with any of that and he set off at a clip for Torphichen Street and the big police station. Helen couldn't help thinking that if they'd found him on one of the lowly streets nearer the scene of the crime he would have blown his whistle and woken every shift worker and baby for a quarter mile around. But here on Palmerston Place he went quietly off, to take the nastiness away from these stately houses and not annoy anyone.

'I really cannot abide this city sometimes,' she said, hardly expecting Dr Sarah to understand what she meant, but needing to let the thought out before it turned her stomach.

'Let's get back and stop them rounding up every woman on the stair,' said Dr Sarah, who might have understood anyway.

★

It was two o'clock in the morning before they finally got away, having been grilled separately and together over and over again about what had brought them to the stair and why they had touched the body and the door handle and the banister, why they had gone traipsing through the streets instead of straight to the station.

It had worsened sharply when one of the many officials milling around – Helen had no idea who he was – finally took a good look at her and said, 'Here! Weren't you at the ice rink on Saturday?'

And then his colleague with the flashing camera clicked a finger at Dr Sarah and said, 'And youse were there at the baths too. What's going on here?'

'Mrs Crowther was at the baths on professional business, assisting a patient,' said Dr Sarah at her snootiest and most English-sounding. 'She rang me because one of you policemen didn't recognise a murder when it was committed under your noses. And I was rung up tonight because I am a doctor whose practice is very close to where that poor man met his sorry end. Of *course* the medical and welfare personnel of Fountainbridge are going to be called upon over murders in Fountainbridge. You Torphichen Street police are too. I might as well suck my teeth and wonder aloud if *you're* all mixed up in this dreadful business.'

'Nonsense!' said the inspector, who'd been listening.

'Agreed,' said Dr Sarah with a sweet smile.

'And the rink?' said the photographer.

'I went skating,' said Helen. 'It was Saturday night and the rink's just down the road.'

'But even so,' said the inspector, 'why did you stop off and collect your secretary before you came down here, *Doctor* Strasser.' The way he said 'doctor' spoke volumes about what he thought of a woman in her profession.

'Mrs Crowther is not a secretary,' said Dr Sarah. 'She is a welfare officer, acquainted with these streets and their residents, ideally placed to assist me in finding the right house.'

'We're not exactly strangers to the back of Haymarket ourselves, on the force,' the inspector said. 'You should have come to us.'

'Should I?' said Dr Sarah, sounding genuine and interested. 'Should I call for police help whenever a summons comes in the night to attend a patient?' The man flushed and turned away. But Dr Sarah was having none of it. 'Would you like to accompany me to confinements?' she said. 'Fever cases? How about whooping cough and colic? I was called to help a man in distress. I took a valued colleague with me. When I found evidence of crime I reported it. What did I do wrong?'

'Aye, aye, all right. Don't lose your shoe kicking me,' the inspector said. He must have meant to ruffle her dignity but Dr Sarah grinned back at him. She was a right one for colourful insults and this example was clearly going to be added to her repertoire immediately.

Helen was half-convinced that the next development was pure spite, because of that smile. The inspector lowered his eyebrows – sparse and no good for glowering with, but he tried anyway – and said, 'Right. I'm finished with you here but I'd like you to go to Torphichen Street and give a set of smudges to the desk sergeant, please.'

'Fingerprints?' said Dr Sarah. '*Our* fingerprints?'

'You've had your mitts all over the place, haven't you?' he shot back. 'Elimination purposes, of course.'

'How thrilling,' said Dr Sarah. 'Something new to put in my letter home this Sunday. My parents will be highly diverted, I'm sure.'

Helen, thinking of *her* parents, couldn't raise more than a sickly grin.

'I rather wonder that you didn't feel the need for Helen's and my prints from the baths,' the doc went on.

'And Helen was at the ice rink too.' Dr Sarah was goading him now. 'Although not in the men's lavatory at Maitland's.'

The inspector's face had been thunderous before but at the mention of the chophouse he lost all semblance of control. He spoke through clenched teeth, flecks of spittle flying out of his mouth at both corners. 'Fingerprints!' he said. 'Do you think you're going to get away with making a fool of me? Of us? What do you know about all this that you're not telling? Eh?'

Even the rest of the coppers turned in his direction, owl-eyed or smirking according to their natures, shocked or amused by their boss's outburst.

'Heavens, Inspector,' Dr Sarah said. 'Mrs Crowther only knows what the rest of the city knows. Whatever do you mean?'

Helen believed that this last piece of pertness sealed their fate. The inspector spoke over his shoulder to one of the constables, saying, 'Right. The whole stair. Over to Torphichen Street now to have prints taken. This pair too.'

'Eh, sir,' said the bobby, then quailed under his boss's glare. 'Right you are, sir.'

'You can't mean . . . ?' Dr Sarah said.

But he did. A pair of constables went up and down all four floors of the tenement knocking and shouting until every one of the girls, some still dressed in their cheap finery, some already in nighties and curlers, and most a long time past being 'girls', stood shivering and grumbling on their landings. And in their midst were Helen and Dr Sarah, like a pair of sparrows amongst a flock of parakeets. The baby was there, screaming lustily at being woken. The old man, although wakened and set to coughing again, was at least let stay in his bed by the constable who knocked up the room he shared with his daughter.

'Ach, we've got his prints already,' he said, in an aside. 'Old Eck's a regular, or he was before his chest packed up.'

'What's going on?' asked a large, high-breasted woman who seemed to be the stair foreman. Helen recognised her from the street, where she was often to be seen with a wall of jet-black hair sticking straight up from her forehead and adding yet more inches to her stature, as did the high heels on her bulging shoes. Tonight, her hair was wrapped in a scarf and her face shone with thickly plastered cold cream. All the same, as she tightened her shawl around her body, she reminded Helen of Greet, ready to go into battle.

'We're being made an example of,' Dr Sarah said, in a ringing voice designed to travel up the stairwell and shame the inspector. 'A very silly policeman thinks it will hurt our tender frailties to be marched through the streets with you all.'

'Ha!' said the large woman. 'He's never met you then, Doc. The things you said to me at that check up? I've never blushed so hard since I wet my knickers at the school when I was seven.'

And so there was something close to a party spirit as the women were shepherded out of the lane and through the quiet streets to the police station. The baby was passed around and soon came to view the outing as an unexpected treat, gurgling and chuckling at each new face. The large woman, who introduced herself as Mary, dropped back and fell into step with Helen as they straggled across the big tram junction.

'Where's Reet?' she said, without moving her lips.

'Safely stowed, with all her belongings,' Helen said. 'The man was nothing to do with her.'

'Oh, I know,' said Mary. 'She was at a do. Specially requested. She can look fourteen when she tries. Men are devils, Mrs C. I know you're married yourself, but men are devils, I'm telling you.'

'I'm lucky,' Helen said and had never meant it more.

The duty sergeant at the desk in Torphichen Street was not best pleased at the influx of extra work in the dead of night, nor at the raucous spirit of the girls, Dr Sarah included by this time. She had told them all about the clothes the corpse was wearing and collectively they seemed to have agreed that he probably deserved his fate.

It was when Helen was having her fingers grabbed and rolled and pinched in a way that was surely not necessary for the procedure that a thought struck her. Fingerprints. She grabbed for the thought before it escaped. It wasn't her being at the baths or rink or the basket tonight that had set the inspector off on this fit of spite. It was the mention of fingerprints. And it wasn't the first time in the last few days that the notion of fingerprints had caused such upset. If only she wasn't so tired she would be able to remember. Maybe when she got out into the fresh air again she could ask Dr Sarah if *she* could bring it to mind.

But, by the time they were trailing home, the bakers and newsboys of the city already awake and en route to their work, the thought had passed again.

Chapter 12

Next morning, Helen was met just inside the basement door by Dr Strasser, dressed for the day apart from his indoor shoes, but with his face still shiny from his morning wash.

'Well, Helen,' he said, as she took off her hat and hung up her raincoat. 'My wife has told me to apply to you for explanation of the sudden addition to the household.'

'Eh?' Helen said. She sat down behind her desk and drew her daily calendar nearer.

'Not that it's not very nice to have a return to the service we enjoyed before the war,' he said. 'Why, in my father's day there were two maids and a cook and he had a driver for his carriage in the very early days. She makes a mean tattie scone too. But who is she?'

'Oh!' said Helen. 'Patricia? Well, Doc, she had to get out of a dangerous fix suddenly last night and she didn't have any money or anywhere to go and so it was either come to stay with me – but you know what a gossip my mother is, not to mention my sister, and how they run in and out of my house like it's a cuckoo clock – so since there was more space here and not a load of people tramping in and out – of the upstairs that is, of course – or if you *did* have guests they wouldn't care who was sleeping in the attic, would they? – we decided she should come here. Just till things settle down again.'

'Oh you did, did you?' he said. 'You decided. And what "things" would these be?'

'Sorry,' Helen said. 'Yes, more like: I asked the doc and I suppose it was hard for her to say no with Rita standing right there on the doorstep.'

'I'm teasing,' he said. 'But who's Rita?'

'Patricia, I mean. And, Doc, as to what things . . . I wonder if you really want to know.'

'Is it related to my wife's avid interest in the recent spate of murders?'

'*You* seemed quite taken up with it too, Doc,' Helen said. She was never very sure where the line was that, once crossed, would have her scolded and punished. Sometimes it seemed to her that she was determined to find it. Right now, she held her breath until Dr Strasser laughed and pushed himself up from where he had been leaning against her doorway.

'So it's four?' he said. 'Just as we prophesied. Which surely makes it well-nigh certain that the police will solve it.'

Helen frowned. 'How do you make that out?'

'Or rather, with that many bodies piling up, the police can be relied upon to do their damnedest to solve it. And there's no need for anyone else to be involved.'

'Ah,' said Helen.

'And certainly no one in her right mind would obstruct them.'

'How do you mean?'

'I want you, as well as my wife, to reassure me that we are not harbouring a criminal.'

'Well,' said Helen. 'Not a murderer anyway.'

Dr Strasser didn't quite laugh this time but only shook his head as he walked away. Helen could hear the first of her morning list coming down the area steps and into the wee waiting room in the old cellar. She put everything out

146

of her mind except how best to help the deserving people of Fountainbridge who, she assumed, cared not a whit for the gore and melodrama gripping the city and filling the newspapers.

She was quite wrong. The patient who came into her office on the last stroke of nine o'clock, was full of it.

'I didn't want to bother the doctor,' she said. It was a sentence Helen heard ten times a day. 'But it's about these killings, you see.'

Helen nodded but said nothing, waiting to hear more. This woman, Mrs King, could usually be relied upon to give every last scrap of detail needed and then some. Today was no exception. 'The thing is, they four men won't be the last of it and mine works at the ice rink, see? I've telt him to get a note off the doctors to say he's off his work till it's all seen to. But he's adamant he's going in. I've telt him to say it's his nerves and he said to me nerves are women's business.'

'Well—'

'As if we didn't all see the shell shock with our own eyes all they years ago.'

It was a good point and Helen couldn't argue.

'So is there anything you can do?'

'To . . . help you stop worrying?' said Helen. 'Or to . . . get a sick note without a consultation? Maybe to the first, Mrs King, but not the second. I'm afraid if your husband wants to go to work there's nothing anyone can do to stop him. But, as I say, I can help you feel better about it and stop fretting. Because I don't think there's any reason to suppose the killer will go back to the same place twice.'

'All *round* here though but.'

'Yes, but I'd be more worried if my husband worked in the dairy than the ice rink.'

'Your man's a scaffie, is he no?'

It wasn't a term Helen cared for even though Sandy didn't seem to mind it. 'I meant, for example,' she said. 'I think nowhere's safer than the ice rink, that chophouse, the baths or— Hang on. Mrs King, how do you know there's four? I had a look at the morning papers first thing and the news wasn't out yet.'

Mrs King stared at Helen very hard while the colour rose in her cheeks. She dipped her head before she spoke. 'My cousin,' she said. 'She's had a hard life and she's gone to the bad, I'm sorry to say. I give her what I can when I can and always on a Tuesday morning, last few scraps left from our big dinner.'

'You're very kind,' Helen said. 'So you'll have heard that I was there too.'

'*Whit?*' Mrs King's voice rang out fit to break the lightbulb and Helen had to bite her lip to save from bursting out in laughter.

'I was called on to help,' she said. 'But then I had to go to Torphichen Street to hand in my fingerprints like everyone else. And I know what you said but if your cousin didn't pass on *that* bit of gossip then she hasn't gone to the bad completely, if you ask me.'

'She's a martyr to the drink,' said Mrs King. 'My auntie won't look at the road she's on. And even I can't have her over the door. My man won't stand for it.'

'Have you ever been to her place?' Helen said, then shushed and soothed as the other woman broke out in spluttering and indignant denials. 'Of course not! Sorry! I didn't mean anything. Only to say that's it's not as bad as you might be imagining. It's single-ends but who's never lived in a single-end? I just meant don't be picturing something from *Oliver Twist.*'

'Aye, fine, okay,' said Mrs King. She tapped her fingertips against her lips, thinking. 'So it's the men at the brewery and distillery and all the pubs and works that haven't been hit yet that need to keep their wits about them, you reckon? Because my oldest nephew is on the goods yard.'

'Not exactly even that,' Helen said. 'The working men have nothing to fear. Don't you know?' She cast her mind back over what had been written in *The Scotsman* the Strassers took every day and the *Daily Record* that Sandy and Gavin passed up to her once they had read it.

'Eh?' said Mrs King.

'The men who were killed weren't folk like us,' Helen said. 'They were gentlemen. Toffs. Or at least they were each found places they'd never been in their lives. They didn't belong with the clothes they wore either.'

'They wore no clothes at all,' said Mrs King. 'That's what I've been hearing. My Tony says the man at the rink was as naked as a newborn baby.'

Helen could have explained the slaughterman's trousers hanging on the cubicle door, the leather apron in the gents' lav and the gauzy linen pinny invisible in the ice, even if she didn't choose to describe the garments worn by last night's victim, but she was suddenly seized by a much better idea.

'Mrs King, was your husband actually working at the rink on Saturday night?'

'No,' she said. 'What are you hinting at? He was not. He was home with his family like every other Saturday night in life. He's a good man. There's not a pub landlord or bookie in the city who knows his name or his face.' She took a breath. 'He was *called* in. Gone ten o'clock it was, and him ready for his bed after a hard week on the day shifts like always, but he was called in to help them deal with clearing up. They made a right mess, did the polis. Ice needs to be handled just so.'

'How terrible for him,' Helen said, feeling a heel for speaking with such a forked tongue. 'I know he's said to you that he's got no such thing as nerves and doesn't need a line, but if I was to come to yours after his shift ends tonight, say, would he talk to me, do you think?'

'That would be very kind,' Mrs King said. 'He must be feeling it even if he says otherwise to me. Thank you, Mrs Crowther.'

'Please don't mention it, Mrs King,' said Helen. She felt guilty enough already without having to accept gratitude as well. She was almost glad that for the rest of the morning, there was nothing but moaner after moaner, unsatisfied and unreasonable, blaming Helen for all their problems and hating all her suggestions.

It didn't take long, Helen thought to herself, for last year's astonished jubilation at the reading spectacles, cough bottles, filled teeth and walking sticks to give way to this. As another knock came at her office door, long past the time when everyone knew her dinner started, she didn't hold out much hope that whoever it was would be different.

When the door opened, though, without her having spoken to invite entry, she saw that she was both wrong and yet more right than she could describe. It was Teenie.

'Why aren't you at school?' Helen said.

'Half-term,' said Teen. 'Mammy told me.'

'Told you what?' said Helen, running through the things Greet might have blabbed to Teenie if she'd a mind. There was no end to the list, since the girls' mother was more than capable of making something up out of whole cloth before sharing it.

'That you're having a party for Halloween to make up for me missing the one at the church hall.'

Halen gaped. Had Greet really built up an order given – to take Teen on a treat sometimes – into a promise received to make that treat a party within days? Or had Teen decided that nothing else would console her and surged ahead as if all she

150

had to do was say it out loud to make it true? Either one was possible.

'Oh, that's just typical,' Teenie said. 'You're as bad as them. All po-faced and holier-than-thou and then dropping anything you don't fancy.'

'I— I— Look, Teenie-bash, you're—'

'Don't call me that when you're being so horrible to me. You saw my dress. What am I supposed to do with it? Give it to the rag and bone man?'

Her voice was rising and Helen stood to go and shut the door. The doctors were kind and all that, but she knew she was different with them than she was with her family and she didn't want to have to try to juggle her two selves if Teenie's ranting brought Dr Sarah down here, nose aquiver.

'Apart from anything else,' she said, giving her sister's shoulder a friendly pat as she passed, 'what about what *they* said?'

Teenie jerked away from Helen's hand as if her touch was a bee sting. 'What *who* said?'

'Your church. If they think it's not right to be having a party and weans out at night to come to it, when there's a dangerous man on the loose in the town, then I shouldn't be having one either.'

'Aye but this lot had a party every Halloween right through the war, even when Elly Ally was happening that minute.'

'El Alamein?'

'When anyone could have got bombed any night at all,' Teen said. 'So don't tell me one wee numpty that thinks he's Auld Nick has floored them. I think it's a story. Anyway, he'd fit right in at Halloween, wouldn't he?'

Helen stared at her sister but decided against arguing. 'Well, whatever the real reason is that they're not to go ahead,' she said instead, 'I'm sure it's a good one.'

'Why would you rather believe them than your own sister? They're just covering their backs, because they've changed their minds or they've run out of money or something. It was gey quiet when I was there on Sunday.'

'Showing your face,' said Helen, still not liking the sound of this at all.

'Same as I'll be at the piskies just before Christmas. Their carol concert is miles better than ours and even Mammy thinks so.'

'Right well, don't come to me if they call that off come December either. Look, be sensible, Teen: where am I supposed to have this party that was going to fill a great big church hall?'

'Tiny toty church hall,' Teen said. 'It's not a real church, Nelly. What have I told you? They're a funny wee bunch, the pee-the-beds.'

'Don't call them that!'

'*Continence*, mind,' said Teenie. 'It's their own stupid fault.'

Helen had a sudden flash of understanding and laughed out loud before she could stop herself. Teenie hated being laughed at. 'It's not "continence", you wee daftie. This is Gilmore Place at the Viewforth crossroads, isn't it? It's "abstinence".'

'What does that mean when it's at home?'

'It means . . . get away with you and let me eat my piece,' Helen said. 'Continence! Aye dear, Teenie, I'll see what I can do about a wee party for you, but it'll be at my house so don't invite the whole world.'

'Halloween night or the Saturday?' Teenie said, quick as a flash.

'Halloween night itself,' Helen said, just as promptly, thinking Monday would be easier to manage.

'No!' Teenie wailed. 'Halloween night itself is for the guising.'

152

'But Mammy'll never let you out guising with a madman on the loose. And you're a bit big for it anyway, are you not?'

'Make your mind up. You're forever telling me I'm a bairn and I shouldn't forget it.'

'We'll see,' Helen said.

'That means "No but I'm not telling you yet",' Teen said. 'Same as when Mammy used to use it. Back when you were on my side. Back when you were fun.'

'Look, you'll have to go! I've got less than half an hour left and I'm needing every minute of it. I'll tell you if it's Saturday or Monday as soon as I can get a minute's peace to think.'

Teenie flounced out, blowing Helen a kiss from the doorway, then poked her head back round and said, 'You're out of luck. There's someone coming already and he looks as sick as a parrot. Rather you than me.'

'Get away and take your nonsense with you!' Helen said, charging towards the door to placate whoever was coming, out of her hours, to seek help.

When she got there, just as Teenie disappeared, it was Billy standing in the passageway.

'Sorry,' he said. 'Is this all right? Can I come in?'

'I'll need to eat my dinner but you can share it,' Helen said, mindful of the time she had been offered a share of the mortuary's daily pie order. It had taken a strong stomach to accept.

'Go ahead,' Billy said. 'I'm not hungry but don't let me stop you. I need to speak to you, see?'

Helen persuaded him to accept a cup of tea and went off to the tap outside the lav to get the water going. She preferred to eat with a glass of water and enjoy her tea afterwards, ever since she had read a pamphlet on digestion written by a Swiss doctor, but she'd have to abandon that healthy habit today. She put two sugars in Billy's cup, returned to her office and set it in front of him. It was odd and unsettling to see him here, in her place, so different from his place. Although, as she had noticed on Saturday night, when he was not dressed in his cotton outfit and red-handed with the rough soap and scalding water, he was a well-looking sort. Neat and clean, without being dapper. Helen couldn't abide dapper men. As she thought this, she remembered that it ought to be of no consequence to her whether Billy was the biggest dandy in Scotland and she cleared her throat and launched into questioning him hoping to distract herself before a blush could overtake her, or to distract him from the surge of colour if she failed, anyway.

'What's the matter then?' she said. 'What brings you here? Is it the new one?'

'Naw. We're doing the . . . fourth one . . . this afternoon. It's hard to know what to call him, isn't it?'

'Boiled, frozen, choked and . . . shamed, maybe.' Helen considered this and nodded. 'Getting him trussed up like that and putting him where he was found? It must have been meant to shame him.'

'Not that the first three were left much dignity either,' Billy said, 'but I know what you mean. Aye right, the shamed man. We're doing him this afternoon, as long as nothing more urgent comes in.'

'It's hard to see what could be more urgent than the fourth victim of a murderous rampage,' Helen said.

'That's the thing though,' Billy said. 'Remember I said there had been a mysterious visit from the Fiscal?' Helen nodded. 'He's been back again. He was there this morning in the boss's office – and he sounded even more keyed up than last time.'

'Did you overhear anything?' Helen said. 'I mean did you happen to be passing and happen to catch any of what they said?'

'No,' said Billy, 'I did not happen to accidentally overhear anything, but I did choose to squeeze into the cupboard that shares an air chute with the office – we need good ventilation in the mortuary – and I did choose to eavesdrop on every word that passed between them.'

'Oh, Billy,' Helen said. Billy flushed and rubbed his hand on the back of his head, mussing the brilliantined perfection he had combed into his hair. 'That's smashing, that is!'

Billy dropped his hand and first gawped then grinned at her. 'That's my girl,' he said. 'You won't feel too squeamish about helping me work it out then?'

'Not me,' Helen said. She brushed the crumbs off her front and screwed up the brown paper bag her piece had been wrapped in, throwing it at the wastepaper basket to clear her desk and therefore her mind.

'The Fiscal said three things that were gey queer, if you ask me,' Billy said. 'He said there was no need to be hasty and no need for alarm—'

'Eh?' Helen said. 'No need for alarm? With a body a day, near abouts, turning up? That's ridiculous. Are you sure, Billy? How clearly can you hear through a ventilation grille, or whatever it is? Are you sure he didn't say there was no point letting alarm spread through the people if it could be helped? I can see the sense in that.'

'Absolutely not,' said Billy. 'Because the next thing he said was that the only real pity was how there was no way of sharing that good news with "the populace".'

Helen frowned, puzzling it out or trying to. When she was quite sure she had failed, she turned to the other bit of the speech. 'I can't deny that bit's a conundrum,' she said. 'But as to the "no need to be hasty", that makes sense, doesn't it? He'll have meant don't be too hasty and get it wrong. He'll have meant do a proper job even if it's not a quick one.'

'And again, no,' said Billy. 'Cos here's the third bit. The Fiscal said to Slice it would be tricky – no, that's not the word he used. What was it? Aha! – it would be "ticklish" to balance not being overly hasty in finding the culprit with stopping any of the good people of the city from thinking the police were dragging their feet.'

'Are you sure?' Helen said. 'No need for alarm, but can't tell anyone that, and no need to be hasty but better look it? That sounds awfy skew-whiff.'

'If you'd heard him, Nelly,' said Billy. 'The way he said "good people" and "populace" and to call anything about this "ticklish"! It stuck in my craw, I can tell you. Him drawling and sneering, but I'll tell you this: I didn't believe a word of it. Oh, he was trying to sound like a gentleman at his club with a double dram and a fat cigar, but he was feart all the same. I could hear it in his voice much as he tried to hide it.'

'Good,' said Helen. 'I hope he's up all night pacing.'

Billy shot her a grin, then sobered again. 'But what do you make of it? I'll admit I came up here hoping I'd lay it all out and you'd go, "Oh aye, that's clear as day".'

'Clear as mud,' said Helen. 'Sorry. The best we can hope is that the Fiscal comes back a third time and says a bit more.'

'Nae chance,' Billy said. 'That was the parting shot. He said to Slice that it had been easy to account for visits to the Cowgate with bodies turning up like something from a penny dreadful, but now that there were to be no more murders, there were to be no more visits either.'

'No more murders?' said Helen.

Billy smacked his head. 'Man, I forgot to tell you. Aye, so four things. That's the last.'

'But no more visits if there's no more murders could be innocent,' Helen said.

'Naw,' said Billy. 'On account of he also said, nothing over the telephone and no letters either. Not a word in writing. That's what he said, Helen. As sure as I'm sitting here.'

'That makes no sense at all,' Helen said. 'And what a scunner that nobody's to know. My wee sister would be thrilled to bits to know it was all over. And my last client too. All the folk in all the places, waiting for another one to turn up. Billy, why would the Fiscal keep good news quiet? And why would your boss agree?'

Chapter 13

Helen thought it all through very carefully. Dr Sallis – she couldn't call him Slice, not even in her own thoughts – and the Fiscal knew it was over but didn't want the public to know the same. Topsy-turvy, any way you looked at it. Maybe they even knew who the killer was but didn't want to arrest him yet. And that was upside down too. Helen was absolutely mystified. She was so mystified that she concluded she must be wrong. She worked back and dismantled her theory, if you could call it that, then tried to think of another one, failed, and fell back on the notion that Billy must have misheard, like he must have misheard 'dentist' the first time.

It was easier to settle on that without Billy there before her, swearing up and down that he had heard it all as clear as day, but she couldn't just keep going round and round: she had a full waiting room of petitioners and complainers and a visit due to an old woman waiting for a room in a nursing home. Afterwards, she hoped that if she'd seemed remote, they would call it 'being professional' and might even prefer it to the way she usually went around chooking babies under the chin and asking for jam recipes.

Maybe, she told herself as she made her way towards the Kings' house after tea, talking to an ice-rink man about *how* one of the murders was done would shoogle something loose and the why and who of it would fall into her lap too. If not, she could always try at the baths next. Surely the attendants couldn't have talked about anything else in their wee net-muffled bothy over the last week since that terrible night for them all. She had cooked her goose at the café but that was the least puzzling of the four anyway, requiring no more than wriggling through a window and undoing the bolt on a door. And restraining a man like a French farmer with his goose, she acknowledged, but that was nothing like rigging up a boiler in a cubicle or doing whatever was done at the rink.

The four murders fell into two pairs, in fact. The café and Rita's room took no kind of special skill or knowledge, just the nerve and the badness required to kill a man. At the rink and the baths, the murderer needed know-how and also had to summon the extra gall to do something that took time and would be impossible to explain away, if interrupted.

The choked man and the shamed man went together in another way too, one that the boiled and frozen men didn't, if only Helen could put her finger on it. She knew there was more sniggering and whispering about them amongst the good folk of Fountainbridge and even the doctors; more genuine horror about the first two. Not that she thought being trussed up in women's unmentionables or suffocated with steak and cake was funny, but it was terrible in a way that extreme heat and extreme cold weren't. It was – she searched for the word – farcical.

Mrs King had given her instructions earlier, but Helen still had to search for the entrance when she arrived. It wasn't a tenement, to her surprise, although she should have twigged when she was told 'the corner of Leven Street and Tarvit Street'. That was the King's Theatre, as everyone on the southside of Edinburgh knew, whether they had ever been taken to a panto or, like Helen, had made do with the coloured posters and a keek in the front lobby at the big Christmas tree. Eventually she found a door with 'A KING' written on a card. It was a long way from the front entrance with all its lights and its brass, got at via a back alley and a rusted metal staircase that made the way up to Rita's single end look swanky.

'Found us then,' Mrs King said, answering the door. 'Cannae miss us, eh?' She chuckled. 'Talk about your name in lights!'

'Do folk not chap this door thinking you're a back way in?' Helen said. She entered the passageway and thought that indeed this house must have been carved out of a bit of the theatre's backstage at some point in the past. There was something both very grand and very makeshift about the way the windows were set so low to the floor, the way carved arches had been cut off to make new walls and smaller rooms.

'Not often enough,' Mrs King said. 'Tony loves it when an artiste rolls up. They're always ready to stay and talk for a cup of tea and a bit toast.'

'I'll have to do today.'

'Aye, come away in,' Mrs King said and led Helen under one of these half arches into a room with open beams and an ornate cast-iron stove, covered with brass twiddles, which sat in the middle of an empty floor. Beyond it, a tall man with jet-black hair and olive skin sat in his shirtsleeves smoking a pipe.

'Are you the private detective?' Mr King said. He had an accent Helen had never heard before; definitely not Scottish and not Irish either but making her think of Irish somehow.

'I'm not!' she said. 'I'm a welfare officer. That's my job. But I've got a bee in my bonnet about all this, Mr King, I don't mind telling you.'

'And am I one of your suspects you've come to interrogate?'

'No,' she said, trying not to yelp it. Mr King had a different way of talking as well as a different sound to his voice, teasing her like a laddie or like some toffs did for their own entertainment sometimes. He didn't sound like any working man

161

Helen had ever heard; completely different from his wife, who was Fountainbridge through and through.

Mrs King was bustling about a sort of camp kitchen they had rigged up on a long table by the back wall, drawing water from a tall jug and setting a kettle onto a wee paraffin stove.

'You'll have a cup of coffee, Mrs Crowther?' she said.

'Or tea,' Helen said.

'I'll put a dash of rum in it and a spoonful of syrup. It's a cold night.'

Helen was speechless. She turned back to the husband, as offering the easier task. 'I don't suspect you of a thing, Mr King. It's just that, as well as not knowing who did these terrible deeds or even who it was they were done to, much less why . . . when it comes to the fro— to the poor man in the ice, I don't even know *how*. Him and the boi— the man in the bath. The pair of them. I just thought you'd be able to work out the . . .'

'Mechanics of it,' he said, nodding. 'Aye, it's been bothering me how it was carried off. One good reason I wouldn't listen to the romni telling me to stay away. Too nosy, like you.'

'Listen to *who*?' said Helen.

'Her there,' said Mr King, jabbing his thumb towards his wife. 'Mrs— Look, I can't keep calling you Mrs Crowther. What's your name, chavi?'

'Stop showing off, Tony,' said Mrs King from the kitchen end of the room. 'He's fair folk, Mrs Crowther, and woe betide anyone who doesnae find out.'

'Fair folk?' said Helen, taking a moment to grasp her meaning. 'Oh, you mean the shows? A funfair? Was—? Is that—? What language is that then? *Chavi* and *romni*?'

'Cut down and driven indoors by the wiles of a woman,' Mr King said. 'Chained to a pay packet and forced to live in the shadows of the world I love.'

162

'Like the phantom of the opera,' Helen said. She had been taken to see it at the New Vic when she was wee and had to sleep in beside Greet and Mack for a week.

Mr King threw back his head and laughed, showing a mouth that was half gold teeth and half bare gums. 'She's a sharp one this, doll,' he said. 'She can stay.'

Mrs King handed Helen a cup and settled down on a chair Helen had thought was a pile of blankets. Or maybe it *was* a pile of blankets, but it looked like the woman's chosen seat.

'How long have you worked at the rink, Mr King?' Helen said.

'I was on an ice show for fifteen years after my old papa died and left the galloper to my brother. The merry-go-round,' he added. 'So when this one—' again he jerked his thumb at his wife '—talked me into bricks, I got a job at the rink, easy as pie.'

Helen nodded and took a sip from her cup, meaning to be polite then put it down. Her eyes opened wide as she felt a delicious, spicy, creamy, warming draught slip down her throat and make her fingertips tingle. 'Thank you,' she said to Mrs King.

Then she turned back to the husband. 'So you know a lot about ice then? How was it done? How long would it take to melt that much of the ice and then freeze it again with him inside? How deep is it anyway?'

Mr King started to laugh and kept on until the guffaws turned to wheezing and then to coughs. 'You—You think that great big block of ice . . . ?' he managed to get out at last. He cleared his throat and blew his nose on a red spotted handkerchief he pulled out of his pocket like a magician's prop. 'Chavi, the ice is about four inches thick on that rink, then it's steel, gravel, sand and stone underneath. If it was thick enough to hide a body in, it would use all the coal from every mine in the country to keep it frozen.'

'Are you saying it was a trick?' Helen said. 'That he wasn't real? I saw him. And the people at the mortuary had to wait till he thawed out before they could do the postmortem.'

'Aye, aye, I saw him too,' said Mr King. 'Him in his wee white pinny all tied up with a bow.' He jabbed a finger at Helen. 'That bit's not been given to the papers, mind. So not a word, eh?'

Helen didn't tell him she already knew; she was too busy puzzling over the huge block of ice, four inches thick. 'I don't understand,' she said.

'Stop teasing her, Tony,' said Mrs King. 'It's *mostly* four inches thick with steel and all that underneath.'

'Aye, aye,' her husband said. 'Mostly. Except there's one place where there's a tray, and under it a pocket, like a hidey-hole, to get down and tinker with the doings.'

'Like a . . . secret drawer in a jewellery box?' said Helen, trying to picture it.

'Exactly. But, sometime before Saturday night, someone lifted out the tray and dropped in a great big square block with a body in it, then they probably heated the join with a blow torch to smooth it over. When we boosted the freezer before the rink opened, it would all firm up again. See?'

'I see that bit,' Helen said, 'but it only makes the rest of it murkier. Where was the big block made? Who could have done that without being seen?'

Mr King shrugged. He finished his coffee with a smack of his lips and set the cup down on the floorboards at his side. 'Nowhere in the rink. That's for sure. We've got no way of making that much ice.'

'And how did they move it into place?'

Again, Mr King just opened his hands wide, looking like those old Sunday school pictures of Jesus preaching. 'We've got dollies,' he said. 'Some of the rig for the summer spectacular is heavier than you'd believe. The Christmas show

164

too but, beyond that, your guess is as good as mine.' He took a long suck on his pipe, drawing his cheeks in until the outline of his teeth and his gaps showed through them. At last, the bowl glowed red and he puffed out a long stream of smoke, coughing a little again.

'And how could anyone break into the rink, hefting that great big lump of ice?' Helen said. 'Don't you have a night-watchman?'

'Aye, there's poor wee Melvin,' Mr King said. 'He's been the nightwatchman at Haymarket all the time I've been there. Strange job for a youngster I always thought, but he's not quite right, is our Mel. He'd be hard-pressed to get anything else and I think he got tooken on as a favour more or less.'

'Favour to who?' said Helen. A simple-minded nightwatch-man sounded like a ridiculous way to keep ne'er-do-wells away, in her opinion.

'Ocht, you know, good works and all that. The manager's not what you'd think, so he's not. Boswell's a grand old gypsy name, but Mr Boswell about as far from . . . I mean to say, it's all flash and fun on the ice but he's a right goody two shoes in his own life.' He seemed to reflect for a moment and then gave a laugh. 'A scaredy-cat too. I went asking fifteen years back, thinking they'd be my people! Ice rink same as a cir-cus or the shows at the end of the pier, you know? Thinking I'd sit and have a drink and find some shared friends and that would get me a job. Mind, doll?' Mrs King nodded, smiling. 'Turned out I got the job out of pity and frilly-anthy-whatsit.'

'Philanthropy?' Helen said.

Mr King chuckled. 'They thought I was Irish and needed a helping hand. I sometimes say – don't I doll? – if I tell them I'm a gypsy I might get a better wage!'

'*Are* you?' Helen said. 'Really and truly? Was that Romany words then? I've never met a gypsy that lived in a— Ohhhh,

165

"into bricks", you said. He must think a lot about you, Mrs King.' Helen knew she was talking more freely than she should but felt unable to do anything about it. The rum-laced coffee had carried her off.

'I am,' said Mr King. 'Full-blooded on both sides and Romany my native tongue, reduced to living above a theatre, the closest I can get to the world where I belong.'

'How ever did you meet?' Helen said, looking between the two of them.

'On the shows,' said Mrs King. 'I was a contortionist before four babies filled up my middle and stopped me.'

Helen had to bite her lip to prevent a plea for a demonstration slipping out. Then, despite the rum, her professional self took over and she looked around the sparse furnishings and the makeshift facilities. 'Four babies?' she said. 'Where are they?'

'Not babies now,' Mrs King said. 'The eldest is running the gallopers for his uncle. They never had any family of their own, so my big girl is with him, taking tickets and cooking for the men. The wee laddies are away in Turkey, training.'

'For *what*?' said Helen.

'Fire eaters,' said their father proudly. 'There's no one on earth for eating fire like the Turks.'

'Well, you're no scaredy-cats, you Kings,' Helen said. She blinked. 'What made you say that, anyway? About your boss?'

'Ocht, that wasn't fair,' said Mr King. 'Just that he's tooken himself off till this murderer's been caught. Haven't seen hide nor hair of him. Typical!'

★

As Helen walked home shortly afterwards, she felt she was making a greater journey than the few streets between their two houses. She felt she was leaving a thrilling world to

166

return to her own much more mundane life. And a rather lonely life. She was no longer in the bosom of her family. She certainly wasn't one of the gang with Sandy and Gavin and, although the Strassers were kind to her, she was on the edge of their life too. This time last year she thought Carolyn was going to fill all the gaps but, as the scandal of the Sinclair family started to fade, some of her own set began to remember how much they missed Carolyn's wit and cheer and, even down in the Botanics – since she didn't have a snobbish bone in her body – she was beginning to make more friends, ones she saw every day and could stop in for a glass of beer with after they hung up their spades. She'd certainly got on like a house on fire with Tam. From Tam, it was a short step in Helen's thoughts to the only person in the whole of the city who seemed to choose Helen first, above all others, and she didn't know what to do about *that*.

So, instead of going straight home, she stopped at the telephone kiosk at Tollcross and rang Carolyn's number. There was a system with the family in the major portion of the house. For them, people rang up; for Carolyn, they rang twice, broke the connection and rang again. It was a boon, this new automatic exchange. Helen would never had had the nerve to ask an operator to do that for her, nor would she have wanted to get the family involved in shouting up the stairs and summoning their lodger to the telephone. This way was easy.

'Nell?' said Carolyn's voice. 'Is everything all right? It's awfully late.'

'Sorry!' Helen said. 'You know what just occurred to me? I don't make enough effort. I always wait for you to get a hold of me, so I thought for once I'd do a bit of the running.'

'You called me and invited me to the morgue not even a week ago,' Carolyn said. 'And it's you I've got to thank for the outing with Tam, my new beau.'

'Aye, right,' Helen said. 'Ocht well. Anyway, this doesn't count either because if you thought getting grabbed by Tam was bad wait till you hear what's next.'

'More corpses?'

'Worse. I said I'd organise a Halloween party for my wee sister. Do you want to come?'

'Fancy dress?'

'Not if you don't wan—'

'Of course I want to! I shall come as . . . Well, I shall have to decide what to come as but I'm a firm yes. When is it?'

'Haven't decided. It was supposed to be this coming Saturday, but the organisers withdrew. Can you face a party on a Monday?'

'Withdrew? That's shabby.'

'Well, it was a church do and the church decided a party wasn't safe with that man out from West House.'

'A good deal safer than children traipsing around in the dark guising,' Carolyn said.

'Or maybe they thought it was poor taste, with all these murders going on.'

Carolyn made a rude noise down the line, making Helen wonder how secluded the telephone was in that big house up in the Grange, and what the family would think if they could overhear.

'Poor taste!' she said. 'They sound like a lot of ninnies. I shall take great pleasure in helping you show the youngsters a good time, Nelly. Why not come up here tomorrow for supper and we can start to plot our triumph.'

★

Before that, though, the next day delivered a chance for Helen to return to the baths, more or less innocently, when a home visit to an overwhelmed young wife in Lochrin Buildings turned up three children in dire need of a good scrub and a nit comb.

'I could murder that besom!' the young woman said, when Helen explained why she was there. It had been the downstairs neighbour who had come slinking into the surgery, with a pious look of concern on her face, saying 'poor Mrs Bell wasn't coping'. 'I had a terrible tummy, Mrs Crowther,' she went on. 'Running at both ends, I was. I couldn't leave the po to get the weans washed and I didn't want them in the sink I kept being sick into.'

Helen couldn't help taking a step backwards, although it was a thing she had strenuously trained herself to stop doing. 'Did any of them come down with it?' she said. 'You should tell the doctor if you think it's contagious.'

'Naw,' said Mrs Bell. 'It was a kipper. I kent it was on the turn but there wasn't enough of anything else to go round so I ate it and gave the weans the eggs. It was as high as a church spire, so it serves me right. And I knew they'd been and got lousy from somewhere too, but I couldn't face them.'

'And how are you feeling now?' Helen said. 'If I make you some tea and toast and you have a good nap in your bed for an hour or two, could you maybe get this place cleaned up and running fair again after?'

'How?' said Mrs Bell, instantly suspicious of any kindness. What a life she must have had to get so wary so young.

'I'll take the wee ones to the baths,' Helen said. 'Give you a chance to get yourself ahead of things. No need for this to go any further, if it was just a kipper.'

Mrs Bell surveyed her three children, who were sitting on the floor playing at chuckies with a handful of wee black stones. Even with the light of maternal love in her eye, she surely couldn't think they were much of a prospect. To Helen's gaze, with their hair knotted up from scratching and their faces grimy with spit and snot and coal dust, they were simply pitiable. She tried not to think about what was under their clothes, since the state of the littlest one's bare feet was enough to soften her gullet.

'Right,' she said, 'You three get clean clothes each out the press. Vest and knickers, leggings, shorts or a skirt, and a jersey each. Then get your shoes on. Coats too and you'll all need a hat you don't want to keep. Where do you keep your towels, Mrs Bell?'

'I've nae clean towels,' she said. 'There was two days I couldn't lift my head, Mrs Crowther, or my behind either.'

Helen swallowed hard. 'Don't wash them,' she said. 'Just wrap them and put them out for the bucket, eh? I'll get new for you. Make up for the three hats I'm cowping.'

'It's no that cold,' said Mrs Bell. 'Hats?'

'That's not the problem,' said Helen. 'Come on, babies! What's your names? Who can run fastest? Come on and show me!'

She shepherded them out of the stair and back to Gardener's Crescent, lining them up on the doorstep and daring them to move and risk not getting a lollipop, while she went inside to the big cupboard of emergency linens Dr Sarah and she had started filling one terrible day when the state of the bedclothes in a patient's house had left them both unable to eat their dinners.

'I'm taking a right bite out of the pile of towels, Doc,' she said, when Dr Sarah came to see what was going on.

'Do I want to know?'

'I wish *I* didn't know,' Helen said. She parcelled up five towels in brown paper and string then went downstairs to her own cupboard for the paraffin oil and fine comb.

'Toffee for Tommy,' she said, back out on the step, handing a lolly to the big boy, 'chocolate for Roy, and strawberry sherbet for Doreen. Or you can swap.'

170

But the children had already unwrapped the lollipops and stuck them into their pursed mouths. They looked like three little old men smoking thin cigarettes and Helen had to smile. She took the hands of the smaller two and ordered Tommy to walk in front where she could keep an eye on him, then marched them off to Caledonian Crescent.

'Now put your hats on tight,' she said, when they arrived, 'tuck your hair up, Doreen. And don't scratch. No scratching, you hear me?' She ushered them inside and up to the ticket desk.

'One shilling and thruppence, please,' she said.

'Are *you* getting in?' said the woman behind the counter, keeping her hand clamped on the ticket dispenser. It wasn't allowed for adults and children to share a bath at Cally Crescent.

'Wi' this shower of wee coal lumps?' said Helen. 'You're kidding me.'

Her effort to be friendly fell flat. The woman just tucked her folded arms more tightly under the bosom that was straining her white overall and said, 'How old are you?' to Tommy.

'Five,' he said, with big innocent eyes that no amount of filth could change. Helen tried not to smile. He was seven, but five was the last age the trams and buses were free and his mammy had him well told.

'Hmph,' the woman said. She had one last arrow in her quiver. 'What's with the hats?'

'They'll get cold on the way home with wet hair and they wanted to wear them on the way here too,' Helen said. 'Save me carrying them.'

'They better have them on when they come back out,' said the woman with a glare.

'How come?' Helen said, trying to look puzzled. She had no intention of hurrying this bath and she was sure the woman would be off her shift when they left. Anyway, what would she do after the fact? It would be too late by then.

She ran the bath far too hot, knowing that it would be a good long while before any of the children got into it, then one after the other as it was cooling, she clamped them between her knees, slicked the paraffin through their hair and combed out their nits.

'That's better,' little Doreen said, as she felt the oil soothing her scratched scalp. She laid a pudgy hand on Helen's knee and patted her like a dog. Helen blew her a kiss – she couldn't contemplate actually touching any part of the little girl with her lips – and then stripped off her clothes, trying not to look too closely, wiped the worst of it off with the cleanest bit of vest and plopped her into the water with her brothers.

'It's rare and deep when we're all in,' said Roy, round his lollipop.

'It's nice and warm,' Tommy added.

'Can Doreen play in the bath without going under?' Helen asked. 'Cos I want to go and speak to the attendants, but I don't want her swallowing half the water if she slips.'

'I'm nearly four!' Doreen said.

'Aye well, don't shout it so loud seeing your big brother up but one is five,' said Helen, but the point was beyond them. 'Lollies out a minute while I dicht your faces,' she said, wringing out a flannel in the hot water and setting to. 'There! Look what was under there! Three wee pink angels!'

'You're daft,' said Roy and put his lollipop back in.

Helen grabbed each of them in turn, soaped up their heads to get rid of the paraffin and then dunked them backwards to rinse it off again.

'Are youse all warm enough?' she said.

'Ah'm beelin,' said Doreen, lifting a chubby leg to show Helen how red it was in the hot water.

'I'll not be long,' she assured them. Then she slipped out of the cubicle and along to the net-curtained door.

She was often to think, in the days following, that had she not had half her mind on the bairns along the balcony in their bath, she would have been able to see the whole case and the shining solution to the mystery in what she heard from the baths attendants that day. But then, there was so much other noise and kerfuffle, what with gossip and local news, with connections made and acquaintance discovered, she might still have missed it.

Chapter 14

Helen had never knocked on this door before. Even when the plug in her bath had crumbled away one time and her precious hot water started to leak down the drain before she had even rinsed the soap out of her hair, Greet had simply wrapped a pair of winter stockings in an odd bit of wax paper she happened to have in her shopping bag and screwed the lump into the plughole. You didn't want to go bothering the attendants was a lesson Helen had learned well.

So her heart was in her mouth as the voice from behind the nets rose in irritation. 'This better be good!'

She had planned her appeal, but whether it was good or not she had no idea.

'Whit is i—? Oh. You again!' It was the attendant who had fainted and fallen into the swimming pond, and clearly he hadn't got over his embarrassment: he flushed a deep painful purple colour when he saw Helen standing there.

'It's me,' Helen agreed, trying to look sheepish. 'I was here on Thursday night when . . .' She fell silent and shuddered, hardly acting.

'What do you want?' the little man said. Behind him, another attendant sat scowling. He hadn't been on that night and he couldn't possibly know who she was but his loyalty was instant and his face seemed to say that if his colleague didn't care for Helen then he loathed her too.

'Well, it's going to sound daft,' Helen said, 'but I just can't get it out of my head. I'm not sleeping and, when I do drop off, I get nightmares. I'm jumping at shadows. I can't eat!'

The man's face softened slightly, He might have swooned and made a laughing stock of himself but he was over it, less than a week later, and could be magnanimous to this member of the weaker sex.

'Aye well,' he said. 'There's some sights not meant for ladies' eyes.'

Helen lowered her 'lady's eyes' so he couldn't see the flash of annoyance in them. 'Anyway,' she went on, 'my boss said – did you know I work at the Gardener's Crescent surgery? – my boss said I should "face it head on" and "do it down". Like I was St Whatsisname slaying a dragon.'

'George,' said the scowling man, still in his seat but leaning forward to be sure and show off his superior knowledge.

'Of course, they two doctors are "European", aren't they?' said the first attendant, standing back a little, not quite inviting Helen in, not yet, but certainly hinting that an invitation might follow. She managed to paste a grin on her face and hoped that the cold fury she felt inside didn't show in her eyes, for Dr Sarah was Manchester through and through and Dr Strasser had been born right here in Edinburgh. And how anyone could talk archly about 'Europeans' that way after what they had all just been through was beyond her.

'Aye, they want me lying on a couch,' she said, with a laugh.

'Well, there's no couch in here,' the wee man said, stepping all the way to the side and ushering Helen in, 'but take a pew.'

'And what is it you want to know?' said the big man.

'I think the doc reckoned if I could understand it, it would be a bit easier to stop dwelling on it,' said Helen, shaking her head at the lifted teapot, for hadn't she just claimed she was so badly shocked she could hardly swallow?

176

'Understand?' said the wee man. 'How could anyone ever understand wickedness like that?'

'No, no, I don't mean understand *why*,' Helen put in hastily, 'but understand *how*. Maybe.'

She was starting to sweat and the act was dwindling by the minute. The heat in this little bothy, the smell of bath soap and floor soap and disinfectant cake, the odour of the big man sitting so close to her was beginning to sicken her. How could a man smell as if he hadn't washed in a month when he worked here?

'You wouldn't understand how, lass,' he said, giving her a broad grin that showed her he didn't clean his teeth any more often than he took a flannel to the rest of him. 'It was cleverness with a portable boiler element. The polis explained it all to Pedy and me but it'll be beyond you, won't it, Peed.'

'It will that, Jappy,' said the wee man, Pedy apparently.

'A portable boiler?' Helen echoed. 'How did anybody manage to smuggle that in? Or do you have it here all the time, likes of in a cupboard?'

'Why would we have such a thing?' said Jappy.

'Likes of if the big boiler went off,' Helen said. 'To heat the water for folk's baths.'

Both men laughed. They probably thought they laughed fondly but Helen wondered how they would like that kind of fondness from *her*, if she treated them to it.

'Do you want to know how many gallons of hot water we use in a day?' said Pedy. 'How much coke it takes our boiler to keep the swimming pool at a temperature the weans can splash about in without chittering? Do you want us to tell you how long you'd have to queue outside if we were heating every drop with the type of wee rig the police think got smuggled in here?'

'Not really,' said Helen. 'It would more'n likely make my head spin.' That pleased them and so she went on. 'So it was a wee contraption. And whoever it was, black-hearted so-and-so that they were, brought it right in rolled up in a towel then?'

They laughed again. 'Oh aye, like a cigarette lighter! That would boil a bath full of water right enough!' said Jappy.

'He should have just struck a match!' added Pedy. Then he sobered. 'Naw, it was quite a size, as best as they can reckon. But . . . eh, dear.'

'Aye,' said Jappy and heaved a sigh.

'What?' Helen said.

'It wasn't Big Florrie that waved him through,' Pedy said. 'It was poor wee Galt, wee Logie Galt covering for her tea. He was on the counter last Thursday night for near on an hour.'

'Aye, Florrie likes to spin her tea out, right enough,' Jappy pitched in. 'It's not like she could get that size nibbling a biscuit.'

Helen was coming to despise these two men, laughing at the counter-woman behind her back. She *was* a fair old size, mind you, but having heard Mrs Hogg's tearful reports of all the unkind things said to *her*, Helen was in a new frame of mind.

'Wee Galt said he let a man in with a pram,' said Jappy.

'So?' Helen said. Greet had brought her girls to the baths in their pram many times. Helen remembered one summer night, riding home standing on the axle and hanging on to the handle, while Mack pushed her as fast as he could go through a blue and gold sunset, Baby Teen chuckling and waving her chubby arms as Helen went 'Wheeeeee!' and Greet shouted from behind that he would cowp the pram and kill her babbies and then she'd swing for him.

'Aye but not a pram with a bairn in,' said Jappy. 'A pram with a bale of washing in, or so he thought.'

'That would be bad enough!' put in Pedy.

178

Helen nodded. The rules against bringing in washing and using the bath water to cut down on your steamie fees were strict and well known.

'But the next day, when the polis were trying to fathom how it was done, Wee Galt admitted that this man – a *man*, mark you – could hardly haul this pram up the steps, never mind he was a big lad with strong arms and should have managed it just dandy.'

'That was stupid,' said Helen, but she was surprised when both men frowned. Maybe *they* were allowed to insult their colleague but she needed to keep a civil tongue in her head, like a family. 'Sorry,' she said. 'So this Mr Galt actually saw . . . the murderer?'

'Mr Galt!' said Jappy. 'I suppose he is, mind you. Aye, he did. Saw him hauling an old pram full of equipment up the steps and said nothing. On account of this big man with his pram was with an old pal.' He shook his head and sucked his teeth.

Pedy joined in. 'I kept my own mother to half-hour baths, before she died,' he said. 'And Big Florrie has never waved a single soul through without a ticket in all her years. Mr Pettit is adamant about that, no matter what kind of soft touch he is elsewise.'

'Is Mr Pettit the manager?' Helen said.

Pedy laughed softly. 'Mr Pettit is the superintendent of the city's baths,' he said. 'But he's not the sort to stay in his office and sign his name. A right one for interfering he is.'

'Aye but, Peed,' said Jappy. 'You see what that means? That means we can chap on his door and tell him all about wee Galt and make sure the blame gets put where it belongs.'

These two men really were among the least appealing Helen had ever come across, she who'd spent many an afternoon in the hostel for the indigent, sometimes – like this last week – after an outbreak of fleas. As fleas crossed her mind, her thoughts returned to the three wee Bells and their nits along the balcony there. She needed to move a bit more briskly here.

'Could I speak to him?' Helen said.

'Mr Pettit?'

'Mr Galt!' she said. 'If he saw the man with the pram and if he could tell me he *was* just a man, maybe I could stop dreaming of monsters every time I lay my head down.'

Pedy shook his head and sucked his teeth. Jappy shook his head and cleared his throat.

'He's more like to think of monsters than you,' said Jappy. 'This has sent him right round the twist.'

'Poor soul,' Helen said. 'But could one of youse not go round and see him? See if you can change his mind? Talk to his wife, maybe?' She was hoping that this was the first step towards persuading the men that this task was right up her street, and thereby getting Galt's address.

'His wife!' said Jappy. 'Imagine Wee Galt married, Peed?'

'You've got the wrong end of the stick, hen,' said Pedy, with a scornful sort of laugh.

Helen, sensitive to any hints in that direction, tried to look mildly interested and said, 'Oh?'

'He's no catch for a good woman,' said Jappy. 'His mammy put him on church steps when he was a baby and he never knew any different. Brought up on their charity and pushed out to make his way in a cold world at fifteen, he was. And now this.'

'But none of it's his fault,' Helen said. 'From his mammy not wanting him, to him being kind to a man with a pram of washing. *He* didn't kill anyone.'

'Aye well,' said Pedy, to which there was no reply.

'I better be getting back,' Helen said, sensing that the useful portion of the conversation was over.

'Are you scrubbing that great big wifie again?' said Jappy.

180

'Naw, different family,' Helen said. 'Three bairns. They've had plenty time to splash about now though.'

Jappy's curranty little eyes narrowed. 'Three bairns?'

'Cousins, aye,' said Helen, knowing fine well there was no way that three siblings young enough to share bathwater didn't have at least one too young to be left unminded. Unless she was going to say they were triplets.

But that wasn't the problem.

'You've been having nightmares and you can't get the pictures out of your head,' Jappy said, 'but you've brought three weans for a bath, have you?'

'It's my job,' Helen said, which wasn't strictly true. 'And I like looking after weans. I'm putting on a Halloween party for a whole load of them come Monday.'

'Get out of it!' Pedy said. 'Coming in here, making eyes, giving out how you're so upset and your tender wee feelings and all the rest of it. Digging away for gossip!'

'For information,' Helen said. 'I'm trying to help.'

'Help with whit?' said Jappy.

'Catch a killer!' Helen said. 'What do you think?'

But the two men set their jaws and wouldn't listen to another word from her.

She got all three Bells out of the water, dried and dressed in record time, bribing them with promises of a banana split if the café was still open or a poke of chips if it was already closed. On her way out, all three little heads bare and all three hats deep in a canvas duffel bag ready for the midden or a good boiling in tar soap anyway, she made sure and kept her eyes down.

'Here! Youse!' shouted the woman on the counter, Big Florrie as Helen now knew. 'Where's their hats? Ah *kent* they were lousy! I'll be watching out for you, Missus. Don't you think you'll be strolling back in here anytime soon.'

She didn't know about Helen's beautiful white bathroom with the soft mat and the pale pink walls. Helen could easy not

181

come back to Cally Crescent till Big Florrie was retired. She'd have to give up bathing Mrs Hogg, but that was no hardship.

The café *was* still open and all three wee Bells ate every scrap of their banana splits, even Doreen, whose belly ended up as tight as a bouncy ball. They talked Helen into letting them take a wandering route back to Lochrin Buildings afterwards, away round by the canal, passing the church with the fire and brimstone words outside.

'Cleanliness and hardiness we've got sorted,' Helen said. 'Just out the baths and full of ice cream on a perishing cold night like this.'

'Eh?' said Tommy.

'Can you read?' Helen said. 'Can you tell me what it says up there on that building?'

'The Edinburgh . . . Ad-Vent-Ist True . . .' Tommy said, looking at the sign instead of the poster.'

'Tabernacle,' Roy finished off.

'Knick knack tabernack, give a dog a bone!' Doreen sang out. She reminded Helen a lot of Teen as a child.

'It's paddywhack, you wee daftie,' said Roy.

And they sang all the way home.

Chapter 15

Carolyn's flat was an almost self-contained portion of the bigger house, on the kind of street Carolyn was used to living on. She had a wooden staircase climbing the outside of the carriage house wall. *That* housed a motorcar now, of course, but what used to be the carriage driver's and then the chauffeur's accommodation had been turned into a cosy wee place smaller even than Helen's house, but ideal for one. There was a tiny wooden porch at the top of the steps then straight into a living room. A few steps up at the back led to a wood-panelled bedroom made from an attic. A few steps down lay the kitchen with hardly room for the sink and cooker, but with a table and two chairs squeezed in somehow. A door led onto the landing of the main staircase and gave access to a bathroom that Carolyn shared with the family. Helen wouldn't have cared for it – the landlord and landlady rattling the door when you were in your bath, or worse – but if Carolyn had been disciplined about her belongings, with a commitment to tidiness and a good cleaning routine, 43A Pitsligo Road could have been a nest and a retreat.

Carolyn, though, had none of what it took to live alone in a small space. She shopped for books and clothes and picked up sticks of 'interesting' furniture in the second-hand shops at Canonmills, leaving all of it strewn about half unwrapped, along with paintbrushes set into pots of hardened paint like the sword in the stone, wilting flowers in jars of stinking green water, and cups with tea evaporating and staining them, coffee grounds sticking to others. Helen was sure, although she tried not to look too closely, that there would be droppings all over the kitchen from the inevitable party after lights out every night when the mice came back to feast on that day's crumbs. If Carolyn had been poor and this flat a room-and-kitchen in Tollcross, Helen's visits would have been weekly and written up in reports after.

On the other hand, Carolyn's collections and her devil-may-care approach to plans made her the perfect choice to help pull off a Halloween party on a few days' notice. When Helen arrived, she had already looked out a bolt of black netting – for cobwebs – a pile of sheets – for ghosts – and a big silver tub that looked like a jeely pan but was far too fancy and had no proper handle.

'It's an ice bucket,' she said, when Helen asked. 'Good and sturdy so it won't get kicked over in the dooking. I think it's silver.'

'These sheets are too good to cut holes in,' Helen said.

'They're ancient,' said Carolyn. 'I think they were Granny's wedding presents. Far too heavy and far too large for modern times.'

'You could take them in,' Helen said. 'Use the rest for cloths.'

Carolyn rolled her eyes and groaned. 'I sleep on flannel all year round in this place, Nell. I swear it's colder here in August than the North Pole at Christmastime. Besides, you're always on at me to clear out. I'm clearing *this* out.'

'Where did you get the net?'

'No idea. It's rather wonderful, isn't it? We can cover up a lot of Bible verses with swags of this – there's yards.'

Helen frowned. 'But we're having it at my house,' she said. 'What Bible verses?'

'Oh! Don't tell me I forgot to say – what a juggins. No, it's back on at the church hall. Such as it is.'

'Have they caught him?'

'Caught who?' said Carolyn. Perhaps Helen hadn't told her what upset the party plans in the first place. 'No, it's more that I can be very persuasive. And I didn't want your lovely house getting covered in treacle.'

'Thanks,' Helen said. 'I forgot about the treacle, right enough. But how did you know who to ask? Did I even tell you where it was?'

'Teenie told me,' Carolyn said.

Helen boggled. She didn't try all that hard to keep the different bits of her life separate for she wasn't ashamed of her family, nor of her friend, but she had never deliberately brought them together and couldn't imagine how Carolyn had managed it.

'She comes to the Bs,' Carolyn said. That was how she referred to the Botanic Gardens, as if it was a cocktail bar, Helen always thought, and as if her job there was a lark. It softened Helen's heart just when Carolyn was at her most irritating, making her think she wasn't the only one not quite ashamed of her life.

'Does she?' she asked. 'Since when does Teenie-bash care about trees and flowers?'

'No, she comes with her "friend",' said Carolyn. 'And don't worry, Nelly. They walk on the paths in a completely respectable fashion, no ducking into the bushes.'

'Are you telling me Teenie's got a boyfriend? Because it's the first I've heard. Is he in her class at the school?'

'Well, promise me you won't leap up and start charging about,' Carolyn said, 'but he's a soldier. From Redford Barracks. So you see—'

'See *what*?' Helen said. She might well have jumped up if she hadn't been warned. 'A soldier? How old is he?'

'Which shows how keen he is,' Carolyn said. 'It's lots of trams from Redford down to Inverleith and there are nearer

185

spots if he wanted to get Teenie alone. Why, the Water of Leith is a perfect glade and it's right there.'

'Or,' Helen said, 'he could sit on the top step of the landing with the door open a crack like Sandy and me did when we were courting. Save a lot of fares. But obviously they think it's worth going all over the town to somewhere no one knows them.'

'She *did* almost faint when I said hello the first time,' Carolyn said, smiling as she remembered. 'But as to the rest of it: I wouldn't have said he was even sixteen if I didn't know he was in the army. Very quiet-looking, with big hands and pink ears. Clearly besotted with your sister.'

'An idiot then,' said Helen. 'Teenie's a rattle and a . . . a . . . flibbertigibbet. And *you* can stop laughing at me too.' Helen fumed in silence for a moment. 'Is he connected to this strange church she's started going to?'

'*This strange church*!' Carolyn said. 'I go to it too. Well, sometimes.'

'The Adventists?'

'What? No! Good Lord. The Anglicans. No, I don't think so, although he's coming to the party.'

'Which *is* at the Adventists', right? On Gilmore Place? Not the piskies.'

'In their teeny-tiny little hall, yes. Odd, isn't it?'

'I'll say,' Helen agreed. 'They claim it's "disrespectful" to *host* a party while Edinburgh's in the grip of this murderer but, oh yes, they'll hand their hall over to . . .'

'The likes of me?' It was just as well Carolyn Sinclair was so hard to offend, for that was exactly what Helen meant. They smiled at one another, in perfect understanding. 'But Teenie was right, Nell. It was nothing to do with the dread murders. They found themselves unable to find the usual volunteers, that's all. And they didn't want to say so – eighth commandment notwithstanding.'

186

'Ninth,' said Helen. 'So why did you say it was odd then, if you never believed the story.'

'Oh, simply that those sorts of Protestants tend towards the joyless, don't you think?'

Helen could not have answered for a pension. She wasn't used to having the word 'Protestants' bandied about so airily. Her mammy would faint if she could hear.

'They never seem to realise that a spoonful of sugar might be a better bet than fire and brimstone,' Carolyn went on. 'And this lot in particular declare their objections to enjoyment right above the front door. Cleanliness, hardiness, abstinence and thrift! I do wonder what sort of party they would have put on with *those* as their watchwords.'

Helen giggled. 'Teenie thought it was "continence".'

'Good Lord,' said Carolyn again. 'No, it's most definitely abstinence. Perhaps that's why they go in for parties for children Teenie's age. To keep them on apples and treacle a bit longer and put off the day they succumb to the demon drink. Speaking of which, would you like a sherry before supper? It's eggs on toast.'

Helen could remember when eggs on toast for tea would come with an apology, not the drumroll Carolyn had just given them. 'Where did you get eggs?' she said.

'We've got chickens at the back of the hothouses at work,' Carolyn said. 'Fed on scraps and thinnings and not officially known about. Look.' She opened up a brown paper bag that was sitting on the table at her elbow and showed Helen four enormous brown eggs nestled in crumpled newspaper. 'Come and keep me company while I poach them,' she said. 'If I promise to concentrate on the party afterwards, can we start with you telling me all the latest about this killer? I can't believe half of what's in the papers. But then my colleagues down at the Bs do tend to take the more lurid of our jour-nalistic organs.'

'I will,' Helen said, although she knew it would have been easier to enjoy her egg tea if she stayed out of the kitchen and didn't see the evidence of Carolyn's housekeeping. 'I'll lay out everything I know, as long as you don't ask me how I know some of it.'

'Billy,' Carolyn said.

Helen said nothing about that. It was Rita she was keeping quiet about, so it did no harm to have all of Carolyn's suspicions pointed elsewhere. 'A boiled man at the public baths, with the clothes of a slaughterman hanging on the back of the cubicle door,' she began. 'The water heater wheeled right in, in a pram, while the usual wifie was on her dinner and the door wasn't half being watched. The choked man at Maitland's Chophouse, locked in the gents in a tanner's apron and the murderer away through a high-up window. And the funny thing is that the man with the pram was a fair size, by all accounts, but the chophouse window is tiny.' She looked expectantly at Carolyn, who only shrugged. 'Then a frozen man at the Haymarket rink,' she went on. 'Wearing a housemaid's pinny and trapped in a block of ice that was frozen who knows where and moved overnight. Nobody's sure how *that* got past the watchman, except to say the rest of them down there don't think he's up to much. And finally, the shamed man, dressed in the clothes of a working girl and found in the house of one too, strangled and battered and left there. All four of them were well-to-do gentlemen, soft hands from soft living, but none of them have had family asking where they are. And every one of them wore a ring that's been pulled off and taken away.'

'Very clear and succinct,' Carolyn said.

'And now for the bit that's got me scratching my head,' Helen said, and launched into the puzzling tale Billy had told, of Slice and the Fiscal and their whispered plans.

188

Carolyn's comeback was the same as Helen's had been. She frowned down into the little pan where the eggs were simmering and said, 'Dr Sallis has that the wrong way round though. They want the public to believe it's over even though they know it's not. They want to proceed with urgency while not looking as if they're panicking. Surely.'

'No,' Helen said. 'The doc and the Fiscal *know* it's over but can't let on. And they *could* tie it all up in a bow right now, but they're lagging.'

'Nonsense,' said Carolyn.

'You'd think,' Helen said. 'Back to front and upside down. Like something from . . .'

'*Alice in Wonderland.*'

'Exactly. But that's good. If it doesn't all add up then we must be missing something. And so we can search it out.'

'And will we know it when we find it?' said Carolyn.

Helen shrugged, then the toast under the grill started smoking and Carolyn couldn't take her eyes off the precious eggs and there wasn't really space in the tiny kitchen for Helen to help and they discussed the case no more that night. If only the bread had been a day fresher so the toast had burned a moment later, one or the other of them might have hit upon it right there.

★

Helen reckoned she had burnt her bridges at the baths and learned all she could about the rink from Mr King. And there was no way she was going back to the café or Jessie Gibb's house to try to find out any more about the choked man. She wasn't even sure there were any more questions to ask. But, regarding the murder of the shamed man, she had an advantage over the police and Dr Sallis and everyone, in the form of Rita, or Patricia, right there in the doctors' house.

First thing on Thursday morning, she found the girl in the ground-floor kitchen, washing up the breakfast plates with a dreamy look on her face.

'I could get used to this,' she said. 'I've always liked nice things, just never had them.'

Helen looked around the green distempered walls, the pot shelves lined with plain brown paper and the red, Cardinal-polished floor. 'What nice things?' she said.

Rita lifted a soapy arm out of the deep sink and held up a milk jug for Helen to admire along with her. The bubbles looked like rainbows in the sunshine peeping in this east-facing window and the jug was a dainty little object, right enough, the handle so refined that Helen wondered if Dr Strasser could even get a finger through it. Maybe Dr Sarah poured his morning coffee.

'When you're finished here,' she said, 'can you come down to my office, please? I want to talk to you.'

'What about?' said Rita, instantly wary. 'Because Mrs Lady Doctor has had a right good go at me already and it wasn't as if I didn't know.'

Helen smiled and shook her head. 'No, nothing like that. It's just I realised that, with every other body, the polis have had the chance to ask all the folk in the baths and the rink and the café to wrack their brains for any wee scrap of evidence, but nobody's questioned you.'

'You're not taking me to the polis!' Rita shrank back.

'No, you daftie,' Helen said. 'I'm going to ask you questions, that's all. If there's anything the police need to know we can decide how to pass it on after.'

'Aw,' said Rita. 'Righto then.' She turned back to her sink. 'Can I bring you a cup of tea down when I come?'

Helen frowned at her back, wondering where that mousy voice had come from and why Rita was using it. 'I'll make a cup for *you*,' she said. 'Ten minutes?'

'Aye, right,' said Rita, her chin dropping as if she was bowing her head under a great weight of sadness. 'I'm a guest. I know.'

She would have to get to the bottom of this, as well as everything else, Helen thought to herself, as she went back down to the basement and set the water to boiling while she made some notes.

She had half a scrawled page when Rita appeared round the office door with two cups – saucers, spoons and all – balanced in one hand and a plate of biscuits in the other.

'You nearly let it boil dry,' she said. 'But I got to it in time.'

'Good girl,' Helen said. 'And you're rare and handy looking there. Have you been a nippy before now?'

Rita scoffed, although she said nothing until she was settled in the patient's chair. 'Right, fire away.' She looked at Helen as though braced against attack.

'You didn't recognise him,' Helen said.

Rita shook her head.

'But that was at the time, on the night, in all the upset. Have you thought back to it again since?'

Rita squeezed her eyes shut and shook her head again. 'I've been trying to forget the sight of it.'

'But with me here, could you try and think now?' Helen spoke gently but firmly.

'How could I recognise him?' Rita said, her voice rising. 'His face was all black and swollen and smeared with blood. And his tongue! And his eyes popping out like that! His own mother wouldn't recognise him!'

'All right, all right,' Helen said. 'Have a wee drink of your tea and forget his face.' She sipped her own and then tried again. 'What about the rest of him? He had grey hair, Rita, and a full head of it.'

'Patricia!'

'Right, right. But what I'm saying is grey hair means he wasn't young. And he wasn't tall, or thin, or hairy or smooth. Do you maybe recognise . . . I don't know.'

'Naw you don't, do you?' Rita said. 'If you think I'd know every inch of him like he was my husband, you know nothing.'

'Well, what about the clothes he had on,' said Helen next. 'Do you know, or have you ever heard of, a man who would be wearing that sort of get-up?'

With a fraction of her old spirit, Rita said, 'I'll start a list for you, will I? You kent I was at a party – that was why I wasn't home for a night or two – so do you want me to tell you what everyone was wearing there? Will I sketch it?'

'Calm down,' Helen said. 'Don't upset yourself.'

'Ah'm not upsetting myself!' said Rita. 'You're upsetting me.' It was a good point. 'Can you not see I'm trying to put that . . . right, well, not behind me, for how can I? . . . but aside. Just away, just a wee while.' She started to breathe raggedly with a hitch in her chest as if she was about to sob. Helen put her cup down and came round the desk to crouch and take the girl's two hands in her own.

'Sorry,' she said. 'I'm sorry. I get a bee in my bonnet and I forget about being kind. I'm sorry, Patricia.'

Rita sniffed and blew out a big breath, heading off the threatened sobs. 'You're as soft as they doctors,' she said. 'Like three babes in the woods, you are. One wee tear and you're grovelling like a kicked puppy.'

Helen stood, stretched and went back to her seat. What a puzzle this girl was. Doing the work she did, but so upset at being asked about it. So sensitive and yet brushing off a kind word.

'Right,' she said. 'Well, here's another notion then. Where was the party and who organised it? Because someone knew you'd be away, didn't they? Someone knew your room would be empty.'

Rita shook her head. 'I never hear any names.' She made it sound like a policy, which Helen supposed it might be.

'Where was it though?'

'A big house somewhere on the southside,' Rita said. 'It was dark when I got there and dark when I left and the curtains were shut the whole time.'

'So you couldn't find it again?' Another shake of the head. 'Did you walk?' A hard stare. 'What bus did you take?' Rita's eyes narrowed.

'We got picked up in a car,' she said. 'Like usual.'

Helen couldn't help herself. 'Where's your family, you wee soul?' she said. 'Could you not just go home?'

Rita laughed and it was a bleaker sound than Helen could ever remember hearing. 'I've no family,' she said. 'And no home to go to, now that my room's not safe for me anymore.'

'There are charitab—'

'Has Dr Sarah told you to get me out?' Rita banged her cup down and looked half bereft but half enraged too.

'No, no, nothing like that. She's not said a word.'

'Because she told me I could go to the synagogue with them on Saturday. I was looking forward to it. She said it would be interesting for me.'

'I could take you to church on Sunday,' Helen said, 'if you're feeling the need.'

'No thanks,' said Rita. 'I've had a bellyful of *that*. I fancy a nice wee change and the doc said it was all right so there's no need for you to look at me so mumpy.'

Helen held up both her hands in surrender. 'I'm sure it will be. A change. I'm jealous.' She wasn't but the whole thing had tumbled her thoughts so much she hardly knew what she was saying.

'Right,' said Rita. 'Well, if that's us done, I'm away to polish silver. It's been in boxes since the doc brought it from her mammy's, seeing she's no time to be at it, but I'm going to

193

polish it up and lay it out on the sideboard where it should be. Silver! Can you credit it?'

She smiled, the sun out again at the thought of playing at houses, and went tripping up the stairs as if she hadn't a care in the world.

Helen had no trouble believing Dr Sarah had brought some posh bits with her when she married, nor even that she had let a street girl like Rita loose with them. There was no way of broaching the subject with either of the Strassers, though, and so she put it out of her mind and for the rest of the day she handed out slips, wrote reports, listened to complaints, and tried to believe everything was all right, like Billy had over-heard the Fiscal tell Dr Sallis: that there was no danger and no hurry and nothing to worry about except keeping the city from panicking.

★

Somebody needed to tell the press that, Helen thought, as she passed the news stand at Tollcross on her outing to fetch buns that afternoon. She had had to wrest the task back to herself after Dr Sarah had given Rita a handful of change and sent *her* to get them.

It was daft, Helen knew, to have a flare of jealousy, to have it on the tip of her tongue that *she* bought the buns for the Strassers, whenever good news or bad made a treat essential. She was a professional welfare officer, with more folk needing her help than she had hours in the day to help them and if she could pass the daily shopping off to Rita for the length of the girl's visit, she should be pleased.

She stole a sideways glance at Rita now, skipping alongside. Helen had suggested they go together, so she could show Rita the bakery. Rita suspected nothing but Dr Strasser gave Helen a grave look as he saw them both

194

leaving, and Helen was still ruffled when they got to the main road. Her thoughts flew to Sandy, as they so often did. He had cut so deep into her, her daily life near him but not with him, a wound that would never heal, it was hardly surprising that she saw usurpers everywhere she looked. Gavin was the worst of them, of course, but there was Teenie with her parents, even Carolyn finding it so easy and funny to go skating with Tam, making Helen feel silly for all her hand-wringing about Billy, and now here was Rita edging into Helen's place at the surgery before she had even stopped feeling awkward about it herself.

'By jings, *she'll* ken us another time!' Rita said, as they crossed the tramlines towards the good baker on Panmure Place. Helen turned to look and saw Jessie Gibb standing outside the chophouse with a pole in her hands, just about to hook the awning and raise it, now the sun had moved round. She was gazing in their direction as though she had seen a ghost.

'It's me she's staring at, not you,' Helen said, and gave Jessie a friendly wave. But the girl stood as though frozen in shock as Helen approached her, the only movement coming from the way the breeze was fluttering the frilled edge of her white apron.

'It's nice to see you on your feet and back at work, Miss Gibb,' Helen said. 'This is—' she turned to introduce Rita but to her astonishment the girl was nowhere to be seen. She had disappeared inside one of the other shops and Helen felt the thrill of being right: Rita couldn't go out to fetch the buns if she was going to be waylaid by the wares in any other window she happened to pass.

'How come you've got *her*?' Jessie said, jerking her head to the empty space beside Helen where Rita should be standing.

'How come you *know* her?' Helen said, astonishment turning her brusque.

'I don't know her or any like her!' Jessie exclaimed. She even went as far as to adjust her grip on the hook pole as if she was going to wield it.

The chophouse door opened and a waiter, still in his shirt-sleeves and without his waistcoat and stiff collar, stuck the top half of his body out. 'Get on with it, lassie,' he said. 'Mr F's in no mood to be crossed.'

Jessie Gibb let go of the hook pole, ignoring it banging against the plate glass of the window and ducked inside, going under the waiter's arm like a little woodland creature popping back into its burrow.

He tutted and stepped outside, twirling the pole with the dexterity of long years and effortlessly pushing the two awnings back until they snecked into place against the wall. 'It's all very well taking on the halt and the lame,' he said over his shoulder to Helen, 'but we've got a dining room to run all the same, haven't we?'

'The halt and the lame?' said Helen. 'Miss Gibb?' She had been laid low by shock the first time Helen had met her but she looked lively enough today.

'I try to be kind,' the waiter said. 'But it's hard to take when you're a trained and experienced professional like me and then the bosses show you exactly what they think of you. How would *you* like it?'

'I'm not with you,' Helen said. 'If you're unhappy with Miss Gibb's work, or if the manager is, I mean, then he could just sack her.'

'Only the owner gets to hire and fire at Maitland's,' the waiter said. 'And as soon as he deigns to show his face, we'll tell him to give her the heave-ho. It's us have got to take up all the slack, like I said.' He gave Helen a dark look and went inside.

Helen puzzled after him a moment or two. She had heard of men who wanted all girls and women back in their own kitchens, or a laundry anyway, once the war was over, but she'd never heard her whole sex called 'the halt and the lame' before.

Putting him out of her mind, she turned to see if she could work out which shop had drawn Rita inside. There was a locksmith, a brush and broom maker and a gents' hatter to choose from. Remembering the pleasure Rita had taken in doing the dishes that morning, Helen headed for the brush shop, but the girl popped out of the hatter's door as Helen passed the window.

'What on earth were you doing in there?' she said.

Rita looked all about herself and then said, 'I wondered if they made they feather scarves. I was thinking we could maybe find out where that one came from.'

'Boas?' Helen said. 'You thought a maker of caps, bowlers and toppers might have a sideline in feather boas?'

'Aye all right,' said Rita. 'I'm not as clever as you but you don't need to rub it in. What harm did I do? They don't make any women's things at all, but it's no skin off anybody's nose for me asking.'

Helen nodded as though in acceptance and continued to the baker's, noting that Rita didn't pop in to ask at the *ladies'* outfitter they passed on the way.

So, at the end of the afternoon, instead of going straight home, Helen paid her own visit to the hatter, who was just closing his door.

'This morning,' she said, 'a girl came in here and left again after a couple of minutes.'

'And now here *you* are,' said the hatter, a fussy little man who, to be fair to him, couldn't have been used to two ladies in one day.

'What did she ask you?' Helen said.

'Ask me?' he echoed. 'She didn't ask me anything. She told me she was hiding from her factor because her father was laid

197

up with his back and they were three weeks' behind on the rent. I told her she wasn't using my shop for a hidey-hole and went to shoo her out, but she was quite a fierce little thing and I retired behind my counter, I can tell you. The better part of valour, I decided.' He was getting het up and he took his spectacles off to polish them on a chamois.

'Probably a good idea,' Helen said and walked home, more mystified than ever.

Chapter 16

'Can I ask you something?' Helen said to Dr Sarah the next morning. They were out in the back garden, looking to see if any of the apples on the single tree there were good enough to take to the Halloween party or if Helen was going to have to get round the fruit seller with the cart on the side road, to let her pick over his stock for bruised and blemished treasure. She knew there was no point asking at the greengrocer's shop. He prided himself on the quality of his stock and Helen's budget for this party didn't stretch to buying best, new-season fruit. Not to tumble into that sturdy ice bucket to get bumped and bitten and slavered on.

'Anything, always,' Dr Sarah said. She inspected a windfall. 'On the bright side, they're quite mushy so they'll be easy for the children to get their teeth into.'

'They might sink,' Helen said, squeezing a fruit that felt heavy and was starting to wrinkle. 'It's about Patricia.' Dr Sarah cocked her head in invitation for Helen to carry on. 'How long did you think she would be here?'

'Why?' said Dr Sarah. 'Is there a problem? You surely can't wish to see her hurry back to her old life.'

'Not me,' Helen said. 'And not her either, I don't think. I was even wondering if you and Dr Strasser were thinking of keeping her on. Permanently. As a kind of a . . .'

'Housekeeper,' said Dr Sarah, nodding. 'We thought that was the best term, although she's very young. Sam said "servant", but really! Even "housekeeper" is too narrow to cover what she's been up to this last week. She was out here sweeping something yesterday.'

Helen cast her eye around the garden. It had its charms – a big old honeysuckle slowly taking over the toolshed, a rambling rose that spilled over the wall from the garden next door and reached the ground on this side, even the apple tree as gnarled and knuckled as it was – but it was never very tidy, what with neither of the Strassers being green-fingered and both of them being short of time. Dr Strasser toiled round with an old mower a couple of times each summer and Dr Sarah would sometimes go out and pull the worst of the weeds, after a heavy rain when the soil was loose enough. When Helen had ever compared it to her own little patch, as neat and pretty as an embroidered hand-kerchief, it was only a disinclination to offend them that had stopped her offering to come round with Sandy one Saturday and put the place to rights.

Rita clearly had no such squeamish concerns about show-ing them up and the garden was indeed looking less unkempt than usual. The rosehips, which grew to the size of walnuts, had been snipped off and the edges of the grass had been sliced through with a blade to leave a neat dark line against the soil of the borders. There was more to be done, but Rita had made a start.

'You wouldn't think she'd know about gardens,' Helen said. 'Has she told you anything about her early years?'

'Nothing beyond saying she'd rather forget them,' said Dr Sarah. 'So do we have your approval to offer her a home here?'

'You're not needing my approval,' Helen said. 'Only . . . something right queer happened yesterday. You know that poor girl that found the choked man?'

'Jessie Gibb,' said Dr Sarah. 'What about her?'

200

'I'm sure Rita knows her and Jessie recognised Rita too. Neither one of them looked very happy about it either, I can tell you.'

'Patricia,' said Dr Sarah, mildly. Helen could have kicked herself. She didn't do it deliberately but she knew that never using the right name made her look petty. 'But why on earth would knowing Jessie Gibb reflect badly on Patricia?' Dr Sarah went on. 'We know the worst of her past already, the poor child. I would say it makes me question *Jessie* and what adventures *she* might have escaped to end up in her respectable job as a waitress.'

'She lives with her mammy!' Helen said. 'She couldn't ever have been a . . . working girl.'

'Prostitute, Nelly,' Dr Sarah said. 'We should call things by their names.'

'Although,' Helen said, 'a waiter at her work did say . . . or no, he didn't quite say it but near enough . . . that his nose was out of joint that the likes of Jessie Gibb got given a job alongside him. I thought he meant all girls, but maybe not.'

'There you go then!' said Dr Sarah.

'I hope she's not still at it,' Helen said. 'No, she can't be. How would she get out from under her mammy's eye to go walking the streets?'

'It might be worth another visit to Mrs Gibb to have a quiet word,' Dr Sarah said. 'A *very* quiet word, mind.'

'Righto, Doc,' said Helen, hoping that no more needed to be said. She should have known better.

'The scourge of prostitution in this country is not a moral one,' Dr Sarah said. 'There are two parties to every transaction, after all. It is a medical matter but, even amongst those so-called forward-thinking doctors who advocate regular health checks for the girls, you can whistle for one who would demand the same of their clients. I say if the girls must be poked, prodded, tested and dosed then so should the men who keep them in business!'

'I know you do, Doc,' said Helen. 'But you don't need to say it so loud and maybe not out in the garden when anyone could be listening over the wall.' Dr Sarah opened her mouth to argue but Helen went on. 'So Patricia's staying?'

'And you, Nelly, can take her the good news.'

'But don't *you* want to?'

Dr Sarah gave Helen a wise sort of look. She was daft in some ways and soft in others, but she was far from stupid. 'That would be a waste of capital,' she said. 'Patricia *already* loves me.'

Right enough, when Helen went into the kitchen for a bucket to collect the apples into, Patricia – as she was going to have to train herself to say – looked up with an expression perfectly balanced between fear and fury.

'What were you and Dr Missus having such a conflab about?' she said, jutting out her chin as if that would hide the fact that she was close to tears. 'Was it me?'

'It was,' said Helen, then took a step back, suddenly remembering how Patricia had made that little hatter man so nervous the previous day. 'What would you think of not going back to your room?' she said. Patricia narrowed her eyes. 'What would you think of staying here for good? Cleaning and gardening and sleeping up in the—?'

The rest of her words were lost and her breath knocked out of her when Patricia barrelled into her at top speed like a dodgem car. She squeezed Helen so tight round the middle that there was not the slightest chance of catching a new breath either.

'All right, all right,' she said, wriggling free. 'I take it that's a yes then.'

'Oh, Mrs Crowther!' Patricia said. 'I can't believe it. I've been hoping and praying. Truly praying down on my knees beside my bed at night.' She broke off and shook herself. 'I didn't think it could happen, but they don't care about all the things I've done, do they? The Strassers. They're taking me to the synagogue with them and they've let me loose on all their lovely things. I never thought I'd ever . . .' Then words failed her and she went back to squeezing Helen and bouncing up and down at the same time.

'Here, I'm not a baby needing burped,' Helen said. 'And listen to this, before you go getting all giddy. It's true they don't care what you might have done in the past, but they care – and so do I – what you do under their roof. So don't you be chucking this new start away if you get bored.'

'I'm getting a library ticket and a cat, Mrs Crowther,' said Patricia. 'I'll not be bored.'

If Patricia was going to be permanent then she should call Helen by her Christian name. Helen told herself she would issue that invitation later, the better to parcel out the good news. She almost believed herself too.

'Right then,' she said. 'After my morning clinic, I'll be out most of the day. If one of the docs asks, tell them I've got a fair few home visits and a bit of business in the Cowgate. And remind them I've to take care of Jessie Gibb too, like we said.'

'Jessie from yesterday?' said Patricia, all the air going out of her as if Helen had pricked her with a pin. 'Taking care of her how? She's got a job and a home. What's left to take care of there?'

'Was she called "Jessie" when you knew her?' Helen said. Rita/Patricia had led her to believe that the girls at the back of Haymarket always gave themselves more glamorous names for work.

'Aye,' Patricia said. 'Not Gibb, obviously. But always Jessie. She'll not thank you, by the way. For "taking care of her".'

'Don't you worry about it,' Helen said, as though she understood.

In truth, she understood nothing; not even why she was returning to the Gibb house in Lady Lawson Street. Only, it seemed a wheen of a coincidence that the shamed man was killed in the room of a working girl, and the choked man was killed where another one was waitressing these days. It got Helen to thinking about the boiled man and the frozen man too. No women at all worked at the ice rink. Even the chips and cocoa were served up by a man in a blue overall and a wee hat. Maybe there were women cleaners. She could perhaps ask that nightwatchman about them. What was his name again? Mr King had laughed about him and called him wee . . . Boswell? No, that was the owner. Wee . . . ? Galt? Melvin, was it? No matter.

As for the baths, she couldn't believe any of the doughty wifies that put in a shift there had ever worn lipstick and high heels and gone looking for trouble on dark streets.

Maybe Jessie and Patricia knowing each other was just a pure fluke. Edinburgh wasn't that big a city and all of these deaths had taken place in one certain patch of it.

On the other hand, the boiled man in the baths had slaughterman's clothes, like Mack, and Mack definitely knew more than he was saying. So, since the frozen man at the rink wore an apron, just like Jessie Gibb, and Jessie Gibb found another man . . . Helen lost her grip on the many threads she was attempting to weave together. Not least because tanners, with their leather and mail, didn't connect to anything else despite the strange garb on the choked man in the café that Jessie had stumbled over.

And now, whether she wanted to or not, Helen had to turn her mind away from all of that and back to the question of how young Jessie knew Patricia, because she was practically at the Gibbs' and wasn't Mrs Gibb herself coming along the street with a full shopping basket? She clocked Helen square on.

'Mrs . . .' she said.

'Crowther,' Helen supplied. 'Can I have a quick word?'

'It took me the rest of the day to calm Jessie down again after your last one,' the woman said. She hefted the basket onto her hip to ease the strain on her arms. Helen wondered what she managed to get on her rations that was such a burden.

'Here let me give you a lift up with that,' she said. 'I deliberately came when Jessie's at her work so's *not* to get her all keyed up again. Just to ask if she's maybe remembered anything new or had any ideas that could help.'

Mrs Gibb relinquished the basket and started off into the close, rubbing her arm through her coat sleeve. Helen peeked under the top poke and saw more turnips than she had ever seen in one place outside of the fields they grew in. Halloween, of course. But why Mrs Gibb was all set to carve this many lanterns Helen couldn't fathom.

'Where did you get so many tumshies?' she said, as she hauled the basket up the stair behind Mrs Gibb, both of them puffing. 'I could do with a few for a party if they're a good price.'

'Aye, these are for a party too,' Mrs Gibb said. 'The weans deserve a treat.'

'Your weans?' said Helen. She had seen no signs of small children when she'd been here before – no wee socks or simmets drying on the pulley, no stack of nappies, no toys lying around in corners – and Jessie had all the marks of an only child, as Helen was starting to learn them.

'All weans deserve a treat at Halloween,' said Mrs Gibb. 'So come on then. Spit it out. You don't fool me.' Helen couldn't help looking startled. 'You've never come here to get Jessie's new memories at second-hand from her mammy. So what are you really after?'

Helen nodded. 'Aye, all right then,' she said. 'It's just to say, Mrs Gibb, how tight a rein do you keep on your lassie?

Ken what I mean? I've a wee sister myself and I don't think my mammy has a notion of what she gets up to half the time.'

'Jessie's a good girl,' said Mrs Gibb. 'I've no call to be holding reins.' Helen smiled to give herself thinking time for what came next but, to her surprise, the woman went on unbidden. 'She's been a bad place and now she's safe at home with me. Why would she ever leave me?'

Helen's mouth hung open. She had badly misjudged this woman, brusque as she might be, tough and harsh as her life had made her. Mrs Gibb had the milk of human kindness pouring out of her, for her own daughter and countless other children too.

'You're a rare kind sort,' Helen said.

'Kind?' said Mrs Gibb. 'Is that what you call it? I love my wee lassie, Mrs Crowther. When you've one of your own you'll know.'

'If,' said Helen, pushed into a moment of honesty by the naked openness of this woman who stood before her. 'I've been wed nigh on two years.'

'Ach.' Mrs Gibb flicked a hand as if to bat away such nonsense. 'I'm fifty. I married at twenty. Jessie's sixteen. The Lord moves in mysterious ways, so he does.'

Helen made her goodbyes and left soon after, walking down the stair to the street, lost in thought. The mills of God grinding slowly would have been more to the point, surely. Unless Mrs Gibb meant to suggest that she got her beloved daughter by roundabout means, by the same means that were Helen's only chance too. Mysterious indeed!

'Penny for them.' The voice at her shoulder made Helen jump and she stumbled a bit; she still wasn't used to these good shoes all day every day and it had been well over a year now of her wearing them.

'Billy!' she said and instantly flushed a deep painful pink from her collar to her hat brim, for here standing in front of her was one way she could discover the joys of motherhood.

'That's a nice colour,' Billy said. 'It suits you.'

'A gentleman would make out like he'd noticed nothing,' Helen said.

'A gentleman wouldn't have been listening in to private conversations all morning. Have you time for a chinwag?'

'How come?' Helen said. 'Hing on, were you coming to see me?'

'I was.'

'Because I was coming to see you.'

'Well there, we've saved each other half a journey. How about a wee cup of tea somewhere?'

Helen looked both ways. She used to know where Sandy would be wheeling his dustcart on any given day but it had been a while since they'd had that sort of chat in the morning. Seeing nothing untoward, she nodded to Billy and then clipped along briskly towards Forrest Road and away from her and Sandy's patch of the town.

'I thought you said the Fiscal was done visiting?' she said, when they had arrived at one of the new coffeehouses that were springing up all around the university. Billy and she squeezed in, all the students giving them curious looks as they did, for she was as out of place with her good serge and nurse's bag as was Billy with a donkey jacket over his cotton outfit and heavy boots he had substituted for the wellingtons he wore on the mortuary floor.

'I've never tasted coffee,' he said, looking up at the waitress who came to serve them. He didn't even drop his voice. As honest as the day is long, Helen thought. An open book.

'I'll get a tea and if you don't like it we can swap,' she said. The waitress looked disdainfully at both of them and walked off.

'Fire away,' Helen said. 'How come the Fiscal came back again?'

'He never,' said Billy. 'But Slice was on the blower for near on an hour and he forgot to keep his voice down.'

'Go on then,' Helen said. 'Don't make me drag it out of you.'

'They're going to make an arrest,' Billy said. 'Like they planned. And the gadgie they're arresting didn't do it. Slice knows. Whoever he was talking to this morning knows. And I know too. I couldn't wait to tell you.'

'I don't understand,' Helen said. 'How's it any of Dr Sal—'

'Wheesht!' Billy said, looking hard all around. 'Mind where we are.'

Helen put her hand over her mouth. Just across the road was the hospital and the medical school and some of these lounging, drawling toffs in the coffeehouse had to be medical students who would know Dr Sallis by reputation at least.

'How's it any of Slice's business?' she said in a low voice. The waitress came back then but she seemed to think that the hunched postures and whispering were tell-tale signs of a love affair rather than of secrets. At least, she raised an eyebrow at Helen's wedding ring and smirked a bit before she left them.

'Best as I can work out,' Billy said, 'Slice had to agree that all the injuries to all four men could have been done by this one wee scapegoat.'

'Wouldn't the PM reports show that?' Helen said, bewildered.

'Hing on, I'm not saying it's right.' Billy took a swig of coffee and opened his eyes very wide. 'By Jove, that'll put hairs on your chest. You're fine, hen. You enjoy your tea.' He dropped in two sugar cubes, stirred vigorously and carried on his tale. 'Slice had to agree what bits of the PM to let out and what to keep mum about, so everyone would swallow the story that this poor wee mannie did the lot.'

'I don't understand,' Helen said. 'And how do you know he's a poor wee mannie anyway?'

'Because it's Martin Nunn.' Helen shrugged. 'Martin Nunn, that escaped from West House a week past Thursday.'

'Is that his name? And they've caught him?'

'Aye, they've caught him and they're not letting him go to waste.'

'What does that mea— Hang on,' Helen said. 'How would he . . . I mean, how could he have escaped from a locked ward on Thursday night and have the water boiler all ready to use? Never mind A road into the ice rink and knowing how to do all that was done there and having time to do it. And somebody would have had to let him into Maitland's too. And how would he know that Rita's room would be empty?'

'The papers are not to find out that the man in the ice was already in the ice when he was moved nor that the apparatus to boil that man was hefted upstairs at the baths by someone muscular. Because their scapegoat is anything but.'

'He could get through the chophouse window, mind you,' Helen said. 'But . . .'

'But there's no way it was all done by the same killer,' said Billy, leaning low over the table and giving Helen an earnest look. 'No way. But that's what they're going to say. Martin Nunn.'

'But . . . it must be one,' Helen said. 'Even if it's not *that* one. One madman. How could a whole lot of different people all work together on something so wicked?'

'Aw hen, it happens all the time,' Billy said. 'Have you forgotten already?' He put his head on one side and gave her a look that was either kind or patronising. She couldn't decide.

209

'You mean the war?' she said. 'The Germans? But that *was* one madman. And then he got round a whole load more somehow.' She nodded firmly, as the matter began to settle down in her mind. 'That's what must have happened here too. And he is *mad*, isn't he? So he's threatened his way in, or slithered his way in, to the rink and the baths and the chophouse . . . He didn't need to wangle himself into Rita's room. He only needed to know she was away. Do you see, Billy? Do you see?'

'I see you buying it,' Billy said. 'Swallowing it. Exactly what Slice and the Fiscal hope everyone does. One madman that persuaded weak-minded people to do his bidding. I mean, he persuaded twelve women to dance around in the hills and drink blood, did he not?'

Helen boggled at him.

'Aye, you're right. He's perfect. It was dead handy that he escaped on Thursday night to sleep in a crypt in Greyfriars Kirkyard.'

Helen's head jerked to look out of the window. They were yards from that kirkyard right now.

'That was Slice's wee addition to the fairytale,' Billy said. 'Nunn was found in a cemetery out Corstorphine way, but it makes more sense for the story if he's been on the spot. So. He's been on the spot. And now he's in the cells.' Billy nodded towards the north where the courts of justice lay at the other end of George IV Bridge. 'Soon we'll get the spectacle of him in the dock, in chains, barking and seething and making sure the newsstands sell out of every copy.'

'Then he'll be back off to the Royal Ed again?' Helen said. 'I suppose, as scapegoats go, he's no worse off than he would have been at least.'

'Aye but he was only at the Royal Ed because the worst of his crimes was public indecency,' said Billy.

210

'Is that what drinking blood is?' Helen said. 'Oh!' She had remembered a bit more. 'They were dancing *naked* in the hills, weren't they?'

'But it'll be the criminal lunatic wing at Perth Prison for poor old Beelzebub now,' Billy said. 'Or maybe this new place they've started, out Carstairs way. But he didn't *do* it, Nelly. I heard them cooking it up together. Or I heard one half of it anyway.'

'But why don't they want to catch the real culprits?' Helen said.

'I'm sure they do.' Billy sounded grave. 'But on the quiet like. Once the newsmen have moved on to other stories and they can deal with it . . . discreetly.'

'Are youse finished?' The waitress was back and Helen could see a queue of people, all young men, waiting to take over their little table. She glanced down and was surprised to see that she had finished every drop of her tea without tasting it.

'Aye, right, we're away,' Billy said, standing and drawing Helen's chair out for her. They emerged into a fading day and Helen looked in a panic at her watch. She only just had time to get back to Gardener's Crescent before her afternoon clinic.

'So we can guess what's at the bottom of it, can't we?' Billy said, when they were underway. 'I mean we can't stick the pin right on the donkey's behind but we're facing the wall and we know where the picture is. Discretion, confidentiality, favours, bent rules, convenient wee stories . . .'

'I suppose so,' Helen said. 'Someone's got friends in high places. Who though?'

'Who do you think?' said Billy. 'The real killer.'

211

Chapter 17

Friday was another busy day for the Gardener's Crescent surgery, and there was no rest to look forward to at the weekend because somehow the party had got itself moved to Saturday night when Helen wasn't looking. It was Carolyn's doing, as best she could make out when she had deciphered the scrawled note pushed through her letterbox. It was waiting for her when she got home in time to ready her house for the Downies' Friday night baths. She went straight back out to the kiosk to ring her friend up and object.

'But they've caught him,' Carolyn said. 'Haven't you seen the papers? Well, lucky you and don't look. It's all rather horrid and a little too seasonal for my liking. Halloween and all that, you know. So neither the church nor anyone else has reason to worry about children out in the dark traipsing around the streets on Monday, see? Or, at least they succumbed to persuasion.'

'*Your* persuasion?' said Helen.

'Who else?' said Carolyn. 'I dropped in on them again yesterday and twisted their arms. Are you wondering why they were there hanging around the church to have their arms twisted on a Thursday? Me too. But they were – a whole gaggle of women, as a matter of fact – and they agreed very readily, both to moving the party night and to letting us help.'

'Teen'll be pleased,' said Helen. 'But you and me have got less than a day to get it all sorted. Why can't they do it themselves? Same as they usually do?'

'No idea,' said Carolyn. 'They were in a bit of a flap, though, I can tell you. Anyway, there's oodles of time. Tomorrow morning: shopping for buns, treacle, something to drink and some pies to heat up for actual sustenance. Tomorrow afternoon: lay out and decorate the hall. Tomorrow evening: host party and clear up after it. Speaking of drinks: do you think they're teetotal?'

'It says "abstinence" on their big sign,' Helen reminded her.

'I'll pack a few bottles of cider and play it by ear.'

'I still say it should have been Monday,' Helen grumbled. 'They would all have been out guising by eight o'clock and we'd have been home in our slippers by the end of the news on the radio.'

'You sound ninety!'

'I'll get the pies,' said Helen, ignoring her. 'I know Barbone the butcher. He's a friend of mine.'

'Should we try to come up with some sort of batting order for the games?' said Carolyn.

'The usual,' said Helen.

'You're assuming I've ever been to a Halloween party,' Carolyn said. 'Wait! Yes, there was one once. We had to hang over the back of a chair with a fork in our mouths and drop it into the apple bath to try to spear one. My mother said it was more hygienic.'

'There'll be a riot if you try to stop the weans dooking tomorrow,' Helen said. 'Hygienic! I was brought up sharing slavers with every bairn on the stair every October and I never even had a cold sore.'

'So the dooking is definite,' Carolyn said. 'What else?'

Helen was glad her friend couldn't see her face. They were more or less the same age and had been born a mile from each other, but their lives had been led worlds apart. 'We need to start with the lantern competition,' she said, 'so we can light them for the rest of the night. And the treacle scones should be before the apples, so's their faces get washed in the water. After that, they can all practice their turns for the guising and get their costumes judged, then, while they're having their pies and a sweetie, we can tell ghost stories. The only thing I'm missing out is the fortunes. That holy lot'll never let us tell fortunes in their church hall, I don't think.'

'Do you *know* any ghost stories?' Carolyn said.

'It was always my mother who told them at ours. I'll see if I can remember any.'

'Or I could do it,' Carolyn said. 'I've a lot of weight still to pull, after you organised the apples and if you're getting the pies.'

'And the neeps,' Helen said. Following Mrs Gibbs' tip, she had plans to negotiate a fair price for some nice soft wrinkly turnips on a fruit seller's barrow.

'Are you dressing up?' Carolyn said. 'I left most of my fancy dress behind when I moved into this mousehole, but I daresay I could pull something together.'

'I'm wearing a pinny for the treacle and bootees for the puddles,' Helen said. 'I'll have come as my own mammy.'

Carolyn giggled and rang off.

As if Helen had summoned them, she saw Mack, Greet and Teenie coming along the pavement towards her, when she left the kiosk. 'Good news,' she called to Teen, waving. 'It's tomorrow right enough. You'll get two wears out of your frock.'

'What's this?' said Mack.

'You could come too,' Helen said. 'Halloween party tomorrow night. It's at a wee church hall on Gilmore Place.'

Mack and Greet, who had been advancing, both stopped dead in their tracks. 'Teen?' said Greet. 'Is *that* where your party was? The Tabernacle? The Adventists? You never said that when you asked if you could go.'

'Did I not?' said Teen, unconvincingly. 'Ocht well, that's where it is. Are you coming then, Daddy?' She swung on Mack's arm, as she was wont to do, the golden child who knew she was adored.

'I'd no more cross that door than—' Mack said, before cutting his words off sharp at a swift gesture from his wife. 'Who are they?'

Helen frowned. Greet had heard of them, had their name ready to hand. And why would Mack be so dead set against 'crossing that door' if he didn't know what door was in question? Helen wasn't used to being puzzled by her father and this was the second time in two weeks now. Although, she reminded herself, the first time was more alarm than puzzlement really.

'What about you, Mammy?' she said. 'Will you come?' She tucked her hand into her mother's arm and, even though she was confused and full of questions, and halfway to acting, trying to winkle something out, still she thought how cosy it was, the four of them walking through the crisp dark streets together, the way they used to, going here and there. She hadn't realised how much she missed it until getting a taste of it again this evening.

'I'm going to your aunties,' Greet said, her voice unsteady and half the strength it should be.

She was lying, Helen was almost sure. Thursday was Greet's night for spending with her sisters, in one of their houses or another. It was every woman in Edinburgh's night for her sisters, seeing it was every working man's night to take his wages to the pub. Why would Greet suddenly rush to Auntie Linda or Auntie Mae at the weekend?

'Is everything all right?' she asked her mother softly. Unless it was her imagination, Greet was breathing more heavily than she should be walking along a flat street.

'Oh! Am I not allowed to see my own sisters now?' Greet said. 'Just cos you're putting on a party?'

216

That was more like her usual self. Helen squeezed her arm and said no more.

'You mind and keep a close eye on her, Nelly,' Mack said. 'Church hall or no church hall. You hear?'

Helen briefly wondered if he had heard about the soldier, then shook the thought out of her head. If he had the faintest inkling, he'd have Teenie locked in her bedroom and be sleeping across the door. She gave him a quizzical look and was unnerved that he turned his head and looked resolutely in the other direction.

'You're needing to get some newspaper on that rhubarb crown before the hard frosts,' he said, as they came through the gate. He had never had so much as a window box of his own but that didn't stop him telling Helen how to care for her garden. The moment, just like the moment with her mother, had passed away.

Sandy must have heard them coming. He opened the front door and stood at the top of the stairs to welcome them. 'The water's rare and hot,' he said. 'And there's three kettles boiling for more.'

'You're letting the heat out,' Helen said. It was getting harder and harder to carry out the performance of young married bliss for her parents every week, and she found herself paying him out with little bouts of scolding and nagging like that one. Greet smiled, reassured by the fact that her daughter was learning to speak to her husband as a wife should. Mack shook his head and clapped Sandy on one shoulder as he passed, in recognition of their shared fate.

Helen tried never to think about the endless affection of the Strassers for one another, except to wonder what her parents would make of it. Even less did she let her mind wander to the quiet talk and easy laughter that came up through the floor when Sandy and Gavin were down there together. She hoped Gavin dreaded Friday nights, and the noise of a family together overhead, as much as she resented every other night of the week and Saturday and Sunday mornings too.

★

At least this Saturday morning, she was up and off with the dawn. First stop was Gardener's Crescent to invite Patricia to the party.

She stared at Helen as if she had been asked to a hanging. Then she shook her head hard enough to make her hair slip out of its pins. 'I told you, I'm going with the Strassers to their synagogue. And it's like a Sunday, except on a Saturday. It would be a kick in the teeth for me to go trotting along there and then turn round and be at a party the same night.'

'But the Strassers don't keep to that,' Helen said. 'They were at the pictures two Saturdays ago. To see a musical!'

'It wouldn't be right,' Patricia insisted. 'I don't want to fling their kindness back in their face.'

Helen left her there on her knees sweeping out under the cooker in the kitchen, even though she was half sure you weren't supposed to *work* on the Sabbath either. She was glad to run into Dr Strasser in the front hall, shrugging on his coat and checking his medical bag for supplies.

'Trouble, Doc?' she said.

'Nothing too terrible,' he said. 'I need to go and replaster an arm. The silly woman dunked her baby into the sink instead of giving it a sponge bath and the cast is sloughing off. The poor little mite is screaming the whole tenement down.'

Helen knew the case. A toddler had rolled off a box bed in Brandsfield Street and landed on the edge of the coal bucket. 'Do I need to maybe have a word with her?' she said. 'She sounds like a right daftie. She might need a class for new mothers.'

'I'll see how I think she's doing on my visit today and let you know,' he said. 'Unless you'd like to come with me, Nell? Are you at a loose end?'

Helen laughed. 'Hardly,' she said. 'I'm birling like a peerie today. Halloween party tonight. I thought Patricia might like it as a wee treat but she's scared of annoying you.'

'Me?' said Dr Strasser.

'Both of you. Offending you. Being ungrateful, likes of.'

'Ah,' said Dr Strasser. 'I would imagine it's less about offending Sarah and me than it is about avoiding the temptation to revert to things she has left behind.'

'But it's in a church hall,' said Helen. 'Not a . . .'

'Bordello?' said Dr Strasser. 'A distinction without a difference where Patricia is concerned.' He caught his lip in his teeth. 'Don't tell Sarah I said that, please Nelly. Patricia has confided in me rather than my wife.'

'Aye?' Helen said, then hoped it wasn't insulting.

Dr Strasser only smiled. 'She seemed to think that I could be prevailed upon to honour her wish for confidence and discretion. She imagined my wife might surge ahead with what she thought was best. You see?'

Yes and no was the honest answer. Helen had no idea what he was talking about, but Dr Sarah did breenge in whenever she thought breenging was needed. 'She means well, Doc,' was all she said. 'And she does a lot of good.'

They parted ways at the bottom of the surgery steps and Helen puzzled over his words halfway to the Cowgate, without ever being able to make head nor tail of them. It was unsettling to hear Dr Strasser talk about 'confidence' and 'discretion' so soon after Billy had done so, but maybe as well to be reminded that sometimes they were a good thing.

★

She had hoped Billy wasn't doing a Saturday shift. For, if he wasn't there, she would have had to ask someone for his home address and go knocking on his door. That would have been a step forward in whatever this was, and no mistake. But he answered the back door when she knocked. The broad grin that spread over his face when he saw her was as good as a note of his address anyway.

'Here's a bright spot on a dark day,' he said.

'Dark? Is there another body?'

Billy winked and said in a loud voice, 'No, thank goodness.' Leaning forward, he whispered, 'I told you: it's over, but that was very convincing, you making out you didn't know.' He straightened again and resumed a normal volume. 'What can I do for you? I'm not asking you in because we got a bloater out of Blackford Pond last night and he's absolutely stinking.'

'Definitely not anoth—' Helen began.

'Fully dressed, pockets stuffed with his belongings, and well known to the police for sleeping out, poor old fella. And his family, that never looked the road he was on when he was alive, are round us like stray cats now, demanding to view the body. I've a good mind to let them.'

'Can you tell me where Barbone's pie shop is?' Helen said, desperate to change the subject. She wasn't as squeamish as she used to be, but she was a long way from Billy's carefree views about the end of human life and what came after.

'That's brought you all the way down here?' said Billy, looking so pleased he was almost smug. 'They're in the Post Office Directory, hen. Abbeyhill.'

'I wondered if I could use your name too, to get an order rushed through for tonight. You're a good customer, aren't you?'

'It's hungry work,' Billy said. 'What's tonight?'

'That's the other thing,' Helen said, hoping she could get through this without blushing. 'Did you want to come to a party?'

'With you there and Barbone's pies? Daft question.'

Helen opened her mouth to say what she was so overdue in saying, but nothing came out.

'So when and where is it we'll be dancing cheek to cheek?' Billy asked.

That was another perfect moment, but all Helen said was, 'It's not that sort of party. It's a Halloween treat for bairns. Carolyn's coming,' she added.

'Can I bring Tam?'

They both laughed and then Helen sobered and nodded gravely. 'You better had,' she said. 'It would gey queer for you to come on your own. You should maybe even make out you've got a bairn at the party.'

'Or bring one,' Billy said. 'I could bring two.'

Helen felt her heart move inside her body, as if she had swallowed it and it was dropping to the pit of her belly. 'Have you got bairns then?' she said. She took a deep breath to carry her through the next question. 'Are you married?'

Billy paused a moment and then said, 'My sister's wee girls.'

'I— I better go,' Helen said. 'I can smell that smell even from here. And I want to get to Barbone's sharp.'

'*I'll* go to Barbone's, at twelve when I get off,' said Billy. 'How many pies and where's he taking them?'

'He'll not know it but there's a funny wee church halfway along Gilmore Place where Viewforth crosses it. It's called the Adventists' True Tabernacle.'

'By crikey,' Billy said. 'I'm guessing there'll be no whisky.'

Helen laughed. 'Naw, they're all for abstinence and a whole lot of other things like that. You don't have to come.'

'Try and stop me,' said Billy. Then he stood staring at Helen, or rather through her as if he wanted to see some distant object and she was in the way.

'Why are you looking at me like that?' she asked eventually.

'I don't know,' Billy said. 'There's something . . .'

'I know,' said Helen. 'There is, isn't there?' They each waited another moment to see if illumination would come. Then Helen broke off the gaze. 'It's more'n likely that smell.'

Billy laughed, leaned forward and pecked her on her cheek right beside her ear and just under the brim of her hat. Helen couldn't tell which one of them scuttled away faster.

It was right loud to be kissed in front of your ear. Helen wanted to put her finger in and wiggle it around to stop the ringing. But, on the other hand, she hoped the ringing would never stop and she hoped the feeling of his lips on her skin would last a good long time too.

*

The rest of the day was a blur of busyness. Helen shopped, driving a good price at the fruit barrow and then going back and offering the wee man another two shillings because the soft turnips were better for carving than fresh would have been and he didn't deserve to be hoodwinked. She looked out all her worst knives that she didn't mind getting broken or lost and sharpened them on the strop. Mack always said a blunt knife was more dangerous than a keen one and she hoped he was right, for she had no idea how many children were invited to this jamboree and she couldn't be watching them all. She had a box of candle ends too, that she'd been saving all the time she'd lived here, not quite ready to believe the sudden blackouts of the war years were a thing of the past.

After a scratch dinner of bread in milk, dotted with the last of her margarine and the last of her sugar ration, then toasted under the grill, she set off to Gilmore Place with all her supplies in the old buggy she kept in the garden hut.

It occurred to Helen that, had it not been for the name – EDINBURGH ADVENTISTS' TRUE TABER-NACLE – on the sign above the door, rendered in the same kind of newsstand screamer letters as the posters – CLEAN-LINESS! HARDINESS! ABSTINENCE! THRIFT! – she could have believed this so-called church was a Scout hut or a Masons' lodge. And, if it was a poor-looking place, the hall at the back of it was even worse. The condensation on the windows promised a damp and chilly interior, at least until it was packed with bairns and their laughter. Helen parked her buggy by the steps and went in.

Carolyn was there already, looking like a pantomime villain swathed in smoke and fog as she unfurled all her black net to drape it in swags around the walls. Five women, dressed severely in fawn-coloured, dowdy clothes and wearing their long hair pinned up in tight buns, looked on with sour expressions. They turned as Helen entered but didn't quite manage to look as welcoming as Christians should when a stranger arrives at their gates.

'I'm Mrs Crowther,' Helen said. 'The welfare officer from Gardener's Crescent. I'm helping my friend here with your party.'

One of the women unbent a little at that – mollified, Helen thought, by the respectable-sounding pedigree; one that she knew she shouldn't have offered, for she was here as Teenie Downie's big sister and nothing else. 'But where do you worship?' said another, older woman, who managed to speak without opening her pursed lips, as far as Helen could see.

'North Morningside,' Helen said. 'My mammy and daddy were married there, since my granny lived at Polwarth, and they've never moved far enough away to make it worth shifting.' That had come out all wrong. She should have said they were lucky enough to have stayed close enough to make the trip every Sunday and not made them sound so lazy.

'Gardener's Crescent though,' the first woman said. 'I had heard they were very ecumenical and not at all . . .' her voice tailed off.

'Ecumenical indeed!' said a third woman. 'And Miss Sinclair here, is an Anglican, she tells us.' The way she pronounced 'Sinclair' told Helen that these women might be plain-dressed and strait-laced but they went about enough in the world to know all the Edinburgh gossip and they had placed Carolyn neatly inside her family scandal of the year before.

'Lovely,' Helen said. She had learned a long list of hearty but empty things to fill a silence with since she started her job. She beamed at the three women who'd spoken, the Gossip, the Tartar and the Peacemaker, nodded towards the other two and then went over to Carolyn, feeling their eyes burning into her back.

'This bloody stuff is going to eat me like a swamp!' Carolyn said. 'Can you grab the loose end and we'll stretch it out and start from scratch?'

'Mind your language!' Helen said.

'Oh, they don't care if the air turns blue about me as long as I do all the work,' said Carolyn. 'I asked them about this on-again-off-again party, and they couldn't even keep their story straight. First it was the murders, then it was church elders being ill and others needing to stay and nurse them, and now the latest is a mission has taken too many of them away from home and it was all too much for those remaining.'

'Well, we're here now,' Helen said, walking backwards away from Carolyn as the netting untangled itself. She got close to the five women again, to where they were huddled together whispering to one another with a desperate vehemence that seemed woefully out of place during the preparations for a party. 'How many children are expected?' she said.

224

'Twenty-five of ours and a dozen extra,' said the eldest, who seemed to be the ringleader. 'As well as anyone you might have invited, Mrs Crowther.'

'Twenty-five!' said Helen. 'Do you mean you have five children each?' Carolyn burst out into cackles of laughter, so undone by this that she had to step back down off the bottom rung of the ladder.

'*Our* children, meaning from *our* foundling home,' said the youngest of the women, blushing bright red as she spoke for the first time.

'Ah, I see,' Helen said. 'I see. Sorry. Yes. And where *is* your . . .' She couldn't bring herself to say 'foundling home' . . . 'Where *is* that? I don't ask out of nosiness, more that it's my job.' Carolyn tugged on the net and Helen was forced to walk away from them again, to keep feeding her friend more yards of the stuff as Carolyn carried on twining and tucking. She was making a lovely job of it, although Helen wondered what the women would make of all their Bible verses being covered up with swathes of black.

'Tell you what, Nelly,' Carolyn said, when she had reached the end of the room. 'I don't care for climbing stepladders all that much, so why don't I take care of everything while I'm up here? Can you lay that down and fetch me the bun rope from the table there? I'll sling it over this . . . Hmmmm, what is this, actually?'

She was sitting on the top step of the ladder looking at a flap high up in the wall that resembled the hayloft door in a barn. There was a protruding iron rod at the top of it, apparently tailor-made for knotting the rope onto, to string up buns the length of the hall. Helen looked to the other end and wondered what they could fasten the thing onto there.

'Here!' came a voice, so loud and harsh it made Carolyn twist on her perch and wobble alarmingly. Helen threw her arms around the stepladder to steady it. The oldest of the women was glaring up at Carolyn.

'It's just that you can't tie a rope to that,' said the fifth woman, who hadn't spoken before this. 'It'll drop down and hang open.'

'Is that a concern, Mrs . . . ?' Carolyn said, looking down. She might have claimed to hate heights but she looked comfortable enough, like a magistrate sitting in judgement.

'Mrs Mann,' said the Gossip. 'That wee hatch gives onto the attics of the church proper. 'No one ever uses it except the rat catcher.'

The young woman who had blushed nodded her head vigorously. 'We've a terrible time with rats in the attic,' she said.

Carolyn let go of the iron rod and edged away from the little door, as far as was possible on the square top step of a ladder. 'Rats?' she said. 'Oh dear. I suppose they're suitably nasty for a night like Halloween, but we don't want them running along the rope and competing for the treacle buns, do we?'

'In the past,' said the blushing woman, 'we've strung the buns side to side instead of along the length. And used that handy beam.' She pointed, first to the blank, long back wall of the hut and then to the front, with all the steamy windows, and right enough there was a joist running along each at exactly the right height.

'Thank you, Mrs . . .' said Helen. It was odd that the five women hadn't introduced themselves to her.

'You could call me Sister Agnes,' the youngster said.

Helen boggled a little. Was she a nun?

'Back to the nets then, Nelly,' said Carolyn, from above. 'I'll come down and move the steps along a bit, if you'll let go. I don't want to have to clamber over you.'

Helen hadn't realised she was still hugging the ladder, but she gave a sheepish laugh and the awkward moment passed by, leaving a less festive mood than ever in its wake. Helen seemed to hear the echo of that harsh 'Here!' reverberating endlessly and tried her best to keep her head down and avoid the woman who had delivered it.

'You look miles away,' said one of the others, at half-past four, as they stood picking over the dooking apples together. The sun was going down and, as the shadows lengthened, Carolyn's black net and crepe paper had come into their own, not to mention the candles stuck in saucers all around the high ledges of the hut, which guttered in stray drafts and made the darkness leap and shudder.

'I've a great deal on my mind,' Helen said. 'Sorry, what's your name? I don't think I heard it.'

'Beth Pettit,' the woman said. A familiar name to Helen, although she couldn't quite place it right now. 'I have a great deal on my mind too. I wish—' But she choked off her words. 'God's will is all,' she said instead. 'What's been troubling *you*, Mrs Crowther.'

'Oh, I was more mixed up than I would have chosen to be in all the terrible business that's been happening,' Helen said.

'Do— Do you concern yourself with that place?' the woman said. Helen shrugged, not knowing what place was meant. 'The Royal Edinburgh?' Mrs Pettit whispered.

'Oh!' said Helen. 'The escaped . . . patient? No, not that. No, I don't. I'm happy to say none of ours have had to go anywhere beyond a rest home since I've been at the surgery. I meant the murders. Although, I suppose, it's the same thing.' Not if Billy knew what he was talking about, she thought, but officially the escapee and the four dead men were the same business exactly.

The young woman was gaping at her. 'Mixed . . . up in . . . murders?' she said. She dropped the apple she was holding and didn't notice as it rolled away under the trestle table.

227

'Not like that!' Helen said. 'That's not what I mean. Just that I was at the baths when the boiled man was found and then, by sheer chance, I was at the rink when the frozen man was seen under the ice. And then . . .' She stopped talking, remembering in time that Patricia's presence in the Strassers' house was a private matter, perhaps even a secret matter, not to be blabbed about to just anyone. The police had no reason to believe the girl's room wasn't a basket, but Helen couldn't take the chance.

'What are you talking about?' said Mrs Pettit. 'A boiled man? Is this a story for Halloween? A frozen man?'

Helen couldn't hide her astonishment. 'It's the talk of the city,' she said. 'It's in all the bulletins.'

'We don't read newspapers,' the young woman said. 'And none of us listen to the wireless, with all its dance music and silliness. *What* do you say happened?'

Helen told her the official details as quickly as she could, practised at it by now.

'They made one look like a glutton, and they made one look lustful?' said Mrs Pettit when she was done.

'By jings!' Helen said. She didn't drop her own apple but she set it down, all her attention shifted. 'That's a thought,' she went on. 'Is that what you reckon? It's the seven deadly sins? And three more to go?' She wished she could put on a bright electric light. These dancing shadows were unsettling and she couldn't read the expression on the younger woman's face.

She *could* tell that there was fear in her voice, as she went on, 'But what sins were a washed man and a h— a h— a robust man supposed to have committed?'

'Beth!' The oldest woman had crept up on them and was standing just at Helen's elbow. 'What are you so deep in conversation about? I hope you're not gossiping with Mrs Crowther. Remember yourself.'

'Of course, Sister,' Beth said.

'Oh,' said Helen, hoping to lighten the mood. 'Are you each *other's* sisters? I've got a wee sister too. She's coming tonight. Wait till you see her fancy dress costume. She's so proud of it. Not . . . sinfully proud, I mean. Just . . .'

'A Biblical scholar, Mrs Crowther?' said the older woman. 'I know the ladies of your church have no humility, but I've never heard any woman set herself above St Paul the Apostle.'

'Eh?' Helen said.

'We're not blood sisters,' said Mrs Pettit. 'We call one another Sister in devoted affection, just as you hold your sister.'

'Right,' Helen said. 'Devoted affection.' Carolyn had drawn near and she made a peculiar sound that Helen knew was a suppressed snort. She hoped the churchwomen took it for a sneeze.

'They're starting to gather outside,' said Carolyn. 'Miles before five but there's quite a queue of little tramps and pirates on the pavement. Shall we let them in?'

'And spoil them?' said the woman that Helen couldn't help thinking of as the Big Sister now. 'No indeed. They can come in when our children arrive.'

There was plenty to do to fill another half hour, truth be told, between the pies arriving and having to get Mr Barbone out of the hall before he said something that offended the sisters. And then the fact that there were more turnips than Helen had ever seen in one place before and so a great hunt began for paring knives and chisels. And it turned out there was no tap in the hall and Helen had to make endless trips to a cold-water pump at the far end of a wee yard to fill the ice bucket as well as four jeely pans the church had provided. She stood taking a break before bringing the last pailful back and listened to five o'clock strike on the proper church just up the road. She leaned back, bracing her arms into the small of her

229

back and looked up into the sky, clear and starry as anything without even the thinnest sliver of a moon to spoil the dark and the fun to be had in it.

From the far side of the hall, she heard a cheer as the door was opened to the bairns. Their feet on the wooden floor sounded like a stampede and she lifted her pail of water again, the thought that had hardly begun to form quite washed away.

Chapter 18

The room rang with children's voices and there was no worry about it being cold now. The boys charged up and down, ghostie sheets held high above their ankles, tramp coats streaming out behind them. The girls paraded more demurely, all the wee witches with grannies' shawls and mammies' brooms, paper hats falling over their eyes, coal dust warts smudging. Teenie caused a stir just as she had hoped to, sailing in through the door like a pleasure steamer on a calm lake. She had to be taking tiny mincing steps under the frilly hem of her frock, to look like she was floating that way.

'Is that a Christmas angel?' said young Beth, who had stuck close by Helen since their earlier chat, clearly yearning to speak but not quite daring to. Time and again, Big Sister drew her off with scoldings and, once, with a shake to her shoulders.

'She's the Good Witch of the North,' Helen said. Then, when no understanding came, she added, 'From a film. What do you do at night, for fun?' She couldn't imagine not having the pictures to go to when life got too much for her, even if not reading newspapers would be a blessing half the time.

'We sew and mend and knit,' Beth said. 'And bake.' No wonder she looked as excited as the youngest child, at the costumes and the candlelight.

The woman she'd called her sister clapped her hands now, and most of the children quietened and gathered around her where she stood at the head of the hall. They must be the

231

'foundlings', Helen reckoned, well versed in the ways of the True Tabernacle. It took quite a bit longer for the local weans to simmer down but they settled eventually.

'Dear Lord,' said the Big Sister, then she stopped and stared at the door. Helen turned in time to see Billy and Tam, both wound around in bandages from head to toe with only their eyes and mouths showing. They were dressed up as the mummy, from the film that had terrified Helen and tickled Teenie no end.

'Why are you not dressed?' Billy said, gaping at Helen in her good skirt and blouse.

'Because I'm grown up,' said Helen. 'Did you steal all those bandages from your work?'

'Borrowed,' said Tam. 'You besom!' he added, pointing at Carolyn who was trying not to giggle. 'You tricked us.'

'Carry on with the prayer, Sister,' Helen said.

'If one of you two gentlemen would like to lead a short devotion,' said the woman, stepping aside.

'Naw, you crack on, hen,' Tam said. 'I'm only here for the pies.'

'But I suffer not a woman to teach, not to have authority over a man,' Big Sister said. Her voice had changed entirely and her gaze was lowered. 'Timothy, Chapter 2, verse 12.'

'Help her out, Billy,' Helen said, nodding him forward.

'I'll get struck down, praying in this get-up,' Billy muttered, but he lumbered his way to the front of the room and creaked his arms painfully into position to pray like a child. Most of the bairns in the room followed suit. 'Our Father,' Billy said, 'thank you for these turnips and pies and apples and scones and all the treacle. Thank you for looking kindly on this party and the happiness of your children.' He paused as if to try to think of something else to say. 'And keep us from evil,' he added at last, then paused again. 'Amen.'

He opened his eyes and gave Helen a desperate look. She tried her best but even while she was nodding as if in approval

232

she could feel her lips twitching. Tam was wiping his eyes and shaking all over like a jelly.

'Right then, little ones,' Carolyn said. 'These swedes won't carve themselves. Over tens only with the knives. Under tens can tidy up the scrapings and sketch faces for inspiration. Come and get paper and crayons from me!'

'She doesn't look it,' Billy said, coming back to Helen's side, 'but she's a natural with them, isn't she?'

'Like *you're* a born preacher,' said Helen, before she could stop herself. She hoped none of the sister-women saw him swat her behind with the back of his hand. It didn't hurt, but just like the peck on the cheek from earlier in the day, she could still feel it an hour later, as if the seat of her skirt was glowing.

Helen's hopes for this party had not been high, what with the children being two-thirds wee mice from the Tabernacle home and one third Fountainbridge tearaways. But it started to work when the turnip lanterns were lit. Billy and Tam spread newspapers over the floor, while Helen and Carolyn rolled up their sleeves and dipped round after round of scones in a shallow basin of treacle, before threading them onto strings across the width of the hall and collapsing into giggles as they got stickier than the bairns.

'I can't keep up!' Carolyn said. 'Some of these urchins must have honed their craft for years. Look at him! He's surely dislocating his jaw like a python!'

'Aye, it's a fair size of a gob right enough,' said Helen, watching the boy, who had eaten his scone in two bites and was now sucking the last of the treacle off the knot in the string.

'Quick,' said Carolyn. 'Hand me another! How did we ever think forty children was anything but madness?'

Soon enough though, they were gathering up the newspapers ready to start the dooking. Helen caught sight of a headline blaring at her from the floorboards: NAKED MAN DEAD AT HAYMARKET— 'Tam!' she said, covering the words with her foot, 'Did youse not watch what was *on* these sheets?'

'Ach, who's looking?' Tam said.

Still, Helen was careful to fold the page in on itself as she bundled it away. None of these children needed to know about the frozen man. The 'robust' man, as Beth had called him, which was a very strange way to describe his unfortunate end.

'You needing another penny in the slot there?' said Billy, suddenly at her elbow. She laughed, for it was true: she had ground to a standstill. 'What is it?' he asked her.

'What does "robust" mean?' she said. 'It's one of they words you hear and you sort of know, but what exactly is it?'

'Robust?' said Billy. He took the bundle of newspapers out of Helen's hands. 'Where's the bins, by the way?' Helen nodded him towards the back of the hall and went to hold the yard door open. Behind them, the dooking began, with splashes and shouts of laughter, cries of 'He's spitting in the watter, Missus! Get him telt!'

'Robust,' Billy said again, when they stood together in the starry darkness by the dustbins, 'is likes of healthy and hearty and well set. Isn't it? What's made you ask?'

'That young one – the Adventist wifie I was talking to, Mrs . . . Pettit, was it she said? I know her from somewhere, I'm sure. Anyway, she heard me say the boiled man and the frozen man – but she called them the washed man and the robust man. She said the gluttonous man and the lustful man for the other two. And that's not fair, is it? He wasn't a glutton. He was choked with food. And number four more'n likely had never been near the back of Haymarket in his life before. He was just killed there and shamed after.'

'Aye well, they're a funny lot,' Billy said. 'What's the be all and end all for them isn't what anyone else would care about. Cleanliness!' He gave a scoffing laugh.

'Hardiness!' said Helen.

'Continence!' Billy said. He had found that as funny as everyone else. But Helen wasn't laughing tonight. Billy leaned in close to try to see her expression in the low light shining out into the yard from the high candles in the hall.

'Isn't "robust" another word for hardy?' Helen said. 'More or less?'

'What are you . . . ?' Billy began, then he fell silent.

'Cleanliness,' Helen said.

'Aye well, getting boiled like a bale of linen would make you clean right enough, while it killed you,' said Billy. 'And you'd have to be gey hardy to thole being frozen in a block of ice.'

'Abstinence,' said Helen.

'Surely means you cannae go wearing cami knickers and a feather whatsit in a prostitute's bedroom.'

'And thrift,' Helen said. 'That's the last word on their signs out front. Thrift.'

'I wouldn't say eating so much good steak and rich cake that it choked you was all that thrifty.'

With an act of willpower that made her think of Casey Jones, pulling on that lever to stop his train just in time, with all his muscles bulging and straining, Helen turned herself away from where they both had been going. She even managed a laugh. 'I think we've got Halloween fever, you and me, Billy. We've made a wee fairytale for ourselves. This lot are gey queer but they've not been running about murdering folk.'

'Not the wives,' Billy said. 'But where are the husbands? That big one that put the fear of God in me was going to have to preach her own self, till I turned up.'

'Aye, there's something awfy no right with her,' Helen admitted. 'But the rest of them are just . . . Anyway, we knew their menfolk are away. On a mission suddenly.'

'Funny sort of mission,' Billy said.

'Oh no! They'd never use that word if it was a killing spree. Or do such dark deeds either. Anyway, I don't believe there's a wheen of them off on a mission. They said it was illness too, according to Carolyn. And they blamed wee Martin Nunn.'

Billy shook his head, solemnly. 'How does changing your story make you innocent?' he said. Then, with a tremendous clang, he dropped the dustbin lid he had been holding and clutched at Helen's arms.

'What? What?' she said, searching his face.

'Mind what I said,' Billy whispered, with a look over his shoulder, 'the first time I listened in this was, when I couldn't quite catch everything? Mind I said they were going on about "a dentist, a dentist"?'

'Adventist!' said Helen. 'Dear God, Billy.'

For a moment, they stood perfectly still, staring at one another, then Helen shook her head. 'I'll have to think this through on my own, nice and slow and steady. Not standing here in the dark with you dressed like that.'

She turned, as the door to the hall opened at her back. Inside there, it had seemed dark and spooky but even candles and turnip lanterns gave more light than the few stars shining down between the high roofs all around, and suddenly they were exposed like slaters when a stone's lifted. Helen sprang away from Billy then felt the flush of shame, knowing that her movement made them look more guilty.

It was Carolyn, thank goodness, and she only laughed. 'Was that a gong? Oh, a dustbin lid? Well, in either case, get yourselves back in here and stop mooning around. We've got a bit of an ethical dilemma. Teenie is wearing the best costume by far. How many people know she's your sister?'

'Depends if she said her name,' Helen said. Then she fell silent.

'What is it?' said Carolyn.

'Mrs Pettit and Mrs Mann,' said Helen, speaking to Billy and frowning at him too. 'Billy, see if you can find out the names of the other women. I'll get the name of Big Sister, when I ask her to do the judging.'

Back inside, she busied herself manhandling the ice bucket and jeely pans out of the front door to sluice the water away across the pavements, like Greet did when cleaning the stair. They were considerably lighter now, with half their contents soaking into the wooden floor of the hall, despite the grim-faced Adventist women mopping hard. Helen noticed the rippling muscles in the forearms of Big Sister, as she screwed her mop down tight into the cone. 'Mrs Mann?' she called out, catching the woman's eye.

'No. What is it you need?'

'Or should I call you Sister?'

There was only silence.

'*My* sister is here, I think I told you,' said Helen, seeing two things: that she would have to be cannier than that to get the woman's name; and that there was no earthly reason for Big Sister to be loath to share it. 'So you see,' she went on, 'I don't want to be judging the fancy dress. Would you do me a big favour and pick the one you like the best? It should be you that does it, anyway. It's your kindness. Your hall. Your generosity, to be laying a party on at a time like this.'

'A time like what?'

'When you're shorthanded, I mean,' Helen said. 'With so many of your menfolk away. On a mission, was it? Or ill? I didn't quite—'

'It's of no matter to you surely, Mrs Crowther.'

'Of course not,' said Helen. 'I didn't mean to pry, Sister . . . I'm sorry, what's your Christian name?' Helen crossed her fingers that this would work. It was the surname she needed.

237

'You may call me Mrs Sallis!' came back the snapped reply.

'Mrs Sallis?' Helen said. Her voice suddenly felt as if it had no power behind it, as if she'd been punctured and might deflate until she fell in a heap on the floor. 'Dr Sallis's . . .'

'Are you quite well, Mrs Crowther?' Mrs Sallis said, with a bite in her voice. 'You seem a wee bit unsettled. Do you *know* my husband?'

'I—I—' Helen said. She was sure that her tumbling thoughts and sinking stomach must be showing on her face and had no way to explain it. 'Not to say, I know him, but I had occasion to be . . . there . . .'

'Indeed?' said Mrs Sallis. Her voice was as cold as the bitterest winter, her face set to match it. It put some mettle back into Helen, thank the Lord. She managed to catch a hold of a thought, form a plan around it and deliver the lot.

'There was a tram accident,' she said, quietly casting up a prayer for forgiveness. 'A small child. I went with the father to view the wee scrap. And, you see, I'm . . .' She trailed off and merely rubbed her stomach gently, giving Mrs Sallis a soupy look and hoping she hadn't over-egged it.

'Ah,' the woman said, unbending a little. Then she mustered herself. 'Well, if God wills a soul to stay, it stays. And if God wills a soul to leave it leaves.'

'That's . . .' monstrous, she wanted to say, '. . . faithful,' she managed instead, but she stumbled over the words and knew that she shouldn't try much more or she would give herself away.

She sidled off towards where Billy, Tam and Carolyn stood watching Teenie, with an angelic look on her face and her gliding gait even smoother than before.

'That wifie's name is Boswell,' Billy said, nodding across the way. 'But the other one wouldn't give it up.'

'Mine wasn't keen either,' said Helen, barely moving her lips. 'But I winkled it out of her. Now, promise me you won't let your mouth drop open.'

238

And then she told him.

'*Whit?*' Billy said, startled enough to make a sharp turn and speak at far too loud a volume. Helen shushed him and kept her eyes trained on the parade. It was the middle-sized bairns now, all the wee ghosts and witches, all the wee pirates and tramps.

'Slice's wife?' Billy was saying now, talking out of the side of his mouth. 'Helen, what's going on here?'

'Pettit and Mann and Boswell too are names that should mean something if I could get my brain working,' Helen said. 'Sallis definitely does. What's going on here? Murder, Billy. We need to get away and get Teenie away too.'

Teenie, on the other side of the room, was watching her closely and would all too happily go back to Greet and Mack and say that her sister was standing gey close to a strange man and talking in whispers. Greet, Helen thought. Mack. Her parents knew something about all of this. And her parents were good people, of that she was sure. Harsh from their lives, and plain compared with the Strassers and the Sinclairs, but decent people underneath their rough ways. So there must be some simple explanation for everything. Somehow.

'How soon can we get out without them twigging?' she said.

Billy was shaking his head. 'We need to caw canny, Nell. We're safe as long as we're all standing here together. Teenie's fine. You and me need to stay here in this hall for as long as we can and find out every last possible thing. Then maybe – maybe, mind – we can make sense of it, between the two of us.'

It was past Casey Jones now; Helen felt as if she was turning a battleship in open sea, making herself smile and look upon the fancy dress parade. The tiny ones were having their moment and, as is the way, having made the least effort they were getting the most admiration, just for being wee and sweet to the eye. A coal wart on a chubby cheek, a cowboy hat on top of a head of downy curls, ragged pirate britches with dimpled knees under the hem – who could resist them? If Mrs Sallis gave the prize to one of these, surely even Teenie couldn't sulk about it.

At long last, after all the children had had their turn, Mrs Sallis strode forward with a big bar of chocolate – surely a whole week's ration for a large family – in her hand. 'Well done, children,' she said, 'As John said—' she broke off and glanced at Billy and Tam. 'I mean, it's a fine thing to see such good boys and girls as we have here tonight. I am awarding the prize for best fancy dress, in God's sight, to the little shepherd.'

She nodded at one of the Home children, who wore a peaked hat made of paper and carried a crook in one hand and a bone horn in the other. Other than that, he was dressed in his school shorts and a knitted jersey.

Teenie's face was thunderous as she glared across the hall at her sister and a few more of the Fountainbridge bairns rumbled and muttered under their breath. But the Tabernacle's own girls and boys clapped politely.

'Would you like your chocolate, Andrew?' Mrs Sallis said.

The little shepherd boy shook his head and muttered something too quiet for Helen to hear.

'There's a godly child,' said Mrs Sallis. 'I will indeed take it and use it to do good. You have made Jesus smile.'

'I say, that's a bit much,' said Carolyn. 'I mean, all very worthy I'm sure but how can greater good be done with a bar of chocolate than by giving it to a kiddy?'

Mrs Sallis must have heard her, and one or two of the younger women gave her a sickly look, but no one said anything.

'I'm away,' said Teenie, marching up to Helen's side, all the gliding quite forgotten. 'Glen's waiting outside.'

'Glen?' Helen said. 'Is that your soldier?'

'I suppose you think you can forbid me,' Teenie said.

'You've never been more wrong. You go to Glen and stick by his side until you're safe home,' said Helen.

'Safe from what?' her sister demanded. 'They caught him.' She turned on her heel and flounced off, helped a lot by the ruffles of her costume. After a moment, Helen followed and stood at the door to witness her greeting her young man. He *was* still a boy, just as Carolyn had said. And she was right about his ears as well. But he didn't hang back when it came to putting his arms round Teen and kissing her. He got a warm reception too and Helen turned away, half ashamed to be peeping at them and half jealous, if she was honest. She would need to tell Greet and Mack, unless she could persuade Teenie to tell them herself and invite 'Glen' round for his tea.

Greet, Helen thought again. Mack. She turned to go back into the hall to something that felt a very long way from an innocent children's party now.

It was about to take an even darker turn, if she only knew.

★

Nothing could spoil a good pie, mind you, and Barbone's meat peas were the best in the city. Helen couldn't resist one, once all the bairns were sitting cross-legged on the floor with their greasy, brown paper bags torn open and spread as plates, their bottles of ginger fizzing at the neck, making little sparkles in the candle and lamplight.

'What's in it?' Carolyn said, as Helen handed a bag to her. 'Fat of some kind, clearly, or the bag wouldn't be going see-through.'

'What's *in* it?' said Tam, who, despite his bandages, was on his second pie after polishing off the first in three bites. 'And here I thought you were an Edinburgh lass!'

'Mutton,' said Helen. 'And if the grease is all on the bag there's less for you to eat, surely.'

Carolyn mustered herself and took a bite. She chewed solidly for a moment and then her eyes lit up, even in the dimness of the hall. 'Golly, this is delicious,' she said. 'And you mean to tell me that every little baker on every street corner in the city has been making these my whole life?'

'Stick with me, princess,' Tam said, 'and I'll show you the world.'

When the bairns had got the length of sucking on their lollipops, all the ginger finished and all the belches delivered and applauded, when all the greasy bags were gathered up and borne away, it was time for the stories at last.

'Have you got stories you always tell?' Helen asked Mrs Sallis. 'You'll have your traditions.' Her mind was reeling, in revolt from the tales she and Billy had spun, the suspicions they had formed. Mrs Sallis's reply made any thought of murderous deeds seem even more outlandish.

'Jonah and the whale,' the woman said. 'Or the plagues of Egypt. If one of the men would like to take the lead.'

Billy shook his head and, despite everything, Helen was tickled to see the look of dread in his eyes. Him that dealt with rotted corpses all day every day, he was trembling at the thought. No such bashfulness for Tam; he settled himself down onto the floor right in amongst the bairns, crossed his legs the same as them and planted his meaty hands on his bandaged knees.

'Gather round,' he said, in a dark and deep voice. Then he broke off to say, in his normal tone, 'not really, but. Stay where youse are if you're comfy. But lend an ear.' Then he cleared his throat and went back to the sepulchral voice he was going to use for his story. 'One market night in old Ayr,' he said, 'there was a man called Tam who stayed too long carousing with his pals and missed his last tram home.'

242

'Tam O'Shanter?' said Helen to Billy.

'It's his party piece,' Billy replied. 'On account of them having the same name, I think. I hope he makes a few changes for the youngsters.'

'I can dance when the moment comes,' Carolyn said. 'Might add to the atmosphere.' Helen looked at her friend as if across a chasm. Carolyn still thought tonight was a rest and respite from the horrors. Thinking that, Helen half convinced herself that it must be. Dr Sallis was protecting *someone*, but need that someone be one of his Adventist brethren? Frozen and hardy were not the same thing. Nor were boiled and clean. Yet again, she willed her thoughts away.

The children were rapt. Their faces shone and their eyes gleamed as they listened to Tam spin the tale of that other Tam, the lonely road, the graveyard, the empty tombs and the dancing ghosties.

Mrs Sallis and the rest of the women shifted their feet about a bit and sent severe looks in Tam's direction, but the peace and quiet was irresistible in the end and they left him to it, bustling around clearing the trestle table and beginning to get rid of the apple cores, already browning, which lay all over the floor.

'And who do you think was playing the bagpipes that all they witches and warlocks and imps and demons were dancing to?' Tam asked the children, who shook their heads and bit their lips.

Tam bent even closer towards them. 'It was Beelzebub himself!' he cried. One of the smallest toddlers started girning but, just as Helen was about to go and gather him up for a cuddle, Billy nudged her in the ribs.

'Look,' he murmured, flashing his eyes at the five church-women, who had stopped their redding and were standing like pillars all facing Tam and gaping at him.

'The word'll be in his brain from the news,' Helen said. 'He didn't mean anything by choosing it. But mighty! *They* don't know that, do they?'

Tam, seeing that he was scaring the wee-est ones, had changed tack a bit, and was back to describing the dancing – the hairy legs of the ugly old witches, the pretty dress of the young one, the knobbly knees and bunions of the warlocks – and the children grew happier again.

So the noise of their laughter might have covered the other sound and the strangest of the night's happenings might have gone unmarked, if it weren't for the draft that guttered and snuffed the high candles all along one end of the hall. The change in light made Helen look up. She gasped and clutched at Billy's bandaged arm. 'Look!' she hissed.

For the little door, high in the wall, the door Mrs Sallis had warned Carolyn away from, the door young Beth thought was closed over nothing worse than rats, the door supposed to lead to empty attics, lay open. There was a dark square now where the painted wood panels should have been and, at one edge there was a hand, clutching the lintel with whitened knuckles. And on that hand, on the littlest finger, there was a large and ostentatious signet ring.

'Oh my good God in heaven,' Billy said. 'Nelly, that's Slice! I'd know his hands anywhere. I watch them for hours every day. What the devil is going on here? Why is Slice hiding in that loft and why the *hell* did he open the door?'

'Because he recognised Tam's voice,' Helen said. 'Thank God you've got they wraps over your face Billy, or he would have clocked you too.'

Chapter 19

'We're going for a drink,' Carolyn said, arm in arm with Tam out on the pavement, once the story was done, the door had creaked closed again, and the smallest children had started to wilt as their bedtime passed and the excitement started to catch up with them. The churchwomen had turned up the gas lamps and put out the high candles with a long-handled snuffer. The turnip lanterns had been dished out to be carried home by those who wanted them and the children from the orphanage, without being told, had lined themselves up in two long snakes, hand in hand, for the journey home again.

'Have they far to go?' Helen had said. 'It's a cold night and as black as pitch out there.'

'Colinton just,' Mrs Boswell had replied, which seemed far enough and then some to Helen, but with 'hardiness' right there on the church sign she supposed she shouldn't be surprised.

'You can't go into a pub like that,' Helen said now, nodding at Tam's unravelling bandages.

'I've a shirt and trousers on underneath,' Tam said, 'and I left my coat behind the bar.'

'Are you sure you know what you're doing?' Helen whispered to Carolyn.

She looked at her friend and then at Tam and then back again. 'Look who's talking! Nelly, I've tried nice boys I went to dance class with, and I've tried dashing chaps in their service uniforms. I'm bored to tears with both and I want a whisky.'

She leaned in and pecked Helen on the cheek then dragged Tam off up the street, both of them bursting out into the kind of laughter that tells the ones left behind they're being talked about.

'She's a big girl,' Billy said. 'And Tam's a right enough sort underneath it all.'

'Stranger things have happened,' Helen said. 'But still they should have come back to mine. He's not safe to be out on these dark streets now that Slice—'

Billy held up a hand and shook his head. 'We're wrong,' he said. 'I worked that much out myself. Slice isn't a killer, Nelly. That's not why he's hiding.'

'What do you mean?'

'Think about it,' said Billy. '*He's* still got his ring.'

Helen gasped and covered her mouth. 'But the other missing Adventists had theirs torn off?'

'Exactly. They're not ill and they're not on a mission either.'

'But— But— why is it being covered up? And how could those women get through a party when men from their church are dead?'

'Not just "men from their church",' Billy said. 'There were five of them tonight, weren't there? Mrs Sallis with her husband in hiding and four other women.'

'With husbands in the cold store at the mortuary?' Helen said, in a desperate whisper. 'But then there's no way they could have got through a party!'

'If they knew,' said Billy. 'If any of them know where their men have got to. If anyone except Sallis and that wife of his actually knows. And didn't you tell me that youngster hadn't even heard about the murders?'

Helen put her hands up to her temples and pressed hard, not caring if she gave herself a headache. 'I can't take this in,' she said. 'I'm reeling with it.'

'Is it too late for me to come back with you?' said Billy. 'Sort it through, like you said? Would your mammy and daddy not like that?'

'My mammy?' Helen said. 'My daddy? Billy, when I first met you that day at the back door at the Cowgate, I introduced myself. I know I did.'

'Aye,' Billy said. 'Mrs Crowther. I remember. Helen came after and now Nelly.'

'*Mrs* Crowther,' Helen said.

'What are you getting at? Do you mean you kept your own place on after your man died?' Helen said nothing. 'Aye well, I can't let your neighbours see me lumbering up your stair right enough.'

Her heart was banging in her chest. She was discreet about Sandy with everyone and she couldn't have sworn that she'd ever said his name to Billy in the year and a bit of their acquaintance. But she definitely hadn't called herself a widow. He had made that up for himself somehow and now she was at a loss about what to do. 'Did *you* leave a coat at the pub?' she said.

'No such luck.'

'Well, away and come round to my mammy's, like you said. You can borrow something from my faither, I'm sure.'

Billy crooked his arm and Helen took it, thinking it was more than likely her last chance. She walked along to the crossroads, with a feeling she couldn't name but one that was very restful. Greet and Mack would tell Billy what she couldn't bring herself to, stop all this nonsense. He wouldn't make a scene in front of them, surely. Then tomorrow, when she met him to get her daddy's coat back, she would decide how much of the rest of it she wanted him to know.

At the stair mouth at Upper Grove Place, they met Mrs Suttie on her way back in from the kludgy on the green. 'Mercy! Whae's that?' she said, her always loud voice ringing out around the stairwell.

'I'm here too, Mrs S,' said Helen. 'We've been at a kiddies' treat at the church for Halloween.' She couldn't think of a better way to make Billy seem respectable in his get-up.

'Oh, Nelly!' Mrs Suttie said, pressing a hand to her heart. She was holding her box of Izal in the same hand. Never one to be embarrassed, Mrs Suttie. 'Sorry, Sandy,' she went on. 'But how was I meant to ken you with all that on?' She squeezed past them and went trotting off up the stair to her own house, no doubt looking forward to turning the encounter into a story she would tell for months, to the same people over and over again.

'Who's Sandy?' Billy said. 'Your brother?'

'Come up and meet the family,' Helen replied and scampered off, making better time even than Mrs Suttie, so as to avoid his questions for even a few minutes more.

'Teen?' came Greet's voice from the kitchen when Helen opened the door.

'It's me, Mammy,' Helen said. 'And a visitor.' There was a scuffle as Greet and Mack prepared themselves, according to the unspoken but well understood Downie code. 'A visitor' wasn't a neighbour, a relation, or an old pal who would take them as they were. 'A visitor' was a stranger, an authority figure, or an enemy. Helen waited for Billy and dawdled taking off her hat and coat at the run of pegs in the hallway, instead of breenging straight into the kitchen and laying all her outerwear over a chair. When her parents had settled and the kitchen was quiet again – hair curlers covered, stockings rolled back up, shirt buttoned, flies buttoned, any shaming signs of the family's private life tidied away – and the completion of all manoeuvres punctuated by the bang of the press door to hide the mess, Helen ushered Billy ahead of her and followed him into the room.

Greet cried out and Helen kicked herself for letting it happen. 'He's dressed up for the party, Mammy.'

'Sandy?' Greet said. She was sitting in the chair nearest the fireside, with the piece of mending in her lap that she'd been saving for 'visitors' for years. It was a tray cloth of snowy linen with a small section of the hem coming undone. Greet always put the socks she was darning into her mending basket and took out that tray cloth.

Billy unwound the bandages from his head and arranged his face in an expression of greeting. He knew enough not to ask who Sandy was again.

'This is Billy . . . from the mortuary,' Helen said, flushing to realise that she didn't know his surname.

'William Forrest,' Billy said. 'Pleased to meet you, Mr Downie, Mrs Downie.'

'Aye well, away in and . . . can you sit down in that?'

'Naw, and if you show me where, I'll go and unwind myself.'

Helen led him through to the big room, unused for weeks on end now that she and Sandy no longer slept in the box bed. She left him there and returned to face the interrogation.

'What's to do?' Greet said. 'Where's Teen? You were supposed to be in charge of her? What's "Billy from the mortuary" doing here? What's going on with you, Nelly?'

'He's needing to borrow a coat to get home in, Daddy,' Helen said. 'Just for tonight and he'll give it back in the morning.'

'And how was your party?' Mack said, avidly. He was on the other side of the fire, with his boots hastily shoved back on though still unlaced. Helen deduced that his slippers must be getting old and Greet didn't want them seen. She would buy him a new pair for his Christmas if she remembered.

'Never mind that now!' Greet hissed.

'"How was my party?" Daddy, you've never asked me such a thing in my life before tonight.'

'Where's *Teen*?' said Greet. 'Who *is* that through there?'

'Teen's away a walk with her felly,' said Helen, aware that she was dropping a bombshell, but judging that her parents would be easier handled if they were rocked by news.

'Whit felly's this?' said Mack, starting forward. 'Not some-one from that place?'

'Naw. A soldier.'

Mack sat back. 'Where's he taken her?'

'He's a nice-seeming laddie,' Helen said, which was true as far as she knew. 'But I want to talk to you about the other thing. The reason you were feart he *was* "from that place".'

'And you let him take her off into the night!' said Greet, like someone from a fairytale.

'It's not eight o'clock yet, Mammy,' Helen said. 'And she's in her fairy frock. He'll not have tooken her round the pubs in that.'

'If he has done, he'll regret it,' Mack declared, although his distraction was in his voice as much as on his face.

Then, before Greet could get in another round of questions or Mack a fresh threat to the absent Glen, Billy reappeared. He was wearing a shirt and collar with a striped tie and his trousers looked surprisingly crisp for having been inside bandages all those hours.

'Sit down, Mr Forrest,' Greet said. 'And you'll take a cup of tea?'

'Daddy,' Helen said, her heart banging at her own temerity. 'I need to ask you something and you're not going to like it. But I won't be stopped.'

Greet tittered, which was a very odd sound to Helen's ears. 'See how our daughter speaks to us Mr Forrest. Have you weans of your own? Just you wait.'

'I've not been blessed,' Billy said, which fell a long way short, to Helen's mind, of what he should have said, regarding being a bachelor.

'No more has our Nelly here,' said Greet, making Helen blush as bright and sudden a red as if a loaded paintbrush had been dipped in a jar of water. The stain deepened and spread and she glared at her mother.

'I blame the war,' said Mack, which could have meant anything at all.

'My wife doesn't keep well,' Billy said. 'She's not lived at home for nine years now.'

'West House!' said Helen, suddenly seeing a great many things very clearly.

Billy gave her a rueful smile. 'I visit her but some days she barely knows me.'

Greet, well practised in the art of receiving bad news, shook her head and said, 'What a cross to bear. What a sair fecht.'

Helen couldn't have spoken if her life depended on it. Her mind was like a warren full of startled rabbits. She knew Billy was looking at her but she couldn't meet his gaze. If his face was triumphant, she would weep.

'But that's not what matters tonight,' Billy said. 'I need to hear your answer to this particular question too, Mr Downie.' He took his brimming teacup from Greet. She had loaded it up with sugar and placed a drop scone in the saucer. It was her way of signalling sympathy and, from the look Billy gave her, Helen reckoned he was brought up in the same tradition. 'What do you know about the Adventists of the True Tabernacle? That's what Helen can't bring herself to ask you.'

Mack said nothing. Greet, as ever, filled the silence.

'Helen!' she said. 'How exactly is it you two know each other?'

'Billy works at the mortuary in the Cowgate like I said, Mammy,' said Helen, finding her voice again. 'We met over that sorry business last year and now he's been dealing with the corpses, this last week. The four men. We need to hear what you know about it.'

'Me?' said Greet. 'How are *you* mixed up in it? I know you were at the baths on Thursday and the rink on Saturday, but why are you meddling in the rest of it?'

Helen ignored her. 'For a week and more we've been trying to work out who they are, Daddy,' she said.

'Who they are that did it?' said Mack, jerking his head up and piercing her with his eyes. 'Leave that to the polis, can't you?'

There was a long silence.

'Who they are that got kilt,' said Helen at last. She stared at Mack while she tried to work out what was wrong with what he'd just said. It was like . . . It was kind of like . . . Did he already *know* who the dead men were and so he wasn't interested in that bit? Not quite, she thought. Or not only, anyway. It was more . . . why would anyone think 'who they are' meant the murderer? 'Who he *is*' that would be.

'Why are you looking at me like that?' said Mack.

'Daddy,' she said. 'What makes you think there's more than one killer mixed up in this?'

'Whit?'

'Aye, you're right,' said Billy, clicking his fingers. 'You're right there, Nell.'

'Nell, is it?' said Greet, desperately trying to get everyone's attention back on wee bits of gossip and scandal instead of this dark bloom of knowledge that was spreading through Helen, so out of place in her parents' kitchen, as familiar to her as any home would ever be.

'You've no call to think it was more than one man,' Helen said, 'unless you *know* it was more than one man. They've worked to keep that out of the papers and secret. But you *do* know, don't you, Daddy? You both know.'

She turned and tried to give her mother the same kind of stern look she gave patients sometimes. Not when they were overwhelmed with the state they'd got in, or even when they'd tried to get something they didn't need from her. Life was hard in this ward and people got hard to match it. But sometimes when they didn't trust her, when they hid small shames to save seeing her judgement – a judgement that would never come if they only but knew – and the hiding stopped the help and it all got worse and in the end she couldn't help at all. Then she glared sometimes. Not that Helen's sternest look would ever make a dent in Greet Downie, who'd taught it to her.

'Everybody knows who it was,' Greet said. 'It's on the news. It was a poor wee mannie not in his right mind that did it. They've caught him now.'

'No,' Billy said, 'but I'll tell you what. Martin Nunn, that they've got jailed for it, that's never lifted a finger against them, he's tailor-made to carry the can if someone's got it in for church types. Him and his devil worship.'

'Poor soul,' said Helen. 'He's no more to be blamed for his state than Billy's wife, I doubt. How can you two let it happen?'

But Mack had reached the end of his resources. 'Leave it, lass,' he said to his wife. Then he turned to Helen. 'You too, Nelly. Leave it. Just leave it, eh?'

Helen could no more have left it there than she could fly. 'This makes no sense to me,' she said, fired up beyond anywhere she'd been before. 'Daddy, I *know* you. Both of you. You're good, honest, kind, decent folk and I'm lucky to be your wee girl out of everyone's in the world I could have been.'

'You couldn't be anyone else's wee girl with your Mammy's hair flaming on your heid like that,' said Mack. He was as sentimental as most men and Helen could always soften his mood without trying too hard.

'So why,' she said, going in for the kill now he was laid open, 'is the murder of four more good, honest, kind, decent folk – church folk! – not a bother to you? Four men that do good work all over this city. I saw it with my own two eyes tonight. They hid their grief and put on a party for orphans, Daddy. Mammy. I mean, aye, they're harsh and gey po-faced too. But good with it. So what's going *on* here?'

'That's not all they hid,' Mack said.

'Wheesht!' said Greet, flicking a hand at him as if to get rid of a fly. 'Your eyes aren't as sharp as you think, Helen. Why can't you let well alone when you don't know the first thing about it anyway?'

'*Well?*' said Billy. 'Let *well* alone? Mrs Downie, four men have been killed and their corpses defiled.' Greet shrank away from his words. But Helen hoped he would drive on. Her mammy was harsh but she was squeamish too. Billy must have read her thoughts. 'Have you any idea what a man looks like who's been boiled in his bath, Mrs Downie? Imagine someone you loved naked and blistered and sticking to the table in the morgue, like some handless cook forgot to grease a roasting pan.'

Greet put her hands up in front of her face.

'And I know you work in the slaughterhouse,' Billy said, rounding on Mack. 'And a carcass in the cold store is a sight you're used to. But not a man frozen solid and thawed over days with his guts still full and his eyeballs rotting before the ice is out of his belly.'

Mack stared back, the only sign of distress the way his jaw was clenched.

'And can you remember when you saw your own faither laid in his coffin, Mrs Downie?' Billy said, rounding on her again. 'All nice and peaceful, his head on a wee lacy pillow and his hands folded. Imagine how you'd feel to see him stripped naked and his eyes popping out his head with terror, food stuck in his teeth and rolling down his front, his hands like claws and cake and gravy under his fingernails from him trying to gouge out what was choking him.'

'That's enough!' Mack thundered.

'Or dressed in tart's rags in a knockin' shop,' Billy said, his voice more bitter yet as he used men's words to talk man-to-man, spitting the ugly terms at Mack's face. 'His tongue like a black ham and his veins like red ropes. You must know, working in an abattoir, that everything lets go when death comes for you. He died in his own muck, in a puddle of his own—'

'I said, enough!' Mack rose up out of his seat and took a step forward. 'Get out of my house, whoever you are. Wherever you've sprung fae. And don't darken my door again.'

Billy stood up and Helen leapt to her feet too.

'Sit down, you,' Mack bellowed at her.

Helen looked up into his face. 'I've just worked out what you were doing at the baths, Daddy,' she said. 'Size of you. You were there to push the pram.'

Greet didn't even try to deny it. She whimpered.

'And that big block of ice, Mr Downie?' Billy said. 'Was it made at the abattoir?'

'I don't answer to you,' Mack said. 'But you, lady' – he jabbed a finger at Helen – 'You answer to me, so don't you shame me by leaving this house with him.'

'You and me have got a different idea of shame, Daddy,' Helen said. 'I'm going home, but I'll see Billy out on my way.'

Before either of them could make for the door though, the sound came along the passageway of Teenie returning. And she wasn't alone.

'Mammy, Daddy,' she said, sidling round the kitchen door with a demure look on her face that didn't match the sparkling frilly dress in the least. 'This is Glen. He's come to meet my fa— Who are you?'

'I'm leaving,' said Billy.

Helen sat down again. If Glen was about to bear the brunt of all the anger that belonged to Billy by rights, she would stay and try to smooth things over.

It soon became clear that Greet and Mack were taking a different tack, though. 'Welcome, lad,' Mack said. 'Teenie's sister tells us you're serving the King. Good on you.'

'Sit down and have a cuppa while Teenie changes out of that daft rig-out,' said Greet, who had to let her anger out somewhere.

Helen nodded at Glen, then left without another word, catching up with Billy halfway down the first flight of stairs. 'What the heck was all that?' she said. 'I mean, aye, it was all true and, aye, there's something far from right going on up there.' She jerked her head back towards her parents' door. 'But why did you tear a strip off them like that, Billy? I was trying to find out what they know.'

'To make it easier,' Billy said.

'How's any of that—?' Helen began, but it was over a year since she'd lived in a tenement and she'd forgotten how the stairwell rang out when you raised your voice. She started again near a whisper. 'How's any of that going to make anything easier? They might have told us what they know if we'd gone in gentle-like.'

'Not easier to solve the murders!' Billy said. 'Easier to stay away. Because you're married. And I know I'm married, before you start shouting me down, but that's different.'

Helen's pulse was going like a music hall ditty, not just fast but all jumbled up and skipping around, it felt like. 'Not as different as you'd think,' she said. 'Look, let's not talk about this in my mammy's stair, eh?'

When they were out on the street, Billy shivering without the promised borrowed overcoat and walking fast to try to warm up, Helen said, 'How did giving my mammy and daddy the sharp edge help with me being married?'

'Burn my boats,' Billy said. 'Make them that angry at me that you'd take agin me and never want to see my face again.'

'Aye well, think again,' Helen said. 'Do you want my scarf?' Billy took it and wound it over his shoulders like a shawl. 'You'll have to whip that off if someone comes up the road,' she told him. But it was that quiet time again, the second time in as many days she had found herself on the streets when everyone else was off them.

'Think again?' said Billy.

'It didn't work. My daddy wasn't really angry. It was an act. He was thinking about what you know, not how you were talking to him. And the thing is, he's a big softie usually but he didn't care a whit about the dead men. He helped whoever killed two of them! And I think I know why, at long last.' She waited, but Billy said nothing. They were down on Morrison Street now, hurrying along to the bottom of Gardener's Crescent. 'He knows something about those four dead churchmen that makes him think they deserved it. And he's not the only one. And the church folk know that. *That's* why they're keeping it so quiet what's happened. Because they fear that the whole city will say they had it coming to them. It makes no sense, but I'm sure it's true.'

'*That's* what you meant then,' said Billy in a flat blank voice. 'When you said trying to make them angry "didn't work". I thought you meant it didn't set you against me.'

Now they were at the place where the Rosemount Cottages led off from the flat side of the crescent. It was time for Helen to turn in and Billy to keep walking. They stood under the streetlamp on the silent street each watching the other's breath pluming out and fading. Billy shivered and began to unwind Helen's woolly scarf from around him.

'Come on,' she said. 'Come and get a warm and let me show you.'

Chapter 20

Billy paused on the top step. 'Is "Sandy" not at home?' he said. 'I was ready for your daddy to punch me in the face but he's a sight older than me. I don't want your husband taking a crack.'

'Sandy *is* at home,' said Helen. 'In his home. This is mine. Look, get in before your teeth chitter themselves to bits.'

She led him into the kitchen, where the fire still had a bit of life in it from earlier and came back to full strength once she'd added a few sticks and given it a good going-at with the bellows. Billy sat briefly, then stood and turned his back to the warmth, with his hands behind him.

'You should have kept your bandages on,' Helen said. 'Where are they? Have you left them in my mammy's big room?'

'I'm not worried about Slice checking the cupboards anymore,' Billy said. 'That was definitely him up in that wee attic place, Nelly. If he's at his work on Monday, I'll get those bandages back from your maw and eat them.'

'So you think he's gone into hiding, good and proper?' Helen said.

'Wouldn't you?' said Billy. 'If you were the last— But put me out of my misery, eh?' He crossed his arms and fixed Helen with a firm look. 'How come your man doesn't live in your house? And how come your mammy doesn't know?'

'Stand up,' Helen said.

'You're turfing me out just for asking?'

'Stand *up*!'

When he was on his feet, Helen moved his chair off the edge of the carpet that took up the middle of the room and rolled it carefully back towards the window, revealing the trap door set into the floorboards.

Billy looked at her in puzzlement.

'My husband, in name and in nothing else, is down there,' she said. Seeing the look of horror on Billy's face, she hurried on, 'Not in a dungeon, you daftie! Not in a prison pit! It's another house the same as this one, with its own front door where he comes and goes. This hatch is to hide the arrangement. Let him come up quick like if my family turn up. And they do.' Her face clouded. 'Or they did until I went and ruined it tonight.'

'In name and nothing else?' Billy said. 'But . . .' he held out his hands as if displaying Helen to herself. 'But *why*?'

Helen couldn't help smiling. 'Thank you,' she said. '"Why" isn't my secret to tell. You'll just have to trust me.'

'And how long has this been going on?'

'Always,' Helen said. 'Since our wedding. I thought it was the war – he had a terrible war – but it's always been like this.' She dreaded what might show on his face, if he caught her meaning, if he understood that she meant to call herself a virgin. For if Billy looked pleased at that news, or even too interested in it, she would think less of him than she had grown to. So it was a struggle to look up and meet his eye. When she did, though, what she saw was sorrow.

'I can't say as much,' he told her. 'We had five good years, Hazel and me. We had a son.'

'You've got a son?' Helen said. 'Where is he? Do you look after him all on your own?'

'He's away,' Billy said, with his throat thickening. 'She put him away. That's why *she's* been put away. She doesn't even

260

know she did it. She's not able, Helen. She's not a grown woman anymore. She's like a baby herself these days.'

Helen had heard the phrase before but until that moment she had never truly felt her heart hurting. 'He's got someone else he lives with down there,' she blurted out. 'That's why.' It took Billy a moment to come back from his memories.

'And you put up with it?' he said at last.

'Aye, I do. Don't ask me why. Like I said. Just trust me.'

She had filled the kettle so full for a hot bottle as well as the tea that it had taken all this time to boil, but now it started to screech and they got the chance to gather themselves back together again, Billy folding away his sorrow as he replaced the carpet and the chair, Helen driving away her hopes and silly dreams as she made the tea and filled the stone pig with the rest of the water, then wrapped it in a towel to hand over.

'So,' she said, when she was sitting in the opposite chair, trying not to think of Mack and Greet sitting like that earlier, 'what do we know?'

'Four elders of a church were killed in ways that thumbed a nose at the church's teachings,' Billy said. 'Now, who would do that?'

'Somebody from another church?' said Helen. 'If he'd lost his mind?'

'This is a grand cup of tea, hen,' Billy said. 'And it's "if *they've* lost *their* minds" according to your faither.'

'I should have offered you a bite to eat too,' said Helen. 'And I agree. Mack knows better than most that it took more than one man to pull it all off. He helped two of them.'

'I ate three pies and a spare scone,' said Billy. 'I'm nearer needing the bicarb than another meal.' He sipped his tea. 'When you think about it, of *course* it's more than one man. Stands to reason. How could one man have clothes from a slaughterhouse and a tannery, and the keys to a café, and all

261

the know-how about an ice rink and a hot-water gubbins as well as knowing about that wee girl's room? What's her name again?'

'Patricia,' said Helen. 'Aye, you're right. The only connection I've been able to make in all my going about and poking my nose in is that Jessie Gibb, from the chop-house, used to be on the game with Patricia, when she was still Rita.'

'Is that right?'

'Oh aye, they knew each other and they did *not* want to see each other.'

'And one of them told you?'

'No, Jessie's mammy told me, more or less. Told me she had saved Jessie from going down a bad road, welcomed her back and all that.'

'That's a good mother,' Billy said. Helen was sure he didn't mean to draw a contrast with Greet and how unlikely she was to forgive Helen for any wrongdoing, but the contrast was drawn all the same. As for the wrongdoing . . . there he was in her house, just the two of them, after dark and the door locked. But, on the other hand, there he was on the far side of the fireplace, drinking tea and talking about murder.

'And fingerprints,' Helen said.

'What about them?'

'Something strange. Jessie Gibb took a tizzy when I mentioned the polis dusting the windowsill of the chophouse lavvy for fingerprints and the inspector sort of laughed – or no, that wasn't it. He thought I was laughing at him when I brought the subject up.'

'Why would he think that?'

Helen shrugged. 'Do you think there's anything to be learned if we think about the clothes?' she said. 'The feather boa and cami knickers went with where the shamed man was found, but the rest of them were just a gallimaufry. An abattoir apron in the baths, a tanner's in the chophouse and a pinny at the ice rink.'

'Aye, that's queer when you put it that way.'

'Maybe what we should do is go to the polis and tell them all this, Billy.'

'What bits of it do you reckon they don't already know?'

'Well, they can't know Dr Sallis is hiding in the loft of his own church hall. Surely.'

'Do you think he's still there?' Billy said.

'I would be, if it was me.' Helen shivered. 'The only reason it's over, like he told the Fiscal, is that four elders are dead and he's not going to be a fifth one. I'll bet my eyes he's in that wee attic still.'

Billy gave Helen a sudden grin, not at all looking like a man who'd been chilled and scared and angered this evening, and all that before he brought his pain out to speak of it. 'You know where he should be tomorrow morning, don't you?'

'No,' said Helen. 'At work, you mean? Is there a body needing seen to?'

'You heathen,' Billy said. 'He should be at church, Nelly. How do you fancy a wee change tomorrow? A visit to the True Tabernacle?'

Helen was shocked but managed not to gasp. Then she grinned back. 'Aye go on then,' she said. 'My mammy can't kill me twice.'

'I'll come round for you at the back of ten,' Billy said. 'Give us plenty time to walk there and get a good pew.'

★

Next morning, Helen tried on and discarded every garment in her wardrobe barring party frocks and cotton summer

263

skirts. In the end, she wore her good lilac wool dress and her good grey coat, same as every other Sunday. She pinned her twenty-first-birthday brooch to the lapel and fastened her hat with the pearl-topped pin that had been her Granny Downie's. She had found it in the button box one rainy afternoon they had all been visiting and been made a gift of it there and then, even though Greet pulled her lips in until they disappeared completely.

When she saw Billy coming along the street, looking for him out of the window, Helen pinched her cheeks, let herself out of the house and went trotting to meet him. It would be just like the thing for Sandy or Gavin to be watching.

'There you are,' Billy said, putting an arm across her back and turning her to the inside of the pavement so he could walk beside her at the kerb. 'You're keen.'

'Good pew, you said,' Helen came back with. 'Do you think we'll see anything to help us?'

'More than we'd see in the same hour if we don't go,' said Billy. 'And you know what? We'll see more of it from the back row than sitting under the pulpit. We could have left it a wee.'

When they slipped inside the front door of the church, though, it was clear that they had their pick of the pews from the front to the back, for there were only a handful of worshippers present. Ten in total, not including Mrs Sallis who was banging out an unfamiliar hymn on a battered wee piano off to the side near the vestry door. She saw them come in and gave them a long and calculating look, making the page-turner beside her, who was already fumbling to keep up with the tempo, glance over and lose her place completely.

As well as a family of four near the front, the children with that spit and scrub look of all bairns on a Sunday, and one old man besides, the congregation comprised no more than the other four women from the party – Mrs Pettit, Mrs Boswell, Mrs Mann and the young woman so far nameless – and Helen nudged Billy and bent towards him to speak softly. 'Do you think those four know their husbands have been murdered? Because I don't. I reckon they've been told the "away on a mission" story and believed it.'

'Aye, you could be right,' Billy said. 'But would they believe it? Folk don't just up and disappear, not usually. What?'

This last was because Helen, fishing around in the back of her brain for an elusive thought, was staring at him. 'I don't know,' she said. 'Something.' She turned to face the front again.

A few more worshippers trickled in as half-past ten grew near, including a woman very heavily pregnant and pasty-looking, who sank into the outside seat of Billy and Helen's pew with a grin of apology.

'I'm as sick as a dog,' she said. 'I daren't go further up in case I need to run.'

'You should surely be over the sickness by now,' Helen said, casting an expert eye over the mound of the woman's belly.

'So they tell me every time,' she said. 'But it's morning, noon, and night sickness for me, whether it's a boy or a girl, and it won't stop till I've got it in my arms.'

'Shame,' said Helen. 'But worth it, eh?'

'I should have adopted an orphan,' the woman said. She swallowed hard and popped a mint into her mouth.

'Are the orphans coming to the service?' Helen said. 'They had a long walk back from the party last night, just to turn round and come back again.' The woman stared at her. 'I didn't mean you'd pick one today like a puppy from a pet shop,' Helen said, finding herself babbling at the oddness of the woman's look. 'It's just that you put me in mind . . .'

But the pregnant woman was sliding back out of the pew and, with one last bewildering glare, she marched out.

'Hope she finds a quiet corner,' Billy said. 'Embarrassing else.'

'She's not gone to be sick,' said Helen. 'She's running away from me and my mouth.'

'How, what did you say?'

The truth was that Helen didn't know, and couldn't think, why her mentioning the orphans from the Adventists' children's home had caused such a stir in a stranger who should surely be proud of what her church was doing. But, before she could begin to pick it over, Mrs Sallis started a new tune, loud and triumphant and familiar enough that there was no need for turned pages. The door to the vestry opened.

Helen and Billy watched as a man in minister's garb emerged and mounted the stairs of the pulpit. He was small and thin and looked over seventy, with dry papery skin and sparse faded hair. His voice, when he asked his meagre congregation to be seated, was a peevish sort of whine with a rattle that sounded like he needed to clear his throat. Billy cleared his, making Helen smile, and bringing the minister's attention onto them.

'I see we have new friends amongst us today,' he said. 'Welcome to the Tabernacle and to the truth of Adventism. We welcome all who are ready to work for the glorious day to come. Let us pray.'

Helen bent her head, only now realising that she had not the faintest clue was Adventism was or what the work might be. Advent, she understood, but that was only at Christmastime. She applied herself to hear the prayer and maybe get a clue that way.

'—shall come in his Glory and all the holy angels with Him,' the minister was saying, which didn't sound like a prayer to Helen. It sounded like a verse from the Bible. She took a sideways look at Billy, who had his eyes screwed tight shut. 'Until that day, whose number in the book is hidden from us, we must walk in the shadow of the valley of death, in sure and certain hope of our Lord's coming.'

Billy's eyes popped open. 'Valley of the shadow of death,' he said, and Helen nodded. It had sounded funny to her too although she couldn't put her finger on it.

'Amen,' said the minister. The small congregation murmured an echo, Mrs Sallis struck up 'To God Be The Glory', and they all began to sing, all except the timid little page-turner who was making a meal of that simple task and had no attention left for anything else.

The sermon took as its text some verses from Psalms Helen couldn't remember ever having heard before, although the bit about the stopped-up ears rang a bell. She had found it strange, as a child, that the Bible would talk about things that had happened to her: Greet pouring in warm oil and clapping a poultice to the side of her head to clear the blockage.

'The wicked are estranged from the womb,' the minister said, 'they go astray as soon as they be born, speaking lies.'

'Gey queer bit to pick, for a church that runs a children's home,' Billy muttered. Helen shushed him. She was watching Mrs Sallis, whose mouth was a grim line as she sat glaring at the preacher from her piano stool. 'Break their teeth in their mouths, O God, in their mouths: break the great teeth of the young lions, O Lord.' The minister paused then and seemed to skim ahead on his page to see what else was written there. He looked up at the old man in the front pew, the only other man except Billy, then swallowed and carried on.

'He didn't write that,' Helen whispered. 'He had no idea what he was going to end up saying.'

'Maybe one of the four that's deid was the right minister,' Billy whispered back. 'And this gadge just picked an odd bit to read. A proper minister wouldn't have got the words wrong, I'm thinking. Oy-oy. Look, Nelly. Mrs Slice is not best pleased with his choice.'

'No wonder,' said Helen. 'They're not putting themselves in a good light to their brand-new recruits.'

It got a bit better once the reading was over and the sermon itself began, although the address was full of big words and twisty arguments, talking about the 'age of accountability' and Jesus' sacrifice and the nature of sin. Helen was soon lost and retired into her own thoughts to wait it out, coming to with a jolt as the piano struck up again, in a tune she didn't know at all. The rest of the congregation sang it lustily enough, but with no numbers posted on any signs, Helen had no hope of finding it in the hymnbook she had brought with her, nor did she want to, what with all the 'crimson stains' and 'weakness of children'. *Jesus paid it all*, went the chorus, and at least that was simple enough that Helen managed to be mumbling along by the time a verse or two had gone by. Billy didn't even try.

Then it was time for the plate to come round and, telling herself that no matter how peculiar these people were they did a lot of good in the city, Helen looked a shilling out from her purse and waited. There were no discreet wee envelopes here, not even for the regulars, and no dark velvet bag to drop your offering into; it really was a plate, held by the mousy woman who had been so clumsily trying to turn Mrs Sallis's pages.

Helen wasn't looking, particularly, but she couldn't help seeing, since the hands held the plate under her nose. And right there was the explanation of the poor soul's trouble with the pages of the music book. Her fingers were missing, or not missing exactly but short and misshapen, gnarled with scar tissue and twisted to near uselessness. Helen stared and then a picture flashed in her mind's eye and her chin jerked up as she looked into the woman's eyes.

'You were at the baths,' she breathed and, although it was only the shock of the moment that made her speak so softly it was lucky she did, for no one else heard. The poor woman herself faltered and the coins on the plate rolled close to the lip and rattled together. Then she turned sharply away and scurried along the pews to go back down the other aisle.

'What happened there?' Billy said.

'Fingerprints,' said Helen. All of a sudden, a great big lump of it had come clear and she could see what she had been missing.

All through the intimations, the final hymn and a blessing, she sat sorting through this new revelation, the minister's voice no more than the drone of a bumblebee. She was quite still, but Billy kept shooting glances her way, knowing something had changed.

That wee woman, she was sure, had been in the same cubicle as Mack, last Thursday night at the Cally Crescent Baths. She had held up the towel to stop Helen seeing her own daddy. And she had climbed through the tiny window in the café's gents, leaving the inspector with the puzzle of why there were no proper prints for him to dust. It was her bloody hand that left such a strange pattern on the shoulder of the shamed man in Rita's room at Haymarket too. And, although she couldn't prove it, Helen was sure the woman had been at the ice rink, or knew ice anyway, because she thought that those strange, twisted stumps weren't God's plan, like the wee girl from Richmond Terrace who had come out of her mammy with no toes but only flippers like a seal. And it wasn't burns either that had done that. Helen knew burns well enough. That, she was sure, was frostbite. She had seen it on the newsreels at the end of the war on the Russian front and who could forget it ever after?

When at last it was time to leave, Helen darted out quickly and made a full circuit of the church's outside, making sure there was no back way into the little bit of ground surrounding it.

'Thank goodness,' she said to Billy, who was at her heel. 'Unless somebody's willing to clamber over a high wall and cross a back green, the front door's the only way out. Let's see if there's anywhere we can tuck ourselves away out the road, Billy, and wait for her.'

'What's going on?' Billy said. 'Wait for who?' He followed Helen across the road to the open gate of a house that looked empty and listened in silence as she told him what she had seen and what she thought and what she still didn't understand.

He had smoked a whole cigarette down to the dout by the time she was finished. 'I reckon she's not ever coming out,' he said, ducking to the side and looking over at the church, undercover of the thick hedge that grew right up over the gate. The others had left already, the minister – if he *was* the minister – and Mrs Sallis coming out last of all. It was getting on for dinnertime now. Helen's family surely couldn't be expecting her after last night's ructions, but Sandy would be wondering where she had got to. 'Is it time to go for the polis?' Billy said.

'And try to explain all this, when we still don't understand half of it?' Helen said, throwing up her hands. Billy gave her an all-too-knowing look, making her blush. 'Aye, aye, and there's my daddy too,' Helen said. 'Right, well come on then. All we'd need to say to the inspector that came to the back of Haymarket is we've found the hands that made all those smudged fingerprints.'

'You sure?'

Helen nodded. 'Let's go.'

'What do you think you're doing there, you pair of filthy articles!' Someone had walked in at the gate and jumped to the obvious conclusion on finding Helen and Billy skulking by her hedge. 'And on the Sabbath!' The woman had clearly come from church herself and the feather in her hat quivered with indignation as she advanced to shoo them away.

They spilled out onto the street and as well they did for there was the mousy little woman with the damaged hands, just right then slipping out of the church door and slinking off up Gilmore Place in the direction of Polwarth.

'Miss?' Helen shouted, breaking into a trot. 'Miss?'

The woman did not turn but she heard them and she too started running.

'Haud my coat,' Billy said, shrugging out of it and stuffing it into Helen's hands. He rose on the balls of his feet and went streaking up the pavement in a sprint, catching the woman easily and laying a firm hand on her arm. Helen, scurrying along after them, fully expected her to call out for help, as any innocent woman would have done, but Billy's prey simply shrank down into her collar and tried to draw to the inside edge of the pavement, out of view.

'Why didn't you shout for the polis?' Helen said, arriving puffing and blowing a moment later.

'Ye ken fine,' the woman said. She had a strange, low honk of a voice that made Helen think of wind howling through a close. 'Leave me alone,' she said. 'It's not my fault. I didn't do anything.'

'You were there though, weren't you?' Helen said.

'Where?' The woman scowled at her, belligerent as a little bantam.

Holding up my daddy's towel, Helen thought, although not strong enough to have wheeled in the apparatus. And she'd left Maitland's Chophouse by the gents' window, although she couldn't have restrained that great big man and forced food down his gullet. And she had left a handprint on the man in Rita's room, although again she couldn't have strangled him with those little misshapen paws of hers.

'At the ice rink,' Helen said at last, perversely enough because that was the only murder site where she hadn't managed to place the girl.

'Aye,' she said. 'Watching the fun.'

'And you know something,' Helen went on. 'You know something about four dead men.'

'Did you know the fifth is hiding in the attics above your church hall?' Billy said. Helen imagined he meant to scare the girl – she was not much more than a girl – but instead the news put a bit of fire in her eyes.

'Is that right?' she said. 'That's good news. If you let me go, I'll pass it on to those as need to hear it.'

'Oh right, and you're innocent, are you?' said Helen. 'Sounds like it!'

'Aye,' said the girl. 'I am and so's all the rest. You heard them with your own ears in there.'

'In the church?' Helen said. 'What do you mean?'

'I've paid for sins that weren't mine and paid ten times over. So I'm not just innocent. What's *more* than innocent? Because that's what I am. I'm *wronged*. We're all wronged.'

'All who?' said Billy.

Helen was beginning to think this girl wasn't right in her head. 'What happened to your hands?' she said.

'Hardiness,' said the girl, spitting the word as if it was poison. 'I was put in the icehouse as punishment for sin. Because some of the boys made a fire in their bedroom and smoked out the corridor. It was freezing cold and so they made a wee fire.'

'And you were put in the icehouse?' Helen said. '*You* were? Not them?'

'Aye, back when I was the one,' she said. 'After the last one and before the next.'

272

'What do you mean?' Billy said. 'When you were the one what?'

'We're all over the city,' she said. 'And we're loyal to each other. So you just watch it, Mister. Or maybe next time we'll come for you.'

She sounded less and less innocent, more and more mad.

'Me?' Billy said. 'What did I do?'

'You think that matters?' she said. 'It's our time now. And they know they started it and they can't go crying. See how they like a taste of their own medicine. See how they like all of it coming home to roost.'

'Let her go, Billy,' Helen said, for she had seen a bobby on the beat, strolling very deliberately towards them and watching with avid interest the tableau they made. Billy saw the constable too and tightened his grip.

'Are you aff your heid?' he said. 'We've caught her and we can hand her over.'

'No,' said Helen. 'Trust me. Let her go.'

'If this is because of your faither—'

'You,' Helen said to the woman who was twisting and struggling like an elver. 'Say the names of the elders and we'll let you go.'

'Sallis, Pettit, Mann, Maitland and Boswell,' she spat.

Billy released his grasp and the little woman took off at full pelt. She was long gone by the time the bobby came within hailing distance.

'Everything all right there?' he said.

'Ach, she took a ten-shilling note out my pocket when I laid my coat down,' Billy said. He gestured at his overcoat, still in Helen's hands. 'But she's more in need of it than me.'

'You should have let me deal with her, pal,' said the constable. 'You can't go taking the law into your own hands like that. What about the next one she thieves from?'

'It's Sunday,' Billy said. 'I decided to show some mercy.'

After delivering another ticking off, the policeman carried on up the street, with measured tread and looks from side to side like a metronome.

'I can't explain why I think this,' said Helen, 'but I hope he doesn't find her.'

'Eh?' said Billy. 'As if what she'd get for petty thieving is worse than what she deserves for what she *has* done!'

'What has she done though? Did any of that make sense to you?'

'Not a word.'

'Me neither,' said Helen. 'Except Maitland. The only other thing that gave me a glimmer is that it's definitely something to do with the church itself. It's not just that four bad men all happen to be elders there.'

'How's that a glimmer?'

'Because I know someone who collects religions like other folk collect stamps. And she won't mind being disturbed on a Sunday. Only you might need smelling salts once she gets going, if you've been brought up right, anyway.'

Chapter 21

The Strassers were having their Sunday lunch and it gave Helen a twinge of conscience to interrupt it. So often one or the other of them was called away to a sickbed, deathbed, or confinement, returning to tough meat and dried-up gravy at teatime. Today they were both sitting at the small table in the breakfast room with a bright fire burning, and she was going to ruin their peace for them.

Or she would have been, if they were ordinary people. With this pair it was hard to say.

'It's cutlets, I'm afraid,' said Dr Sarah, when Helen and Billy arrived in the doorway having let themselves in. 'And the cabbage isn't a source of joy. I must speak to Patricia sometime about *steaming* the vegetables. But you can dunk some bread in the sauce, and we can all share the suet roll after.'

'It's Billy, from the mortuary, isn't it?' Dr Strasser said, rootling around in the sideboard for plates and cutlery. He set out two glasses by the seats Helen had in no way accepted and said, 'Wine?'

'I've never tasted the stuff, Doc,' Billy said, dropping into the seat and folding his overcoat over its back. 'But I'm willing to start.'

'You look quite ... animated, Helen,' said Dr Sarah, chewing a mouthful of cutlet but manging to grin nevertheless. 'What's going on?'

'What do you know about Adventists?' Helen said, by way of reply.

Dr Strasser groaned. 'I don't share my wife's fascination with the more exotic forms of Christianity, Billy,' he said. 'And I can only apologise for what's coming.'

'What *is* coming, Sam?' said Dr Sarah. 'I take a healthy anthropological interest in all of humanity. That's all.'

'You act as if you're walking round a zoo sometimes!'

'If the cap fits,' said his wife.

'I like the wine,' said Billy. 'I've always enjoyed cough mixture.'

'A true diplomat,' Dr Sarah said. 'Now then, Adventists, Adventists. They share a central tenet with us Jews, of course.'

'Oh?' said Helen.

'Well sort of, if you half shut your eyes. They look forward to the Advent the way we look forward to the Messiah. Not the yearly anniversary of the Advent of Christ's birth, you understand. But the next Advent.'

'Ohhhh!' said Helen. 'The second coming? I see.' She turned to Billy. 'That makes sense of some of it.'

'What on earth have you been up to?' Dr Sarah said. 'Some sense of what? Is this to do with the murders?'

Helen thought for a moment about how much had changed since she last spoke to the docs about the murders. They didn't even know who the victims were. Rather than try to rehash it all in a nutshell, she said, 'And what about the Adventists of the True Tabernacle?'

To her surprise, Dr Sarah's mouth turned down. 'Well now, they are a different story altogether. They are rather a nasty lot, I always thought.'

'I've never even heard of them,' said Dr Strasser.

'They're not very successful,' said his wife. 'As you can well imagine.' She looked around at them all. 'Well, I suppose you can't until I tell you. They believe the new Messiah is coming any minute and when he does, he, like Christ, will take all the sins of the world unto himself.'

'That's right there in the Bible, isn't it?' said Billy. 'Don't we all believe that?'

'Well, the New Testament,' said Dr Sarah, which made Billy gulp a bit. Helen was used to it. 'The difference is that they start hares running. Do you see?'

Helen shook her head and Billy shrugged. Even Dr Strasser looked puzzled. 'They keep a sort of a scapegoat on the go at all times, one per congregation I believe, a candidate to be the new Messiah, so all the sins of the other Adventists are dealt with.'

'Hence empty pews?' said Dr Strasser. 'No wonder. Not sure I'd go rushing along to be punished for the next man's fornication and gambling.'

'But that's the worst thing of all,' said Dr Sarah. 'They don't ask for volunteers among the adults. Because Jesus was a newborn babe when he came to light up the world, they look for an infant. And, naturally, they don't have many parents willing to offer their infants for the role.'

'Oh my God,' said Helen. Her mammy would have given the back of her hand if she had heard the words slip out, and on a Sunday too. 'What if they ran an orphanage though?'

'Good Lord,' said Dr Strasser. 'Isn't there a congregation in Edinburgh, Sarah? And not too far from here?'

'Gilmore Place,' Billy said.

'But it's all ceremonial these days,' said Dr Sarah. 'I find it misguided and, as I say, most parents' instincts would be to protect their children from such a confusing experience, but I don't think actual punishments are exacted.'

'Punishments like being locked in an icehouse until you lose fingers to frostbite, because some other boys lit a fire?' Billy said.

Dr Sarah simply gaped at him. 'No,' she said.

'Yes,' said Helen. 'We are almost completely sure that the four dead men are elders of the Tabernacle Church: a Mr Boswell, a Mr Pettit, a Mr Mann and a Mr Maitland.'

'Maitland?' said Dr Sarah. 'Like the chophouse.'

'Yes,' said Helen. 'And do any of the other names . . . ?'

'Isn't Mr Mann a landlord?' said Dr Strasser. 'I would believe it of the fellow that he owned that tenement where poor Patricia lived.'

Dr Sarah was thinking furiously, but in the end she had to wait for Helen to speak again. 'We think, don't we Billy, that one of the scapegoats is fighting back.'

'What?' said Dr Strasser. 'One of the children?'

'Let me lay it all out first, Doc,' Helen said. 'The powers that be think it's all over. And not because they've caught themselves another scapegoat in poor wee Martin Nunn, you understand.'

'But because there's four . . . pillars . . . ?' said Billy.

'Of their faith?' said Dr Sarah. 'Continence and what have you?'

'But there's five elders,' Helen said. 'And the last one's in hiding.'

'Because one of the orphans is meting out justice?' said Dr Strasser.

There was a moment of perfect silence and then a crash sounded in the breakfast room doorway as Patricia, standing there with a pure white face, let the dish of suet roll slip to shatter on the floor.

Billy leapt up and took her by the arm as she stood swaying, then led her back to the table and held his own wine glass to her lips.

'You didn't meet Jessie Gibb at the back of Haymarket, did you?' Helen said. 'You knew her from the children's home.'

Patricia nodded.

'And her mother didn't take her back after she'd been working,' Helen went on, with sudden clarity. 'She took her in from being abandoned.'

'Were *you* a scapegoat?' said Dr Sarah. 'Oh Patricia, you poor little love.'

Patricia shook her head and managed to find her voice. 'Only boys were possibles,' she said. 'Logie and Melvin and—'

'Melvin from the ice rink!' said Helen. 'The nightwatchman. And Logie Galt went to work at the baths?'

'I think so,' Patricia said. 'We're all over Edinburgh, in the tannery and the brewery, and in service.'

'Wearing mail gloves, and wee white pinnies,' said Billy, nodding as it all started to fall into place.

'And Maitland's Chophouse!' said Helen.

'And Mr Boswell's ice rink!' Billy said. 'Those names, Nelly, those names.'

'Who is Mr Pettit?' Helen said.

'There's a Mr Pettit on the council,' said Dr Strasser. 'What's his area, Sarah dear?'

'Isn't he the baths superintendent?'

'Yes!' chorused Billy and Helen. 'Yes, he is.' They sat back, beaming. Then Helen could feel the smile die on her face.

'And the slaughterhouse?' she said. 'My daddy works with one of youse, doesn't he?'

'Mack Downie's a good man,' Patricia said. 'He covered for Peter, when he made a bad mistake one time, and kept him his job. Cos there's limits. Even for the do-gooders.'

'Do-gooders?' said Dr Sarah. It was a term that had been flung at her a fair few times.

'Aye. The elders are good at persuading folk to give us all a chance,' said Patricia. 'We're good workers and we take low wages.'

'What happened to *you* then?' said Dr Sarah. 'Sorry,' she added, as the girl cringed. 'Don't answer that, my dear. Rude of me.'

'How come there's none of you ever come to work at the mortuary?' said Billy. 'As far as I know anyway.'

'Elder Sallis wouldn't want the reminder,' said Patricia. 'Last thing he'd care for at his work would be one of the boys he gave up on, hanging around making him feel bad.'

'Boys,' said Helen. 'Patricia, that wee woman at the church wasn't a boy. You know the girl with the frostbitten fingers. Was she there at the same time as you?'

'Aye, he was,' Patricia said. 'They really thought they'd found the one with him. His name was Keith. I don't know what he calls himself now. But he never grew, because of the *thrift*, and he was damaged like you saw from being *hardy*. I wasn't there the first time he put on a skirt and jersey and went out skipping with the girls, but it made their minds up sharpish that he wasn't the second coming.'

'Good for Keith!' said Dr Sarah. 'I should jolly well think so too. I wonder if we might be of any help to him, Sam dear? Once all of this is over and done.'

'Once justice is done, you mean?' said Patricia. 'Once the innocents have been rounded up and the monsters have been soothed.'

'Monster,' said Billy. 'There's only one left. The other four are in the morgue. So "innocents" isn't the word you're after. Not the right word at all.'

'Patricia,' Helen said. 'Is the church hall usually locked when there's nothing on?'

Patricia shrugged.

'What are you thinking, Nell?' said Billy.

'Come with me,' Helen asked him. 'It's worth a try.'

★

280

The door was open and the same hall that had rung with laughter last night was now like a crypt, deadening their footsteps as they walked to the far end, under the high hatch.

'Are you up there, Dr Sallis?' Helen said. 'Give me a sign that you can hear us or we'll go and tell every bit of it right now.'

'And not to the polis, Doc,' Billy chipped in. 'You've got the polis wrapped round your little finger, haven't you? The Fiscal too. Businessmen that you are. Councilmen and property owners. A doctor no less! Naw, we'll go to the press. It'll be the biggest story Edinburgh's ever seen. And that's saying something.'

Helen jumped and grabbed Billy's arm as the door high above them swung open and the hand with the enormous signet ring came into view.

'What do you want?' The voice was unfamiliar to Helen. She had only ever been to the mortuary by the back door and usually after hours, but Billy knew it well and she felt a shiver pass through him.

'What *do* we want?' he whispered.

'For a start, I'd like you to show your face,' Helen said to the dark square in the wall. The hand withdrew but the rest of the man did not appear. 'As well as that,' said Helen, 'I want to ask you if those four women know that they're widows and they're so in thrall that they threw a party anyway. Or if you've got them duped about this "mission".'

'Duped?' came the voice, with a bit more strength behind it. 'Blasphemous female! "Wives, submit yourselves to your own husbands as you do to the Lord. For the husband is the head of the wife as *Christ* is the head of the church."'

'Aye but, Doc,' said Billy. 'It looked to me like four wee women were submitting to the plans of you and *your* wife. Last night, that's how it struck me.'

'They don't know yet,' said Dr Sallis, grudgingly. 'If the rings had been left on . . . But they weren't. As if it's some kind of game!' He was almost comical in his grievance, at least to anyone who knew what he and his church had done.

'I want to ask you something else, Dr Sallis,' Helen said. 'Why are you happy to have that poor wee Martin Nunn pay the price for what he didn't do?'

'He did!' said Dr Sallis.

'Away, Doc, you're havering. He never got out in time to do a quarter of it.'

'He was out in plenty time,' said Dr Sallis. 'And he deserves what's coming. He went from being our best and brightest hope to summoning the devil himself.'

'He— What?' Helen said. 'Martin Nunn was one of your children? One of your *chosen* children?'

'Who turned to the dark and stayed there. So, who better than him to bear the sins of the others?'

Helen's mind was reeling. 'Do you mean to tell me that someone at West House *let* him out? Late that Thursday? When you knew what was happening?'

'The Lord works in mysteri—'

'Blasphemy yourself!' said Helen. 'You, Dr Sallis, are off your rocker.'

'How dare you?' hissed the voice quietly but with a menace that made Helen want to cry. Instead, she raised her chin and spoke as fiercely as she ever had in her life.

'Here's how I dare. Because I'm in charge now. I want to see this building and the one next door empty and up for rent by the end of the year. I want to see whoever's in charge of your children's home in my office tomorrow morning to meet me and my opposite number from out Swanston way – whichever ward that is – to start discussing who's taking over when you step away. And then I want the whole boiling of you out of this city. And poor wee Martin Nunn can go back to West House to be tooken care of like he should be.'

'Who do you think you are?' The voice came thundering down.

'I'm a professional welfare officer for the National Health Service of Scotland,' Helen said. 'And I'm standing here in the middle of the floor giving you a chance you don't deserve. You're a jumped-up, kiddy-on holy man in a church you made up your own self, that's got fifteen members if you're lucky, and you're cowering in an attic so you don't reap what you sowed. Monday morning, Dr Sallis, or you'll be sorry.'

He hadn't had the courage to face her when she asked but he had enough front to show himself when he wanted to. He now appeared, poking his head out into the light, with his mouth turned down as though he smelled something rotten and his eyes pinched up as if he thought someone might be cheating him. It was one of the least attractive faces Helen had ever seen and she turned to look at Billy for sheer respite from it.

'Can you go and get the ladder from where Carolyn left it last night?' she said. 'And let him get down.'

But Dr Sallis had climbed out and was dangling down the wall by his fingertips. He craned over his shoulder to check the drop and then let go, landing neatly on both feet with his knees bent. When he straightened to his full height, Helen took a step back. He was well over six foot tall and broad with it. She glanced back at Billy and was reassured to see the cocky look on his face.

'You've got yourself in a right old fankle, boss.'

'And you've fallen in with some very dubious company,' Dr Sallis said, sneering at Helen. 'Pray tell, young lady, what are your intentions for the true villains in the current matter?'

'True villains?' Helen said. 'You mean the worms that turned?'

'If you will. Do you plan to mete out rough justice to them too?'

Helen said nothing. She hadn't thought that far before she came charging round here.

'You can't mean to let them get away with it?' said Dr Sallis. 'Cold-blooded murder?'

'*You* were,' Billy pointed out. 'You were going to blame Martin Nunn and run away.'

Dr Sallis gave an unpleasant laugh. 'Run away? Whatever gave you that idea? No indeed. We were going to round them up and have them dealt with. Once the scandal had died down, of course.'

'Oh, of *course*,' Helen said. 'You and another doctor were going to declare them all unfit, were you? And then they'd live out the rest of their lives in some locked ward and nobody would believe their wild tales?'

'The new hospital at Carstairs is going to have a very secure wing, they tell me.' He was practically drawling and Helen remembered Billy telling her how the doctor had said 'populace' and 'ticklish'.

'But who's "we"?' she asked him, wondering if he meant the Fiscal, who after all was neck-deep in all of this. 'There's only you left, isn't there?'

Dr Sallis didn't answer, but the outside door opened just then and Mrs Sallis strode in with a basket over her arm. She was looking up at the open loft door and didn't see the three of them standing down among the shadows. 'Thomas?' she said. 'Lunch, my dear.'

'Ah,' said Helen, making Mrs Sallis jump. 'I see. "We". Right.'

'What in the name of glory are you *doing*?' Mrs Sallis said. She was still addressing her husband, years of disappointments and frustrations turning her voice harsh.

'Yes, he's mucked the whole thing up,' Helen said. 'He peeked out last night and we saw him. Husbands, eh?' Billy

284

snorted. 'So you knew about all of it? And was it your idea to hide him?'

'My idea?' said Mrs Sallis. 'I submit to my husband as to the Lord.'

'Aye, sure you do,' Billy said. 'How is the way you treat those poor bairns submitting to the God that loves them? "Suffer the little children" means "put up with them", Mrs Sallis. Not "make their lives a misery".'

'I don't care to discuss Scripture with an orderly,' Mrs Sallis said. 'I want you out of here. I don't understand what you're doing here in the first place.'

'An orderly?' said Helen. 'A humble orderly like Jesus thinks will inherit the earth?' She held up her hand. 'No, don't bother thinking up a smart-aleck comeback. We're leaving. Your husband will tell you what he's got to do and, like you said, you'll have to obey him. But, before we go, I bet there's something in that picnic that I'm going to take with me.'

She strode up, whipped off the teacloth that covered the top of the wicker basket and discovered that her hunch had been spot-on. She plucked the bar of chocolate out from among the sandwiches and slipped it into her pocket.

'I'll see that wee Andrew gets his prize,' she said. 'And one of these days, like it says in the Bible, you'll face your Maker and get what's coming to you too. The pair of you.'

Then she swept out, her stomach churning and her knees knocking. Billy, following on behind her, was swearing under his breath.

'That bloody bar of chocolate!' she heard him say. 'I'm madder about that bar of chocolate than any of the rest of it. Daft, eh?'

'I know what you mean though,' Helen said. 'It's so . . . What's the word?'

'I know,' said Billy. 'I can't think of it either. Let's go and ask your lady doctor. I bet she'll tell us it.'

'But can we stop off somewhere first?' Helen said. 'I need a brandy. Because they're right about one thing, aren't they? We need to decide what to do.'

*

It wasn't *quite* true that the decision was taken out of Helen's hands but, by the time she and Billy had finished their double brandies in Bennet's and got back to Gardener's Crescent, matters had moved along.

'They must be having a drinks party,' Helen said, cocking her head as they came in the front door. There was a murmur of voices from the drawing-room floor.

'Drinks party!' said Billy.

Helen flushed. 'Folk in for a jar,' she said. 'I'm just calling it what they call it.'

Billy was listening too. 'They're not having much of a laugh,' he said.

The drawing-room door opened then and, right enough, what came out was far from the chatter and tinkle of the Strassers' usual gatherings.

'Is that you, Helen?' Dr Strasser said, leaning over the banister so that the long swoop of hair that topped off his short back and sides fell down over his face. 'We were starting to worry about you. Come up here, please. You're needed.'

It was Patricia whose face struck Helen as she and Billy entered the Strassers' drawing room. She was perched on the low armless chair by the fire, where Dr Sarah sat to toast crumpets, and she looked as if she'd seen a ghost.

Jessie Gibb was there too, on the other side of the fireplace, and the woman who was called Keith as a child was pressed into Dr Strasser's usual armchair, hugging her knees in her arms with her strange little hands clasped tight shut. On the

286

two-seater studio couch under the window, two small men sat with their shoulders round their ears and their hands clutching the knees of their trousers up into a sweaty mess. They must have been taught, as little boys, to sit straight and neat and make no noise. One of them, Helen reckoned, was Logie Galt and the other was probably Melvin. That left just one remaining stranger, a great big loaf of a man, with hulking shoulders and the same brawny forearms as Mack, from hard work year after year.

'Are you—' Helen began, but Dr Sarah stopped her.

'Best not,' she said, mildly.

Helen thought for a moment and realised the doc was right. This *was* more than likely Peter from the slaughterhouse, the one Mack had protected from a sacking that time. He and he alone of all of them was strong enough to strangle a man, hold a man underwater, restrain a man one-handed while he stuffed his gullet, or force a man into ice-cold water and keep him there while he froze. But, if Helen didn't know his name, she couldn't go and report him. Of course, 'Peter from the slaughterhouse' would be enough for the coppers to go on, but clearly Dr Sarah was doing the same mental somersaults, or she wouldn't have shushed Helen that way.

'How did you all get here?' she said instead.

Patricia nodded at the little woman hugging her knees in Dr Strasser's armchair. 'She knew I was here and she rallied the rest of them.'

'How did you know it was safe?' Helen asked the woman.

It was Dr Strasser who answered. 'We have a reputation, it seems. My wife's disregard for society's rules seems to be common knowledge.'

'Society's rules is one thing,' Helen said. 'Murder is God's rules, though.'

'Ask how many graves are in the grounds out at that home,' said Patricia. 'And then talk about God's rules.'

Helen thought hard for a long while. She looked at Dr Sarah to see if there was help to be had there, but her boss offered back the blankest of looks. Dr Strasser was sitting with his head back and his eyes closed. When she turned to Billy, he opened up his hands and shrugged.

'Well, tell me this,' she said, at last. 'Is it over?'

'Not while Sallis is alive,' said the strange little woman with the honking voice. 'Think I've put in my years in that church, biding my time, making my plans, just to stop before he's seen to?'

'But that leaves us with a bit of a problem,' Dr Sarah said. 'We can't sit idly by and let such a thing happen. No matter the rights and wrongs of it. Do you see?'

'So why no names no pack drill, Doc?' said Helen. 'If you're turning them all in anyway?'

'A rather big "if",' said Dr Sarah. 'I was hoping you'd have news from Gilmore Place that might persuade our guests to call it quits.'

'I might well,' Helen said. 'What if the children's home is closed and the church is closed and the Adventists leave Edinburgh? Would that do you? Could you let them go?' She wasn't sure who she was asking. 'Mr and Mrs Sallis, stuck together for the rest of their lives, with her biting her lip because she's not supposed to say boo to her lord and master and him knowing she thinks nocht of him. Wouldn't that be enough punishment for any man as proud as him? Not a doctor anymore either? Not a pillar of Edinburgh? Not an elder, nor a friend of the Fiscal, and just waiting for the second coming like the rest of us?' She still didn't know who she was asking. Which one of these veterans – these survivors of the True Tabernacle – had the final say?

'Can you leave us a wee while and let us chew it over?' Patricia said, to nods from the others. 'We need to decide if

288

what matters more is bringing them down or being free of them. It looks like we can't get both.'

'You might get neither,' Helen said. 'Jail for you lot but a nod and a wink for Sallis. Edinburgh-style. You know this city.'

'The Sallises certainly have friends in high places,' said Dr Sarah. 'But you all have friends too now.' She smiled kindly as she stood. 'Let us know what decision you come to.'

The doctors went upstairs to their bedroom to wait and Helen took Billy down to the basement to sit in her office, the only room in this big house that she could invite him into. As they got to the bottom of the basement staircase, he clutched her arm and swung her round until she was facing him.

'I think I love you, Helen Crowther,' he said.

'Oh, Billy,' said Helen. 'There's plenty else going on this weather. Let's just wait and see.'

Facts and Fictions

The geography of Edinburgh in this book is my best attempt at accuracy. Certainly, all of the streets and most of the institutions are real. Fountainbridge in the 1940s was home to a tannery, a slaughterhouse, a distillery, a brewery, a sweet factory and the Co-op dairy stables. It's an ongoing annoyance that I can't justify a handsome milkman by the name of Sean Connery putting in an appearance.

The Caledonian Cresent Baths, the Haymarket ice rink and the Cowgate mortuary are taken from life too, although Maitland's Chophouse, while typical, is imaginary.

The back of Haymarket was once as I depict it here but it had changed by the time I lived in the city and I added a lot of the detail to suit myself.

The Adventists' True Tabernacle buildings never existed on Gilmore Place and, as far as I know, the Adventists of the True Tabernacle themselves never existed anywhere. I made them up. But it wasn't a stretch.

The story itself, of course, I made up in its entirety but I will say that these truly were very Edinburgh murders.

Acknowledgements

I would like to thank: Lisa Moylett, Zoe Apostolides, Elena Langtry and Jamie McLean at CMM Literary Agency; Kate Norman, Jo Dickinson, Allyssa Ollivier-Tabukashvili, David Wardie, Kate Keehan, and all at Hodder and Stoughton; my friends and family – the Americans who ask all the questions and the Scots who help me answer them; and the librarians, booksellers, reviewers, bloggers, podcasters, readers and fellow crime-fiction fans who are the best co-nerds I could ever ask for.